THE BOOK OF SNOBS

WILLIAM MAKEPEACE THACKERAY

THE BOOK OF SNOBS

KÖNEMANN

Notes (on pp. 221 to 229)
are keyed thus in the margin

© 1999 for this edition
Könemann Verlagsgesellschaft mbH
Bonner Straße 126, D–50968 Köln

Series and volume editor: Michael Hulse
Cover design: Peter Feierabend
Layout and typesetting: Birgit Beyer
Printed in Hungary
ISBN 3-8290-3102-5
10 9 8 7 6 5 4 3 2 1

CONTENTS

Chapter	Page

THE BOOK OF SNOBS

BY ONE OF THEMSELVES

PREFATORY REMARKS

[The necessity of a work on Snobs, demonstrated from History, and proved by felicitous illustrations:—I am the individual destined to write that work—My vocation is announced in terms of great eloquence—I show that the world has been gradually preparing itself for the WORK *and the* MAN—*Snobs are to be studied like other objects of Natural Science, and are a part of the Beautiful (with a large B). They pervade all classes—Affecting instance of Colonel Snobley.]*

We have all read a statement, (the authenticity of which I take leave to doubt entirely, for upon what calculations I should like to know is it founded?)—we have all, I say, been favoured by perusing a remark, that when the times and necessities of the world call for a Man, that individual is found. Thus at the French Revolution (which the reader will be pleased to have introduced so early), when it was requisite to administer a corrective dose to the nation, Robespierre was found; a most foul and nauseous dose indeed, and swallowed eagerly by the patient, greatly to the latter's ultimate advantage: thus, when it became necessary to kick John Bull out of America, Mr. Washington stepped forward, and performed that job to satisfaction: thus, when the Earl of Aldborough was unwell, Professor Holloway appeared with his pills, and cured his lordship, as per advertisement, &c. &c. Numberless instances might be adduced to show that when a nation is in great want, the relief is at hand; just as in the Pantomime (that microcosm), where when *Clown* wants anything—a warming-pan, a pump-handle, a goose, or a lady's tippet—a fellow comes sauntering out from behind the side-scenes with the very article in question.

Again, when men commence an undertaking, they always are prepared to show that the absolute necessities of the world demanded its completion.—Say it is a railroad: the directors begin by stating that "A more intimate communication between Bathershins and Derrynane Beg is necessary for the advancement of civilization, and demanded by the multitudinous acclamations of the great Irish people." Or suppose it is a newspaper; the prospectus states that "At a time when the Church is in danger, threatened from without by savage fanaticism and miscreant unbelief, and undermined from within by dangerous Jesuitism and suicidal Schism, a Want has been universally felt—a suffering people has looked abroad—for an Ecclesiastical Champion and Guardian. A body of Prelates and Gentlemen have therefore stepped forward in this our hour of danger, and determined on establishing the *Beadle* newspaper," &c. &c. One or other of these points at least is incontrovertible: the public wants a thing, therefore it is supplied with it; or the public is supplied with a thing, therefore it wants it.

I have long gone about with a conviction on my mind that I had a work to do—a Work, if you like, with a great W; a Purpose to fulfil; a chasm to leap into, like Curtius, horse & foot; a Great Social Evil to Discover and to Remedy. That Conviction Has Pursued me for Years. It has Dogged me in the Busy Street; Seated Itself By Me in The Lonely Study; Jogged My Elbow as it Lifted The Wine-cup at The Festive Board; Pursued me through the Maze of Rotten Row; Followed me in Far Lands. On Brighton's Shingly Beach, or Margate's Sand, the Voice Outpiped the Roaring of the Sea; it Nestles in my Nightcap, and It Whispers, "Wake, Slumberer, thy Work Is Not Yet Done." Last Year, By Moonlight, in the Coliseum, the Little Sedulous Voice Came To Me and Said, "Smith, or Jones" (The Writer's Name is Neither Here nor There), "Smith or Jones, my fine fellow, this is all very well, but you ought to be at home writing your great work on SNOBS."

When a man has this sort of vocation it is all nonsense attempting to elude it. He must speak out to the nations; he must *unbusm* himself as Jeames would say, or choke and die. "Mark to yourself," I have often mentally exclaimed to your humble servant, "the gradual way in which you have been prepared for, and are now led by an irresistible necessity to enter upon your great labour. First, the World was made: then, as a matter of course, Snobs; they existed for years and years, and were no more known than America. But presently,—*ingens patebat tellus*—the people became darkly aware that there was such a race. Not above five-and-twenty years since, a name, an expressive monosyllable, arose to designate that race. That name has spread over England like railroads subsequently; Snobs are known and recognized throughout an Empire on which I am given to understand the Sun never sets. *Punch* appears at the ripe season, to chronicle their history: and the individual comes forth to write that history in *Punch*.

I have (and for this gift I congratulate myself with a Deep and Abiding Thankfulness) an eye for a Snob. If the Truthful is the Beautiful, it is Beautiful to study even the Snobbish; to track Snobs through history, as certain little dogs in Hampshire hunt out truffles; to sink shafts in society and come upon rich veins of Snob-ore. Snobbishness is like Death in a quotation from Horace, which I hope you never have heard, "beating with equal foot at poor men's doors, and kicking at the gates of Emperors." It is a great mistake to judge of Snobs lightly, and think they exist among the lower classes merely. An immense percentage of Snobs, I believe, is to be found in every rank of this mortal life. You must not judge hastily or vulgarly of Snobs: to do so shows that you are yourself a Snob. I myself have been taken for one.

When I was taking the waters at Bagnigge Wells, and living at the 'Imperial Hotel' there, there used to sit opposite me at breakfast, for a short time, a Snob so insufferable that I felt I should never get any benefit of the waters so long as he remained. His name was Lieutenant-Colonel Snobley, of a certain dragoon regiment. He wore japanned boots and moustaches: he lisped, drawled, and left the "r's" out of his words: he was always flourishing about, and smoothing his lacquered whiskers with a huge flaming bandanna, that filled the room with an odour of musk so stifling that I determined to do battle with that Snob, and that either he or I should quit the Inn. I first began harmless conversations with him; frightening him exceedingly, for he did not know what to do when so attacked, and had never the slightest notion that anybody would take such a liberty with him as to speak *first*: then I handed him the paper: then, as he would take no notice of these advances, I used to look him in the face steadily and— and use my fork in the light of a toothpick. After two mornings of this practice, he could bear it no longer, and fairly quitted the place.

Should the Colonel see this, will he remember the Gent who asked him if he thought Publicoaler was a fine writer, and drove him from the Hotel with a four-pronged fork?

CHAPTER I

The Snob playfully dealt with

There are relative and positive Snobs. I mean by positive, such persons as are Snobs everywhere, in all companies, from morning till night, from youth to the grave, being by Nature endowed with Snobbishness—and others who are Snobs only in certain circumstances and relations of life.

For instance: I once knew a man who committed before me an act as atrocious as that which I have indicated in the last chapter as performed by me for the purpose of disgusting Colonel Snobley; viz. the using the fork in the guise of a toothpick. I once, I say, knew a man who, dining in my company at the "Europa Coffee-house," (opposite the Grand Opera, and, as everybody knows, the only decent place for dining at Naples,) ate peas with the assistance of his knife. He was a person with whose society I was greatly pleased at first—indeed, we had met in the crater of Mount Vesuvius, and were subsequently robbed and held to ransom by brigands in Calabria, which is nothing to the purpose—a man of great powers, excellent heart, and varied information; but I had never before seen him with a dish of peas, and his conduct in regard to them caused me the deepest pain.

After having seen him thus publicly comport himself, but one course was open to me—to cut his acquaintance. I commissioned a mutual friend (the Honourable Poly Anthus) to break the matter to this gentleman as delicately as possible, and to say that painful circumstances—in nowise affecting Mr. Marrowfat's honour, or my esteem for him—had occurred, which obliged me to forego my intimacy with him; and accordingly we met, and gave each other the cut direct that night at the Duchess of Monte Fiasco's ball.

Everybody at Naples remarked the separation of the Damon and Pythias—indeed, Marrowfat had saved my life more than once—but, as an English gentleman, what was I to do?

15

My dear friend was, in this instance, the Snob *relative*. It is not snobbish of persons of rank of any other nation to employ their knife in the manner alluded to. I have seen Monte Fiasco clean his trencher with his knife, and every Principe in company doing likewise. I have seen, at the hospitable board of H. I. H. the Grand Duchess Stephanie of Baden—(who, if these humble lines should come under her Imperial eyes, is besought to remember graciously the most devoted of her servants)—I have seen, I say, the Hereditary Princess of Potztausend-Donnerwetter (that serenely-beautiful woman) use her knife in lieu of a fork or spoon; I have seen her almost swallow it, by Jove! like Ramo Samee, the Indian juggler. And did I blench? Did my estimation for the Princess diminish? No, lovely Amalia! One of the truest passions that ever was inspired by woman was raised in this bosom by that lady. Beautiful one! long, long may the knife carry food to those lips! the reddest and loveliest in the world!

The cause of my quarrel with Marrowfat I never breathed to mortal soul for four years. We met in the halls of the aristocracy—our friends and relatives. We jostled each other in the dance or at the board; but the estrangement continued, and seemed irrevocable, until the fourth of June, last year.

We met at Sir George Golloper's. We were placed, he on the right, your humble servant on the left of the admirable Lady G. Peas formed part of the banquet—ducks and green peas. I trembled as I saw Marrowfat helped, and turned away sickening, lest I should behold the weapon darting down his horrid jaws.

What was my astonishment, what my delight, when I saw him use his fork like any other Christian! He did not administer the cold steel once. Old times rushed back upon me—the remembrance of old services—his rescuing me from the brigands—his gallant conduct in the affair with the Countess Degli Spinachi—his lending me the £1,700. I almost burst into tears with joy—my voice trembled with emotion. "George, my boy!" I exclaimed, "George Marrowfat, my dear fellow! a glass of wine!"

Blushing—deeply moved—almost as tremulous as I was myself, George answered, "*Frank, shall it be Hock or Madeira?*" I could have hugged him to my heart but for the presence of the company. Little did Lady Golloper know what was the cause of the emotion which sent the duckling I was carving into her ladyship's pink satin lap. The most good-natured of women pardoned the error, and the butler removed the bird.

We have been the closest friends ever since, nor, of course, has George repeated his odious habit. He acquired it at a country school, where they cultivated peas and only used two-pronged forks, and it was only by living on the Continent, where the usage of the four-prong is general, that he lost the horrible custom.

In this point—and in this only—I confess myself a member of the Silver-Fork School; and if this tale but induce one of my readers to pause, to examine in his own mind solemnly, and ask, "Do I or do I not eat peas with a knife?"—to see the ruin which may fall upon himself by continuing the practice, or his family by beholding the example, these lines will not have been written in vain. And now, whatever other authors may be, I flatter myself, it will be allowed that *I*, at least, am a moral man.

By the way, as some readers are dull of comprehension, I may as well say what the moral of this history is. The moral is this—Society having ordained certain customs, men are bound to obey the law of society and conform to its harmless orders.

If I should go to the British and Foreign Institute (and heaven forbid I should go under any pretext or in any costume whatever)—if I should go to one of the tea-parties in a dressing-gown and slippers and not in the usual attire of a gentleman,—viz., pumps, a gold waistcoat, a crush hat, a sham frill, and a white choker—I should be insulting society, and *eating peas with my knife*. Let the porters of the Institute hustle out the individual who shall so offend. Such an offender is, as regards society, a most emphatical and refractory Snob. It has its code and police as well as governments, and he must conform who would profit by the decrees set forth for their common comfort.

I am naturally averse to egotism, and hate self-laudation consumedly; but I can't help relating here a circumstance illustrative of the point in question, in which I must think I acted with considerable prudence.

Being at Constantinople a few years since—(on a delicate mission),—the Russians were playing a double game, between ourselves, and it became necessary on our part to employ an *extra negotiator*—Leckerbiss Pasha of Roumelia, then Chief Galeongee of the Porte, gave a diplomatic banquet at his summer palace at Bujukdere. I was on the left of the Galeongee, and the Russian agent, Count de Diddloff, on his dexter side. Diddloff is a dandy who would die of a rose in aromatic pain: he had tried to have me assassinated three times in the course of the negotiation; but of course we were friends in public, and saluted each other in the most cordial and charming manner.

The Galeongee is—or was, alas! for a bowstring has done for him—a staunch supporter of the old school of Turkish politics. We dined with our fingers, and had flaps of bread for plates; the only innovation he admitted was the use of European liquors, in which he indulged with great gusto. He was an enormous eater. Amongst the dishes a very large one was placed before him of a lamb dressed in its wool, stuffed with prunes, garlic, asafœtida, capsicums, and other condiments, the most abominable mixture that ever mortal smelt or tasted. The Galeongee ate of this hugely; and pursuing the Eastern fashion, insisted on helping his friends right and left, and when he came to a particularly spicy morsel, would push it with his own hands into his guests' very mouths.

I never shall forget the look of poor Diddloff, when his Excellency, rolling up a large quantity of this into a ball and exclaiming, "Buk Buk" (it is very good), administered the horrible bolus to Diddloff. The Russian's eyes rolled dreadfully as he received it: he swallowed it with a grimace that I thought must precede a convulsion, and seizing a bottle next him, which he thought was Sauterne, but which turned out to be French brandy, he drank off nearly a pint before he knew his error. It finished him; he was carried away from the dining-room almost dead, and laid out to cool in a summer-house on the Bosphorus.

When it came to my turn, I took down the condiment with a smile, said "Bismillah," licked my lips with easy gratification, and when the next dish was served, made up a ball myself so dexterously, and popped it down the old Galeongee's mouth with so much grace, that his heart was won. Russia was put out of court at once, *and the treaty of* Kabobanople *was signed.* As for Diddloff, all was over with *him*: he was recalled to St. Petersburg, and Sir Roderick Murchison saw him, under the No. 3967, working in the Ural mines.

The moral of this tale, I need not say, is, that there are many disagreeable things in society which you are bound to take down, and to do so with a smiling face.

CHAPTER II

The Snob Royal

Long since, at the commencement of the reign of her present Gracious Majesty, it chanced "on a fair summer evening," as Mr. James would say, that three or four young cavaliers were drinking a cup of wine after dinner at the hostelry called the "King's Arms," kept by Mistress Anderson, in the royal village of Kensington. 'Twas a balmy evening, and the wayfarers looked out on a cheerful scene. The tall elms of the ancient gardens were in full leaf, and countless chariots of the nobility of England whirled by to the neighbouring palace, where princely Sussex (whose income latterly only allowed him to give tea-parties) entertained his royal niece at a state banquet. When the caroches of the nobles had set down their owners at the banquet-hall, their varlets and servitors came to quaff a flagon of nut-brown ale in the "King's Arms" gardens hard by. We watched these fellows from our lattice. By Saint Boniface 'twas a rare sight!

The tulips in Mynheer Van Dunck's gardens were not more gorgeous than the liveries of these pie-coated retainers. All the flowers of the field bloomed in their ruffled bosoms, all the hues of the rainbow gleamed in their plush breeches, and the long-caned ones walked up and down the garden with that charming solemnity, that delightful quivering swagger of the calves, which has always had a frantic fascination for us. The walk was not wide enough for them as the shoulder-knots strutted up and down it in canary, and crimson, and light blue.

Suddenly, in the midst of their pride, a little bell was rung, a side door opened, and (after setting down their Royal Mistress) her Majesty's own crimson footmen, with epaulets and black plushes, came in.

It was pitiable to see the other poor Johns slink off at this arrival! Not one of the honest private Plushes could stand up before the Royal Flunkeys. They left the walk; they sneaked into dark holes and drank their beer in silence. The Royal Plush kept possession of the garden until the Royal Plush dinner was announced, when it retired, and we heard from the pavilion where they dined, conservative cheers and speeches, the Kentish fires. The other Flunkeys we never saw more.

My dear Flunkeys, so absurdly conceited at one moment and so abject at the next, are but the types of their masters in this world. *He who meanly admires mean things is a Snob—* perhaps that is a safe definition of the character.

And this is why I have, with the utmost respect, ventured to place The Snob Royal at the head of my list, causing all others to give way before him, as the Flunkeys before the royal representative in Kensington Gardens. To say of such and such a Gracious Sovereign that he is a Snob, is but to say that his Majesty is a man. Kings, too, are men and Snobs. In a country where Snobs are in the majority, a prime one, surely, cannot be unfit to govern. With us they have succeeded to admiration.

For instance, James I. was a Snob, and a Scotch Snob, than which the world contains no more offensive creature. He appears to have had not one of the good qualities of a man— neither courage, nor generosity, nor honesty, nor brains; but read what the great Divines and Doctors of England said about him! Charles II., his grandson, was a rogue, but not a Snob; whilst Louis XIV., his old squaretoes of a contemporary,—the great worshipper of Bigwiggery—has always struck me as a most undoubted and Royal Snob.

I will not, however, take instances from our own country of Royal Snobs, but refer to a neighbouring kingdom, that of Brentford—and its monarch, the late great and lamented Gorgius IV. With the same humility with which the footmen at the "King's Arms" gave way before the Plush Royal, the aristocracy of the Brentford nation bent down and truckled before Gorgius, and proclaimed him the first gentleman in Europe. And it's a wonder to think what is the gentlefolks' opinion of a gentleman, when they gave Gorgius such a title.

What is it to be a gentleman? Is it to be honest, to be gentle, to be generous, to be brave, to be wise, and, possessing all these qualities, to exercise them in the most graceful outward manner? Ought a gentleman to be a loyal son, a true husband, and honest father? Ought his life to be decent—his bills to be paid—his tastes to be high and elegant—his aims in life lofty and noble? In a word, ought not the Biography of a First Gentleman in Europe to be of such a nature that it might be read in Young Ladies' Schools with advantage and studied with profit in the Seminaries of Young Gentlemen? I put this question to all instructors of youth—to Mrs. Ellis and the Women of England; to all schoolmasters, from Doctor Hawtrey down to Mr. Squeers. I conjure up before me an awful tribunal of youth and innocence, attended by its venerable instructors (like the ten thousand red-cheeked charity-children in Saint Paul's), sitting in judgment, and Gorgius pleading his cause in the midst. Out of Court, out of Court, fat old Florizel! Beadles, turn out that bloated, pimple-faced man!——If Gorgius *must* have a statue in the new Palace which the Brentford nation is building, it ought to be set up in the Flunkeys' Hall. He should be represented cutting out a coat, in which art he is said to have excelled. He also invented Mareschino punch, a shoe-buckle (this was in the vigour of his youth and the prime force of his invention), and a Chinese pavilion, the most hideous building in the world. He could drive a four-in-hand very nearly as well as the Brighton coachman, could fence elegantly, and, it is said, played the fiddle well. And he smiled with such irresistible fascination, that persons who were introduced into his august presence became his victims, body and soul, as a rabbit becomes the prey of a great big boa-constrictor.

I would wager that if Mr. Widdicomb were, by a revolution, placed on the throne of Brentford, people would be equally fascinated by his irresistibly majestic smile, and tremble as they knelt down to kiss his hand. If he went to Dublin they would erect an obelisk on the spot where he first landed, as the Paddylanders did when Gorgius visited them. We have all of us read with delight that story of the King's voyage to Haggisland,

22

where his presence inspired such a fury of loyalty; and where the most famous man of the country—the Baron of Bradwardine—coming on board the royal yacht, and finding a glass out of which Gorgius had drunk, put it into his coat-pocket as an inestimable relic, and went ashore in his boat again. But the Baron sat down upon the glass and broke it, and cut his coat-tails very much; and the inestimable relic was lost to the world for ever. O noble Bradwardine! what old-world superstition could set you on your knees before such an idol as that?

If you want to moralise upon the mutability of human affairs, go and see the figure of Gorgius in his real, identical robes, at the waxwork.—Admittance one shilling. Children and flunkeys sixpence. Go, and pay sixpence.

CHAPTER III

The Influence of the Aristocracy on Snobs

Last Sunday week, being at church in this city, and the service just ended, I heard two Snobs conversing about the Parson. One was asking the other who the clergyman was? "He is Mr. So-and-so," the second Snob answered, "domestic chaplain to the Earl of What-d'ye-call'im." "Oh, is he!" said the first Snob, with a tone of indescribable satisfaction—the Parson's orthodoxy and identity were at once settled in this Snob's mind. He knew no more about the Earl than about the Chaplain, but he took the latter's character upon the authority of the former; and went home quite contented with his Reverence, like a little truckling Snob.

This incident gave me more matter for reflection even than the sermon: and wonderment at the extent and prevalence of Lordolatry in this country. What could it matter to Snob whether his Reverence were chaplain to his Lordship or not? What Peerage-worship there is all through this free country! How we are all implicated in it, and more or less down on our knees.—And with regard to the great subject on hand, I think that the influence of the Peerage upon Snobbishness has been more remarkable than that of any other institution. The increase, encouragement, and maintenance of Snobs are among the "priceless services," as Lord John Russell says, which we owe to the nobility.

It can't be otherwise. A man becomes enormously rich, or he jobs successfully in the aid of a Minister, or he wins a great battle, or executes a treaty, or is a clever lawyer who makes a multitude of fees and ascends the bench; and the country rewards him for ever with a gold coronet (with more or less balls or leaves) and a title, and a rank as legislator. "Your merits are so great," says the nation, "that your children shall be allowed to reign over us, in a manner. It does not in the least matter that your eldest son be a fool: we think your services so remarkable, that he shall have the reversion of your honours when death vacates your noble shoes. If you are poor, we will give you such a sum of money as shall enable you and the eldest-born of your race for ever to live in fat and splendour. It is our wish that there should be a race set apart in this happy country, who shall hold the first rank, have the fist prizes and chances in all government jobs and patronages. We cannot make all your dear children Peers—that would make Peerage common and crowd the House of Lords uncomfortably—but the young ones shall have everything a Government can give: they shall get the pick of all the places: they shall be Captains and Lieutenant-Colonels at nineteen, when hoary-headed old lieutenants are spending thirty years at drill: they shall command ships at one-and-twenty, and veterans who fought before they were born. And as we are eminently a free people, and in order to encourage all men to do their duty, we say to any man of any rank—get enormously rich, make immense fees as a lawyer, or great speeches, or distinguish yourself and win battles—and you, even you, shall come into the privileged class, and your children shall reign naturally over ours."

How can we help Snobbishness, with such a prodigious national institution erected for its worship? How can we help cringing to Lords? Flesh and blood can't do otherwise. What man can withstand this prodigious temptation? Inspired by what is called a noble emulation, some people grasp at honours and win them; others, too weak or mean, blindly admire and grovel before those who have gained them; others, not being able to acquire them, furiously hate, abuse, and envy. There are only a few bland and not-in-the-least-conceited philosophers, who can behold the state of society, viz., Toadyism, organised:—base Man-and-Mammon worship, instituted by command of law:—Snobbishness, in a word, perpetuated,—and mark the phenomenon calmly. And of these calm moralists, is there one, I wonder, whose heart would not throb with pleasure if he could be seen walking arm-in-arm with a couple of dukes down Pall Mall? No: it is impossible, in our condition of society, not to be sometimes a Snob.

On one side it encourages the commoner to be snobbishly mean, and the noble to be snobbishly arrogant. When a noble marchioness writes in her Travels about the hard necessity under which steam-boat travellers labour of being brought into contact "with all sorts and conditions of people:" implying that a fellowship with God's creatures is disagreeable to her Ladyship, who is their superior:—when, I say, the Marchioness of — writes in this fashion, we must consider that out of her natural heart it would have been impossible for any woman to have had such a sentiment; but that the habit of truckling and cringing, which all who surround her have adopted towards this beautiful and magnificent lady,—this proprietor of so many black and other diamonds,—has really induced her to believe that she is the superior of the world in general: and that people are not to associate with her except awfully at a distance. I recollect being once at the city of Grand Cairo, through which a European Royal Prince was passing India-wards. One night at the inn there was a great disturbance: a man had drowned himself in the well hard by: all the inhabitants of the hotel came bustling into the Court, and amongst others your humble servant, who asked of a certain young man the reason of the disturbance. How was I to know that this young gent was a prince? He had not his crown and sceptre on: he was dressed in a white jacket and felt hat: but he looked surprised at anybody speaking to him: answered an unintelligible monosyllable, and—*beckoned his aide-de-camp to come and speak to me*. It is our fault, not that of the great, that they should fancy themselves so far above us. If you *will* fling yourself under the wheels, Juggernaut will go over you, depend upon it; and if you and I, my dear friend, had Kotoo performed before us every day,—found people whenever we appeared grovelling in slavish adoration, we should drop into the airs of superiority quite naturally, and accept the greatness with which the world insisted upon endowing us.

Here is an instance, out of Lord L —'s Travels, of that calm, good-natured, undoubting way in which a great man accepts the homage of his inferiors. After making some profound and ingenious remarks about the town of Brussels, his lordship says:—"Staying some days at the Hôtel de Belle Vue—a greatly overrated establishment, and not nearly so comfortable as the Hôtel de France—I made acquaintance with Dr. L——, the physician of the Mission. He was desirous of doing the honour of the place to me, and he ordered for us a *dîner en gourmand* at the chief restaurateur's, maintaining it surpassed the Rocher at Paris. Six or eight partook of the entertainment, and we all agreed it was infinitely inferior to the Paris display, and much more extravagant. So much for the copy."

And so much for the gentleman who gave the dinner. Dr. L—— desirous to do his lordship "the honour of the place," feasts him with the best victuals money can procure—and my lord finds the entertainment extravagant and inferior. Extravagant! it was not extravagant to *him*.—Inferior! Mr. L—— did his best to satisfy those noble jaws, and my lord receives the entertainment, and dismisses the giver with a rebuke. It is like a three-tailed Pasha grumbling about an unsatisfactory backsheesh.

But how should it be otherwise in a country where Lordolatry is part of our creed, and where our children are brought up to respect the "Peerage" as the Englishman's second Bible?

CHAPTER IV

"The Court Circular," and its Influence on Snobs

Example is the best of precepts; so let us begin with a true and authentic story, showing how young aristocratic snobs are reared, and how early their Snobbishness may be made to bloom. A beautiful and fashionable lady—(pardon, gracious madam, that your story should be made public; but it is so moral that it ought to be known to the universal world)—told me that in her early youth she had a little acquaintance, who is now indeed a beautiful and fashionable lady too. In mentioning Miss Snobky, daughter of Sir Snobby Snobky, whose presentation at Court caused such a sensation, need I say more?

When Miss Snobky was so very young as to be in the nursery regions, and to walk of early mornings in St. James's Park, protected by a French governess and followed by a huge hirsute flunkey in the canary-coloured livery of the Snobkys, she used occasionally in these promenades to meet with young Lord Claude Lollipop, the Marquis of Sillabub's younger son. In the very height of the season, from some unexplained cause, the Snobkys suddenly determined upon leaving town. Miss Snobky spoke to her female friend and confidante. "What will poor Claude Lollipop say when he hears of my absence?" asked the-tender-hearted child.

"Oh, perhaps he won't hear of it," answers the confidante.

"My dear, he will read it in the papers," replied the dear little fashionable rogue of seven years old. She knew already her importance, and how all the world of England, how all the would-be-genteel people, how all the silver-fork worshippers, how all the tattle-mongers, how all the grocers' ladies, the tailors' ladies, the attorneys' and merchants' ladies, and the people living at Clapham and Brunswick Square,—who have no more chance of consorting with a Snobky than my beloved reader has of dining with the Emperor of China—yet watched

the movements of the Snobkys with interest, and were glad to know when they came to London and left it.

Here is the account of Miss Snobky's dress, and that of her mother, Lady Snobky, from the papers:—

"Habit de Cour, composed of a yellow nankeen illusion dress over a slip of rich pea-green corduroy, trimmed en tablier, with bouquets of Brussels sprouts: the body and sleeves handsomely trimmed with calimanco, and festooned with a pink train and white radishes. Head-dress, carrots and lappets.

"Costume de Cour, composed of a train of the most superb Pekin bandannas, elegantly trimmed with spangles, tinfoil, and red-tape, Bodice and under-dress of sky-blue velveteen, trimmed with bouffants and nœuds of bell-pulls. Stomacher, a muffin. Head-dress, a bird's nest, with a bird of paradise, over a rich brass knocker en ferronnière. This splendid costume, by Madame Crinoline, of Regent Street, was the object of universal admiration."

This is what you read. Oh, Mrs. Ellis! Oh, mothers, daughters, aunts, grandmothers of England, this is the sort of writing which is put in the newspapers for you! How can you help being the mothers, daughters, &c. of Snobs, so long as this balderdash is set before you?

You stuff the little rosy foot of a Chinese young lady of fashion into a slipper that is about the size of a salt-cruet, and keep the poor little toes there imprisoned and twisted up so long that the dwarfishness becomes irremediable. Later, the foot would not expand to the natural size were you to give her a washing-tub for a shoe, and for all her life she has little feet, and is a cripple. Oh, my dear Miss Wiggins, thank your stars that those beautiful feet of yours—though I declare when you walk they are so small as to be almost invisible—thank your stars that society never so practised upon them; but look around and see how many friends of ours in the highest circles have had their *brains* so prematurely and hopelessly pinched and distorted.

How can you expect that those poor creatures are to move naturally when the world and their parents have mutilated them so cruelly? As long as a *Court Circular* exists, how the deuce are people whose names are chronicled in it ever to believe themselves the equals of the cringing race which daily reads that abominable trash? I believe that ours is the only country in the world now where the *Court Circular* remains in full flourish—where you read, "This day his Royal Highness Prince Pattypan was taken an airing in his go-cart," "The Princess Pimminy was taken a drive, attended by her ladies of honour, and accompanied by her doll," &c. We laugh at the solemnity with which Saint Simon announces that *Sa Majestè se médicamente aujourd hui*. Under our very noses the same folly is daily going on. That wonderful and mysterious man, the author of the *Court Circular*, drops in with his budget at the newspaper offices every night. I once asked the editor of a paper to allow me to lie in wait and see him.

I am told that in a kingdom where there is a German King-Consort (Portugal it must be, for the Queen of that country married a German Prince, who is greatly admired and respected by the natives), whenever the Consort takes the diversion of shooting among the rabbit-warrens of Cintra, or the pheasant-preserves of Mafra, he has a keeper to load his guns, as a matter of course, and then they are handed to the nobleman, his equerry, and the nobleman hands them to the Prince, who blazes away—gives back the discharged gun to the nobleman, who gives it to the keeper, and so on. But the Prince *won't take the gun from the hands of the loader*.

As long as this unnatural and monstrous etiquette continues, Snobs there must be. The three persons engaged in this transaction are, for the time being, Snobs.

1. The keeper—the least Snob of all, because he is discharging

his daily duty; but he appears here as a Snob, that is to say, in a position of debasement, before another human being (the Prince), with whom he is only allowed to communicate through another party. A free Portuguese gamekeeper, who professes himself to be unworthy to communicate directly with any person, confesses himself to be a Snob.

2. The nobleman in waiting is a Snob. If it degrades the Prince to receive the gun from the gamekeeper, it is degrading to the nobleman in waiting to execute that service. He acts as a Snob towards the keeper, whom he keeps from communication with the Prince—a Snob towards the Prince, to whom he pays a degrading homage.

3. The King-Consort of Portugal is a Snob for insulting fellow-men in this way. There's no harm in his accepting the services of the keeper directly; but indirectly he insults the service performed, and the two servants who perform it; and therefore, I say, respectfully, is a most undoubted, though royal SN-B.

And then you read in the *Diario do Goberno*—"Yesterday, his Majesty the King took the diversion of shooting in the woods of Cintra, attended by Colonel the Honourable Whiskerando Sombrero. His Majesty returned to the Necessidades to lunch, at," &c. &c.

Oh! that *Court Circular*! once more, I exclaim. Down with the *Court Circular*—that engine and propagator of Snobbishness! I promise to subscribe for a year to any daily paper that shall come out without a *Court Circular*—were it the *Morning Herald* itself. When I read that trash, I rise in my wrath; I feel myself disloyal, a regicide, a member of the Calf's Head Club. The only *Court Circular* story which ever pleased me, was that of the King of Spain, who in great part was roasted, because there was not time for the Prime Minister to command the Lord Chamberlain to desire the Grand Gold Stick to order the first page in waiting to bid the chief of the flunkeys to request the Housemaid of Honour to bring up a pail of water to put his Majesty out.

I am like the Pasha of three tails, to whom the Sultan sends *his Court Circular*, the bowstring.

It *chokes* me. May its usage be abolished for ever.

CHAPTER V

What Snobs Admire

Now let us consider how difficult it is even for great men to escape from being Snobs. It is very well for the reader, whose fine feelings are disgusted by the assertion that Kings, Princes, Lords, are Snobs, to say, "You are confessedly a Snob yourself. In professing to depict Snobs, it is only your own ugly mug which you are copying with a Narcissus-like conceit and fatuity." But I shall pardon this explosion of ill-temper on the part of my constant reader, reflecting upon the misfortune of his birth and country. It is impossible for *any* Briton, perhaps, not to be a Snob in some degree. If people can be convinced of this fact, an immense point is gained, surely. If I have pointed out the disease, let us hope that other scientific characters may discover the remedy.

If you, who are a person of the middle ranks of life, are a Snob,—you whom nobody flatters particularly; you who have no toadies; you whom no cringing flunkeys or shopmen bow out of doors; you whom the policeman tells to move on; you who are jostled in the crowd of this world, and amongst the Snobs our brethren: consider how much harder it is for a man to escape who has not your advantages, and is all his life long subject to adulation; the butt of meanness; consider how difficult it is for the Snobs' idol not to be a Snob.

As I was discoursing with my friend Eugenio in this impressive way, Lord Buckram passed us, the son of the Marquis of Bagwig, and knocked at the door of the family mansion in Red Lion Square. His noble father and mother occupied, as everybody knows, distinguished posts in the Courts of late Sovereigns. The Marquis was Lord of the Pantry, and her Ladyship, Lady of the Powder Closet to Queen Charlotte. Buck (as I call him, for we are very familiar) gave me a nod as he passed, and I proceeded to show Eugenio how it was impossible that this nobleman should not be one of ourselves, having been practised upon by Snobs all his life.

His parents resolved to give him a public education, and sent him to school at the earliest possible period. The Reverend Otto Rose, D.D., Principal of the Preparatory Academy for young noblemen and gentlemen, Richmond Lodge, took this little Lord in hand, and fell down and worshipped him. He always introduced him to fathers and mothers who came to visit their children at the school. He referred with pride and pleasure to the most noble the Marquis of Bagwig, as one of the kind friends and patrons of his Seminary. He made Lord Buckram a bait for such a multiplicity of pupils, that a new wing was built to Richmond Lodge, and thirty-five new little white dimity beds were added to the establishment. Mrs. Rose used to take out the little Lord in the one-horse chaise with her when she paid visits, until the Rector's lady and the Surgeon's wife almost died with envy. His own son and Lord Buckram having been discovered robbing an orchard together, the Doctor flogged his own flesh and blood most unmercifully for leading the young Lord astray. He parted from him with tears. There was always a letter directed to the Most Noble the Marquis of Bagwig, on the Doctor's study table, when any visitors were received by him.

At Eton, a great deal of Snobbishness was thrashed out of Lord Buckram, and he was birched with perfect impartiality. Even there, however, a select band of sucking tuft-hunters followed him. Young Crœsus lent him three-and-twenty bran new sovereigns out of his father's bank. Young Snaily did his exercises for him, and tried "to know him at home;" but Young Bull licked him in a fight of fifty-five minutes, and he was caned several times with great advantage for not sufficiently polishing his master Smith's shoes. Boys are not *all* toadies in the morning of life.

But when he went to the University, crowds of toadies sprawled over him. The tutors toadied him. The fellows in hall paid him great clumsy compliments. The Dean never remarked his absence from Chapel, or heard any noise issuing from his rooms. A number of respectable young fellows, (it is among the respectable, the Baker Street class, that Snobbishness flourishes, more than among any set of people in England)—a number of these clung to him like leeches. There was no end now to Crœsus's loans of money; and Buckram couldn't ride out with the hounds, but Snaily (a timid creature by nature) was in the field, and would take any leap at which his friend chose to ride. Young Rose came up to the same College, having been kept back for that express purpose by his father. He spent a quarter's allowance in giving Buckram a single dinner; but he knew there was always pardon for him for extravagance in such a cause; and a ten-pound note always came to him from home when he mentioned Buckram's name in a letter. What wild visions entered the brains of Mrs. Podge and Miss Podge, the wife and daughter of the Principal of Lord Buckram's College, I don't know, but that reverend old gentleman was too profound a flunkey by nature ever for one minute to think that a child of his could marry a nobleman. He therefore hastened on his daughter's union with Professor Crab.

When Lord Buckram, after taking his honorary degree, (for Alma Mater is a Snob, too, and truckles to a Lord like the rest,)—when Lord Buckram went abroad to finish his education, you all know what dangers he ran, and what numbers of caps were set at him. Lady Leach and her daughters followed him from Paris to Rome, and from Rome to Baden-Baden; Miss Leggitt burst into tears before his face when he announced his determination to quit Naples, and fainted on the neck of her mamma; Captain Macdragon, of Macdragonstown, county Tipperary, called upon him to "explene his intintions with respect to his sisther, Miss Amalia Macdragon, of Macdragonstown," and proposed to shoot him unless he married that spotless and beautiful young creature, who was afterwards led to the altar by Mr. Muff, at Cheltenham. If perseverance and forty thousand pounds down could have tempted him, Miss Lydia Crœsus would certainly have been

Lady Buckram. Count Towrowski was glad to take her with half the money, as all the genteel world knows.

And now, perhaps, the reader is anxious to know what sort of a man this is who wounded so many ladies' hearts, and who has been such a prodigious favourite with men. If we were to describe him it would be personal. Besides, it really does not matter in the least what sort of a man he is, or what his personal qualities are.

Suppose he is a young nobleman of a literary turn, and that he published poems ever so foolish and feeble, the Snobs would purchase thousands of his volumes: the publishers (who refused my Passion-Flowers and my grand Epic at any price) would give him his own. Suppose he is a nobleman of a jovial turn, and has a fancy for wrenching off knockers, frequenting gin-shops, and half murdering policemen: the public will sympathize good-naturedly with his amusements, and say he is a hearty, honest fellow. Suppose he is fond of play and the turf, and has a fancy to be a blackleg, and occasionally condescends to pluck a pigeon at cards; the public will pardon him, and many honest people will court him, as they would court a housebreaker if he happened to be a Lord. Suppose he is an idiot; yet, by the glorious constitution, he is good enough to governs *us*. Suppose he is an honest, high-minded gentleman; so much the better for himself. But he may be an ass, and yet respected; or a ruffian, and yet be exceedingly popular; or a rogue, and yet excuses will be found for him. Snobs will still worship him. Male Snobs will do him honour, the females look kindly upon him, however hideous he may be.

CHAPTER VI

On Some Respectable Snobs

Having received a great deal of obloquy for dragging monarchs, princes, and the respected nobility into the Snob category, I trust to please everybody in the present chapter, by stating my firm opinion that it is among the *respectable* classes of this vast and happy empire that the greatest profusion of Snobs is to be found. I pace down my beloved Baker Street, (I am engaged on a life of Baker, founder of this celebrated street,) I walk in Harley Street (where every other house has a hatchment), Wimpole Street, that is as cheerful as the Catacombs—a dingy Mausoleum of the genteel:—I rove round Regent's Park, where the plaster is patching off the house walls; where Methodist preachers are holding forth to three little children in the green inclosures, and puffy valetudinarians are cantering in the solitary mud:—I thread the doubtful zig-zags of May Fair, where Mrs. Kitty Lorimer's brougham may be seen drawn up next door to old Lady Lollipop's belozenged family coach;—I roam through Belgravia, that pale and polite district, where all the inhabitants look prim and correct, and the mansions are painted a faint whitey-brown: I lose myself in the new squares and terraces of the brilliant bran-new Bayswater-and-Tyburn-Junction line; and in one and all of these districts the same truth comes across me. I stop before any house at hazard, and say, "O house, you are inhabited—O knocker, you are knocked at—O undressed flunkey, sunning your lazy calves as you lean against the iron railings, you are paid—by Snobs." It is a tremendous thought that; and it is almost sufficient to drive a benevolent mind to madness to think that perhaps there is not one in ten of those houses where the "Peerage" does not lie on the drawing-room table. Considering the harm that foolish lying book does, I would have all the copies of it burned, as the barber burned all Quixote's books of humbugging chivalry.

Look at this grand house in the middle of the square. The Earl of Loughcorrib lives there! he has fifty thousand a year. A *déjeûner dansant* given at his house last week cost, who knows how much? The mere flowers for the room and bouquets for the ladies cost four hundred pounds. That man in drab trousers, coming crying down the steps, is a dun! Lord Loughcorrib has ruined him, and won't see him: that is, his lordship is peeping through the blind of his study at him now. Go thy ways, Loughcorrib, thou art a Snob, a heartless pretender, a hypocrite of hospitality; a rogue who passes forged notes upon society;—but I am growing too eloquent.

You see that fine house, No. 23, where a butcher's boy is ringing the area-bell. He has three mutton-chops in his tray. They are for the dinner of a very different and very respectable family; for Lady Susan Scraper, and her daughters, Miss Scraper and Miss Emily Scraper. The domestics, luckily for them, are on board wages—two huge footmen in light blue and canary, a fat steady coachman who is a Methodist, and a butler who would never have stayed in the family but that he was orderly to General Scraper when the General distinguished himself at Walcheren. His widow sent his portrait to the United Service Club, and it is hung up in one of the back dressing-closets there. He is represented at a parlour window with red curtains; in the distance is a whirlwind, in which cannon are firing off; and he is pointing to a chart, on which are written the words "Walcheren, Tobago."

Lady Susan is, as everybody knows by referring to the "British Bible," a daughter of the great and good Earl Bagwig before mentioned. She thinks everything belonging to her the greatest and best in the world. The first of men naturally are the Buckrams, her own race: then follow in rank the Scrapers. The General was the greatest general: his eldest son, Scraper Buckram Scraper, is at present the greatest and best; his second son the next greatest and best; and herself the paragon of women.

Indeed, she is a most respectable and honourable lady. She

goes to church of course: she would fancy the Church in danger if she did not. She subscribes to the church and parish charities; and is a directress of many meritorious charitable institutions—of Queen Charlotte's Lying-in Hospital, the Washerwomen's Asylum, the British Drummers' Daughters' Home, &c. &c. She is a model of a matron.

The tradesman never lived who could say that his bill was not paid on the quarter-day. The beggars of her neighbourhood avoid her like a pestilence; for while she walks out, protected by John, that domestic has always two or three mendicity tickets ready for deserving objects. Ten guineas a year will pay all her charities. There is no respectable lady in all London who gets her name more often printed for such a sum of money.

Those three mutton-chops which you see entering at the kitchen-door will be served on the family-plate at seven o'clock this evening, the huge footman being present, and the butler in black, and the crest and coat-of-arms of the Scrapers blazing everywhere. I pity Miss Emily Scraper—she is still young— young and hungry. Is it a fact that she spends her pocket-money in buns? Malicious tongues say so; but she has very little to spare for buns, the poor little hungry soul! For the fact is, that when the footmen, and the ladies'-maids, and the fat coach-horses, which are jobbed, and the six dinner-parties in the season, and the two great solemn evening-parties, and the rent of the big house, and the journey to an English or foreign watering-place for the autumn, are paid, my lady's income has dwindled away to a very small sum, and she is as poor as you or I.

You would not think it when you saw her big carriage rattling up to the drawing-room, and caught a glimpse of her plumes, lappets, and diamonds, waving over her ladyship's sandy hair and majestical hooked nose;—you would not think it when you hear "Lady Susan Scraper's carriage" bawled out at midnight so as to disturb all Belgravia:—you would not think it when she comes rustling into church, the obsequious John behind with the bag of Prayer-books. Is it possible, you would say, that so grand and awful a personage as that can be hard-up for money? Alas! so it is.

She never heard such a word as Snob, I will engage, in this wicked and vulgar world. And, oh stars and garters! how she would start if she heard that she—she, as solemn as Minerva—she, as chaste as Diana (without that heathen goddess's unladylike propensity for field-sports)—that she too was a Snob!

A Snob she is, as long as she sets that prodigious value upon herself, upon her name, upon her outward appearance, and indulges in that intolerable pomposity; as long as she goes parading abroad, like Solomon in all his glory; as long as she goes to bed—as I believe she does—with a turban and a bird of paradise in it, and a court train to her night-gown; as long as she is so insufferably virtuous and condescending; as long as she does not cut at least one of those footmen down into mutton-chops for the benefit of the young ladies.

I had my notions of her from my old schoolfellow,—her son Sydney Scraper—a Chancery barrister without any practice—the most placid, polite, and genteel of Snobs, who never exceeded his allowance of two hundred a year, and who may be seen any evening at the "Oxford and Cambridge Club," simpering over the *Quarterly Review*, in the blameless enjoyment of his half-pint of port.

CHAPTER VII

On Some Respectable Snobs

Look at the next house to Lady Susan Scraper's. The first mansion with the awning over the door: that canopy will be let down this evening for the comfort of the friends of Sir Alured and Lady S. de Mogyns, whose parties are so much admired by the public, and the givers themselves.

Peach-coloured liveries laced with silver, and pea-green plush inexpressibles, render the De Mogyns' flunkeys the pride of the ring when they appear in Hyde Park, where Lady de Mogyns, as she sits upon her satin cushions, with her dwarf spaniel in her arms, only bows to the very selectest of the genteel. Times are altered now with Mary Anne, or, as she calls herself, Marian de Mogyns.

She was the daughter of Captain Flack of the Rathdrum Fencibles, who crossed with his regiment over from Ireland to Caermarthenshire ever so many years ago, and defended Wales from the Corsican invader. The Rathdrums were quartered at Pontydwdlm, where Marian wooed and won her De Mogyns, a young banker in the place. His attentions to Miss Flack at a race ball were such that her father said De Mogyns must either die on the field of honour, or become his son-in-law. He preferred marriage. His name was Muggins then, and his father—a flourishing banker, army-contractor, smuggler, and general jobber—almost disinherited him on account of this connection. There is a story that Muggins the Elder was made a baronet for having lent money to a R-y-l p-rs-n-ge. I do not believe it. The R-y-l Family always paid their debts, from the Prince of Wales downwards.

Howbeit, to his life's end he remained simple Sir Thomas Muggins, representing Pontydwdlm in Parliament for many years after the war. The old banker died in course of time, and, to use the affectionate phrase common on such occasions, "cut up" prodigiously well. His son, Alfred Smith Mogyns, succeeded to the main portion of his wealth, and to his titles and the bloody hand of his scutcheon. It was not for many years after that he appeared as Sir Alured Mogyns Smyth de Mogyns, with a genealogy found out for him by the Editor of "Fluke's Peerage," and which appears as follows in that work:—

"De Mogyns.—Sir Alured Mogyns Smyth, 2nd Baronet. This gentleman is a representative of one of the most ancient families of Wales, who trace their descent until it is lost in the mists of antiquity. A genealogical tree beginning with Shem is in the possession of the family, and is stated by a legend of many thousand years' date to have been drawn on papyrus by a grandson of the patriarch himself. Be this as it may, there can be no doubt of the immense antiquity of the race of Mogyns.

"In the time of Boadicea, Hogyn Mogyn, of the hundred Beeves, was a suitor and a rival of Caractacus for the hand of that Princess. He was a person gigantic in stature, and was slain by Suetonius in the battle which terminated the liberties of Britain. From him descended directly the Princes of Pontydwdlm, Mogyn of the Golden Harp (see the Mabinogion of Lady Charlotte Guest), Bogyn-Merodac-ap-Mogyn (the black fiend son of Mogyn), and a long list of bards and warriors, celebrated both in Wales and Armorica. The independent Princes of Mogyn long held out against the ruthless Kings of England, until finally Gam Mogyns made his submission to Prince Henry, son of Henry IV., and under the name of Sir David Gam de Mogyns, was distinguished at the battle of Agincourt. From him the present Baronet is descended. (And here the descent follows in order until it comes to) Thomas Muggins, first Baronet of Pontydwdlm Castle, for 23 years Member of Parliament for that borough, who had issue, Alured Mogyns Smyth, the present Baronet, who married Marian, daughter of the late General P. Flack, of Ballyflack, in the Kingdom of Ireland, of the Counts Flack of the H. R. Empire. Sir Alured has issue, Alured Caradoc, born 1819, Marian, 1811, Blanche Adeliza, Emily Doria, Adelaide Obleans, Katinka Rostopchin, Patrick Flack, died 1809.

"Arms—a mullion garbled, gules on a saltire reversed of the second. Crest—a tom-tit rampant regardant. Motto—*Ung Roy ung Mogyns.*"

It was long before Lady de Mogyns shone as a star in the fashionable world. At first, poor Muggins was in the hands of the Flacks, the Clancys, the Tooles, the Shanahans, his wife's Irish relations; and whilst he was yet but heir-apparent, his house overflowed with claret and the national nectar, for the benefit of his Hibernian relatives. Tom Tufto absolutely left the street in which they lived in London, because he said "it was infected with such a confounded smell of whisky from the house of those *Iwish* people."

It was abroad that they learned to be genteel. They pushed into all foreign courts, and elbowed their way into the halls of Ambassadors. They pounced upon the stray nobility, and seized young lords travelling with their bear-leaders. They gave parties at Naples, Rome, and Paris. They got a Royal Prince to attend their *soirées* at the latter place, and it was here that they first appeared under the name of De Mogyns, which they bear with such splendour to this day.

All sorts of stories are told of the desperate efforts made by the indomitable Lady de Mogyns to gain the place she now occupies, and those of my beloved readers who live in middle life, and are unacquainted with the frantic struggles, the wicked feuds, the intrigues, cabals, and disappointments which, as I am given to understand, reign in the fashionable world, may bless their stars that they at least are not *fashionable* Snobs. The intrigues set afoot by the De Mogyns to get the Duchess of Buckskin to her parties, would strike a Talleyrand with admiration. She had a brain fever after being disappointed of an invitation to Lady Aldermanbury's *thé dansant*, and would have committed suicide but for a ball at Windsor. I have the following story from my noble friend Lady Clapperclaw herself,—Lady Kathleen O'Shaughnessy that was, and daughter of the Earl of Turfanthunder:—

"When that ojous disguised Irishwoman, Lady Muggins, was struggling to take her place in the world, and was bringing out her hidjous daughter Blanche," said old Lady Clapperclaw— "(Marian has a hump-back and doesn't show, but she's the only lady in the family)—when that wretched Polly Muggins was bringing out Blanche, with her radish of a nose, and her carrots of ringlets, and her turnip for a face, she was most anxious—as her father had been a cow-boy on my father's land—to be patronized by us, and asked me point-blank, in the midst of a silence at Count Volauvent's, the French Ambassador's dinner, why I had not sent her a card for my ball?

"'Because my rooms are already too full, and your ladyship would be crowded inconveniently,' says I; indeed she takes up as much room as an elephant: besides I wouldn't have her, and that was flat.

"I thought my answer was a settler to her: but the next day she comes weeping to my arms—'Dear Lady Clapperclaw,' says she, 'it's not for *me*; I ask it for my blessed Blanche! a young creature in her first season, and not at your ball! My tender child will pine and die of vexation. *I* don't want to come. *I* will stay at home to nurse Sir Alured in the gout. Mrs. Bolster is going, I know; she will be Blanche's chaperon.'

"'You wouldn't subscribe for the Rathdrum blanket and potato fund; you, who come out of the parish,' says I, 'and whose grandfather, honest man, kept cows there.'

"'Will twenty guineas be enough, dearest Lady Clapperclaw?'

"'Twenty guineas is sufficient,' says I, and she paid them; so I said, 'Blanche may come, but not you, mind:' and she left me with a world of thanks.

"Would you believe it?—when my ball came, the horrid woman made her appearance with her daughter! 'Didn't I tell you not to come,' said I, in a mighty passion. 'What would the world have said?' cries my Lady Muggins: 'my carriage is gone for Sir Alured to the Club; let me stay only ten minutes, dearest Lady Clapperclaw.'

"'Well, as you are here, madam, you may stay and get your

supper,' I answered, and so left her, and never spoke a word more to her all night.

"And now," screamed out old Lady Clapperclaw, clapping her hands, and speaking with more brogue than ever, "what do you think, after all my kindness to her, the wicked, vulgar, odious, impudent upstart of a cowboy's granddaughter has done?—she cut me yesterday in Hy' Park, and hasn't sent me a ticket for her ball tonight, though they say Prince George is to be there."

Yes, such is the fact. In the race of fashion the resolute and active De Mogyns has passed the poor old Clapperclaw. Her progress in gentility may be traced by the sets of friends whom she has courted, and made, and cut, and left behind her. She has struggled so gallantly for polite reputation that she has won it: pitilessly kicking down the ladder as she advanced degree by degree.

Her Irish relations were first sacrificed; she made her father dine in the steward's room, to his perfect contentment: and would send Sir Alured thither likewise, but that he is a peg on which she hopes to hang her future honours; and is, after all, paymaster of her daughters' fortunes. He is meek and content. He has been so long a gentleman that he is used to it, and acts the part of governor very well. In the day-time he goes from the "Union" to "Arthur's," and from "Arthur's" to the "Union." He is a dead hand at piquet, and loses a very comfortable maintenance to some young fellows, at whist, at the Travellers'."

His son has taken his father's seat in Parliament, and has, of course, joined Young England. He is the only man in the country who believes in the De Mogynses, and sighs for the days when a De Mogyns led the van of battle. He has written a little volume of spoony puny poems. He wears a lock of the hair of Laud, the Confessor and Martyr, and fainted when he kissed the Pope's toe at Rome. He sleeps in white kid-gloves, and commits dangerous excesses upon green tea.

CHAPTER VIII

Great City Snobs

There is no disguising the fact that this series of papers is making a prodigious sensation among all classes in this Empire. Notes of admiration (!), of interrogation (?), of remonstrance, approval, or abuse, come pouring into *Mr. Punch's* box. We have been called to task for betraying the secrets of three different families of De Mogyns; no less than four Lady Susan Scrapers have been discovered; and young gentlemen are quite shy of ordering half-a-pint of port and simpering over the *Quarterly Review* at the Club, lest they should be mistaken for Sydney Scraper, Esq. "What *can* be your antipathy to Baker Street?" asks some fair remonstrant, evidently writing from that quarter.

"Why only attack the aristocratic Snobs?" says one estimable correspondent: "are not the snobbish Snobs to have their turn?"—"Pitch into the University Snobs!" writes an indignant gentleman (who spells *elegant* with two *l*'s).—"Show up the Clerical Snob," suggests another.—"Being at 'Meurice's Hotel,' Paris, some time since," some wag hints, "I saw Lord B. leaning out of the window with his boots in his hand, and bawling out, '*Garçon, cirez-moi ces bottes.*' Oughtn't he to be brought in among the Snobs?"

No; far from it. If his lordship's boots are dirty, it is because he is Lord B., and walks. There is nothing snobbish in having only one pair of boots, or a favourite pair; and certainly nothing snobbish in desiring to have them cleaned. Lord B., in so doing, performed a perfectly natural and gentlemanlike action; for which I am so pleased with him that I should like to have him designed in a favourable and elegant attitude, and put at the head of this Chapter in the place of honour. No, we are not personal in these candid remarks. As Phidias took the pick of a score of beauties before he completed a Venus, so have we to examine, perhaps, a thousand Snobs, before one is expressed upon paper.

Great City Snobs are the next in the hierarchy, and ought to be considered. But here is a difficulty. The great City Snob is commonly most difficult of access. Unless you are a capitalist, you cannot visit him in the recesses of his bank parlour in Lombard Street. Unless you are a sprig of nobility there is little hope of seeing him at home. In a great City Snob firm there is generally one partner whose name is down for charities, and who frequents Exeter Hall; you may catch a glimpse of another (a scientific City Snob) at my Lord N—'s *soirées*, or the lectures of the London Institution; of a third (a City Snob of taste) at picture-auctions, at private views of exhibitions, or at the Opera or the Philharmonic. But intimacy is impossible, in most cases, with this grave, pompous, and awful being.

A mere gentleman may hope to sit at almost anybody's table—to take his place at my lord duke's in the country—to dance a quadrille at Buckingham Palace itself—(beloved Lady Wilhelmina Waggle-wiggle! do you recollect the sensation we made at the ball of our late adored Sovereign Queen Caroline, at Brandenburg House, Hammersmith?) but the City Snob's doors are, for the most part, closed to him; and hence all that one knows of this great class is mostly from hearsay.

In other countries of Europe, the Banking Snob is more expansive and communicative than with us, and receives all the world into his circle. For instance, everybody knows the princely hospitalities of the Scharlaschild family at Paris, Naples, Frankfort, &c. They entertain all the world, even the poor, at their *fêtes*. Prince Polonia, at Rome, and his brother, the Duke of Strachino, are also remarkable for their hospitalities. I like the spirit of the first-named nobleman. Titles not costing much in the Roman territory, he has had the head clerk of the banking-house made a Marquis, and his Lordship will screw a *bajocco* out of you in exchange as dexterously as any commoner could do. It is a comfort to be able to gratify such grandees with a farthing or two; it makes the poorest man feel that he can do good. The Polonias have intermarried with the greatest and most ancient families of Rome, and you see their heraldic cognizance (a mushroom *or* on an azure field) quartered in a hundred places in the city, with the arms of the Colonnas and Dorias.

Our City Snobs have the same mania for aristocratic marriages. I like to see such. I am of a savage and envious nature,—I like to see these two humbugs, which, dividing as they do the social empire of this kingdom between them, hate each other naturally, making truce and uniting, for the sordid interests of either. I like to see an old aristocrat, swelling with pride of race, the descendant of illustrious Norman robbers, whose blood has been pure for centuries, and who looks down upon common Englishmen as a free-born American does on a nigger,—I like to see old Stiffneck obliged to bow down his head and swallow his infernal pride, and drink the cup of humiliation poured out by Pump and Aldgate's butler. "Pump and Aldgate," says he, "your grandfather was a bricklayer, and his hod is still kept in the bank. Your pedigree begins in a workhouse; mine can be dated from all the royal palaces of Europe. I came over with the Conqueror; I am own cousin to Charles Martel, Orlando Furioso, Philip Augustus, Peter the Cruel, and Frederick Barbarossa. I quarter the Royal Arms of Brentford in my coat. I despise you, but I want money; and I will sell you my beloved daughter, Blanche Stiffneck, for a hundred thousand pounds, to pay off my mortgages. Let your son marry her, and she shall become Lady Blanche Pump and Aldgate."

Old Pump and Aldgate clutches at the bargain. And a comfortable thing it is to think that birth can be bought for money. So you learn to value it. Why should we, who don't possess it, set a higher store on it than those who do! Perhaps the best use of that book, the "Peerage," is to look down the list, and see how many have bought and sold birth,—how poor sprigs of nobility somehow sell themselves to rich City Snobs' daughters, how rich City Snobs purchase noble ladies—and so to admire the double baseness of the bargain.

Old Pump and Aldgate buys the article and pays the money. The sale of the girl's person is blessed by a Bishop at St. George's, Hanover Square, and next year you read, "At Roehampton, on Saturday, the Lady Blanche Pump, of a son and heir."

After this interesting event, some old acquaintance who saw young Pump in the parlour at the bank in the City, said to him, familiarly, "How's your wife, Pump my boy?"

Mr. Pump looked exceedingly puzzled and disgusted, and, after a pause, said, "*Lady Blanche Pump* is pretty well, I thank you."

"*Oh, I thought she was your wife!*" said the familiar brute, Snooks, wishing him good-bye; and ten minutes after, the story was all over the Stock Exchange, where it is told, when young Pump appears, to this very day.

We can imagine the weary life this poor Pump, this martyr to Mammon, is compelled to undergo. Fancy the domestic enjoyments of a man who has a wife who scorns him; who cannot see his own friends in his own house; who having deserted the middle rank of life, is not yet admitted to the higher; but who is resigned to rebuffs and delay and humiliation, contented to think that his son will be more fortunate.

It used to be the custom of some very old-fashioned clubs in this city, when a gentleman asked for change for a guinea, always to bring it to him in *washed silver*; that which had passed immediately out of the hands of the vulgar being considered "as too coarse to soil a gentleman's fingers." So, when the City Snob's money has been washed during a generation or so; has been washed into estates, and woods, and castles, and town-mansions, it is allowed to pass current as real aristocratic coin. Old Pump sweeps a shop, runs of messages, becomes a confidential clerk and partner. Pump the Second becomes chief of the house, spins more and more money, marries his son to an Earl's daughter. Pump Tertius goes on with the bank; but his chief business in life is to become the father of Pump Quartus, who comes out a full-blown aristocrat, and takes his seat as Baron Pumpington, and his race rules hereditarily over this nation of Snobs.

CHAPTER IX

On Some Military Snobs

As no society in the world is more agreeable than that of well-bred and well-informed military gentlemen, so, likewise, none is more insufferable than that of Military Snobs. They are to be found of all grades, from the General Officer, whose padded old breast twinkles over with a score of stars, clasps, and decorations, to the budding cornet, who is shaving for a beard, and has just been appointed to the Saxe-Coburg Lancers.

I have always admired that dispensation of rank in our country, which sets up this last-named little creature (who was flogged only last week because he could not spell) to command great whiskered warriors, who have faced all dangers of climate and battle; which, because he has money to lodge at the agent's, will place him over the heads of men who have a thousand times more experience and desert; and, which, in the course of time, will bring him all the honours of his profession, when the veteran soldier he commanded has got no other reward for his bravery than a berth in Chelsea Hospital, and the veteran officer he superseded has slunk into shabby retirement, and ends his disappointed life on a threadbare half-pay.

When I read in the *Gazette* such announcements as "Lieutenant and Captain Grig, from the Bombardier Guards, to be Captain, vice Grizzle, who retires," I know what becomes of the Peninsular Grizzle; I follow him in spirit to the humble country town, where he takes up his quarters, and occupies himself with the most desperate attempts to live like a gentleman, on the stipend of half a tailor's foreman; and I picture to myself little Grig rising from rank to rank, skipping from one regiment to another, with an increased grade in each, avoiding disagreeable foreign service, and ranking as a colonel at thirty;—all because he has money, and Lord Grigsby is his father, who had the same luck before him. Grig must blush at first to give his orders to old men in every way his betters. And as it is very difficult for a spoiled child to escape being selfish and arrogant, so it is a very hard task indeed for this spoiled child of fortune not to be a Snob.

It must have often been a matter of wonder to the candid reader, that the army, the most enormous job of all our political institutions, should yet work so well in the field; and we must cheerfully give Grig, and his like, the credit for courage which they display whenever occasion calls for it. The Duke's dandy regiments fought as well as any (they said better than any, but that is absurd). The great Duke himself was a dandy once, and jobbed on, as Marlborough did before him. But this only proves that dandies are brave as well as other Britons—as all Britons. Let us concede that the high-born Grig rode into the entrenchments at Sobraon as gallantly as Corporal Wallop, the ex-ploughboy.

The times of war are more favourable to him than the periods of peace. Think of Grig's life in the Bombardier Guards, or the Jackboot Guards; his marches from Windsor to London, from London to Windsor, from Knightsbridge to Regent's Park; the idiotic services he has to perform, which consist in inspecting the pipeclay of his company, or the horses in the stable, or bellowing out "Shoulder humps! Carry humps!" all which duties the very smallest intellect that ever belonged to mortal man would suffice to comprehend. The professional duties of a footman are quite as difficult and various. The red-jackets who hold gentlemen's horses in St. James's Street could do the work just as well as those vacuous, good-natured gentlemanlike, rickety little lieutenants, who may be seen sauntering about Pall Mall, in high-heeled little boots, or rallying round the standard of their regiment in the Palace Court, at eleven o'clock, when the band plays. Did the beloved reader ever see one of the young fellows staggering under the flag, or, above all, going through the operation of saluting it? It is worth a walk to the Palace to witness that magnificent piece of tomfoolery.

I have had the honour of meeting once or twice an old gentleman, whom I look upon to be a specimen of army-training, and who has served in crack regiments, or commanded them, all his life. I allude to Lieutenant-General the Honourable Sir George Granby Tufto, K.C.B., K.T.S., K.H., K.S.W., &c. &c. His manners are irreproachable generally; in society he is a perfect gentleman, and a most thorough Snob.

A man can't help being a fool, be he ever so old, and Sir George is a greater ass at sixty-eight than he was when he first entered the army at fifteen. He distinguished himself everywhere; his name is mentioned with praise in a score of Gazettes: he is the man, in fact, whose padded breast, twinkling over with innumerable decorations, has already been introduced to the reader. It is difficult to say what virtues this prosperous gentleman possesses. He never read a book in his life, and, with his purple, old gouty fingers, still writes a schoolboy hand. He has reached old age and grey hairs without being the least venerable. He dresses like an outrageously young man to the present moment, and laces and pads his old carcass as if he were still handsome George Tufto of 1800. He is selfish, brutal, passionate, and a glutton. It is curious to mark him at table, and see him heaving in his waistband, his little bloodshot eyes gloating over his meal. He swears considerably in his talk, and tells filthy garrison stories after dinner. On account of his rank and his services, people pay the bestarred and betitled old brute a sort of reverence; and he looks down upon you and me, and exhibits his contempt for us, with a stupid and artless candour which is quite amusing to watch. Perhaps, had he been bred to another profession, he would not have been the disreputable old creature he now is. But what other? He was fit for none; too incorrigibly idle and dull for any trade but this, in which he has distinguished himself publicly as a good and gallant officer, and privately for riding races, drinking port, fighting duels, and seducing women. He believes himself to be one of the most honourable and deserving beings in the world. About

Waterloo Place, of afternoons, you may see him tottering in his varnished boots, and leering under the bonnets of the women who pass by. When he dies of apoplexy, *The Times* will have a quarter of a column about his services and battles—four lines of print will be wanted to describe his titles and orders alone—and the earth will cover one of the wickedest and dullest old wretches that ever strutted over it.

Lest it should be imagined that I am of so obstinate a misanthropic nature as to be satisfied with nothing, I beg (for the comfort of the forces) to state my belief that the army is not composed of such persons as the above. He has only been selected for the study of civilians and the military, as a specimen of a prosperous and bloated army Snob. No: when epaulets are not sold; when corporal punishments are abolished, and Corporal Smith has a chance to have his gallantry rewarded as well as that of Lieutenant Grig; when there is no such rank as ensign and lieutenant (the existence of which rank is an absurd anomaly, and an insult upon all the rest of the army), and should there be no war, I should not be disinclined to be a major-general myself.

I have a little sheaf of Army Snobs in my portfolio, but shall pause in my attack upon the forces till next week.

CHAPTER X

Military Snobs

Walking in the Park yesterday with my young friend Tagg, and discoursing with him upon the next number of the Snob, at the very nick of time who should pass us but two very good specimens of Military Snobs,—the Sporting Military Snob, Capt. Rag, and the "larking" or raffish Military Snob, Ensign Famish. Indeed you are fully sure to meet them lounging on horseback, about five o'clock, under the trees by the Serpentine, examining critically the inmates of the flashy broughams which parade up and down "the Lady's Mile."

Tagg and Rag are very well acquainted, and so the former, with that candour inseparable from intimate friendship, told me his dear friend's history. Captain Rag is a small dapper north-country man. He went when quite a boy into a crack light-cavalry regiment, and by the time he got his troop, had cheated all his brother officers so completely, selling them lame horses for sound ones, and winning their money by all manner of strange and ingenious contrivances, that his Colonel advised him to retire; which he did without much reluctance, accommodating a youngster, who had just entered the regiment, with a glandered charger at an uncommonly stiff figure.

He has since devoted his time to billiards, steeple-chasing, and the turf. His head-quarters are "Rummer's," in Conduit Street, where he keeps his kit; but he is ever on the move in the exercise of his vocation as a gentleman-jockey and gentleman-leg.

According to *Bell's Life*, he is an invariable attendant at all races, and an actor in most of them. He rode the winner at Leamington; he was left for dead in a ditch a fortnight ago at Harrow; and yet there he was, last week, at the Croix de Berny, pale and determined as ever, astonishing the *badauds* of Paris by the elegance of his seat and the neatness of his rig, as he took a preliminary gallop on that vicious brute "The Disowned," before starting for "the French Grand National."

He is a regular attendant at the Corner, where he compiles a limited but comfortable libretto. During the season he rides often in the Park, mounted on a clever, well-bred pony. He is to be seen escorting that celebrated horsewoman, Fanny Highflyer, or in confidential converse with Lord Thimblerig, the eminent handicapper.

He carefully avoids decent society, and would rather dine off a steak at the "One Tun" with Sam Snaffle the jockey, Captain O'Rourke, and two or three other notorious turf robbers, than with the choicest company in London. He likes to announce at "Rummer's" that he is going to run down and spend his Saturday and Sunday in a friendly way with Hocus, the leg, at his little box near Epsom: where, if report speak true, many "rummish plants" are concocted.

He does not play billiards often, and never in public: but when he does play, he always contrives to get hold of a good flat, and never leaves him till he has done him uncommonly brown. He has lately been playing a good deal with Famish.

When he makes his appearance in the drawing-room, which occasionally happens at a hunt-meeting or a race-ball, he enjoys himself extremely.

His young friend is Ensign Famish, who is not a little pleased to be seen with such a smart fellow as Rag, who bows to the best turf company in the Park. Rag lets Famish accompany him to Tattersall's, and sells him bargains in horse-flesh, and uses Famish's cab. That young gentleman's regiment is in India, and he is at home on sick leave. He recruits his health by being intoxicated every night, and fortifies his lungs, which are weak, by smoking cigars all day. The policemen about the Haymarket know the little creature, and the early cabmen salute him. The closed doors of fish and lobster shops open after service, and vomit out little Famish, who is either tipsy and quarrelsome–when he wants to fight the cabmen; or drunk and helpless–when some kind friend (in yellow satin) takes care of him. All the neighbourhood, the cabmen, the police, the early potato-men, and the friends in yellow satin, know the young fellow, and he is called Little Bobby by some of the very worst reprobates in Europe.

His mother, Lady Fanny Famish, believes devotedly that Robert is in London solely for the benefit of consulting the physician; is going to have him exchanged into a dragoon regiment, which doesn't go to that odious India; and has an idea that his chest is delicate, and that he takes gruel every evening, when he puts his feet in hot water. Her Ladyship resides at Cheltenham, and is of a serious turn.

Bobby frequents the "Union-Jack Club" of course: where he breakfasts on pale ale and devilled kidneys at three o'clock; where beardless young heroes of his own sort congregate, and make merry, and give each other dinners; where you may see half-a-dozen of young rakes of the fourth or fifth order lounging and smoking on the steps; where you behold Slapper's long-tailed leggy mare in the custody of a red-jacket until the Captain is primed for the Park with a glass of curaçoa; and where you see Hobby, of the Highland Buffs, driving up with Dobby, of the Madras Fusiliers, in the great banging, swinging cab, which the latter hires from Rumble of Bond Street.

In fact, Military Snobs are of such number and variety, that a hundred weeks of *Punch* would not suffice to give an audience to them. There is, besides the disreputable old Military Snob, who has seen service, the respectable old military Snob, who has seen none, and gives himself the most prodigious Martinet airs. There is the Medical Military Snob, who is generally more outrageously military in his conversation than the greatest *sabreur* in the army. There is the Heavy-Dragoon Snob, whom young ladies admire, with his great stupid pink face and yellow moustaches—a vacuous, solemn, foolish, but brave and honourable Snob. There is the Amateur Military Snob, who writes Captain on his card because he is a Lieutenant in the Bungay Militia. There is the

Lady-killing Military Snob; and more, who need not be named.

But let no man, we repeat, charge *Mr. Punch* with disrespect for the Army in general—that gallant and judicious Army, every man of which, from F.M. the Duke of Wellington, &c., downwards—(with the exception of H.R.H. Field-Marshal Prince Albert, who, however, can hardly count as a military man,)—reads *Punch* in every quarter of the globe.

Let those civilians who sneer at the acquirements of the Army read Sir Harry Smith's account of the Battle of Aliwal. A noble deed was never told in nobler language. And you who doubt if chivalry exists, or the age of heroism has passed by, think of Sir Henry Hardinge, with his son, "dear little Arthur," riding in front of the lines at Ferozeshah. I hope no English painter will endeavour to illustrate that scene; for who is there to do justice to it? The history of the world contains no more brilliant and heroic picture. No, no; the men who perform these deeds with such brilliant valour, and describe them with such modest manliness—*such* are not Snobs. Their country admires them, their Sovereign rewards them, and *Punch*, the universal railer, takes off his hat and says, Heaven save them!

CHAPTER XI

On Clerical Snobs

After Snobs Military, Snobs Clerical suggest themselves quite naturally, and it is clear that, with every respect for the cloth, yet having a regard for truth, humanity, and the British public, such a vast and influential class must not be omitted from our notices of the great Snob world.

Of these Clerics there are some whose claim to snobbishness is undoubted, and yet it cannot be discussed here; for the same reason that *Punch* would not set up his show in a Cathedral, out of respect for the solemn service celebrated within. There are some places where he acknowledges himself not privileged to make a noise, and puts away his show, and silences his drum, and takes off his hat, and holds his peace.

And I know this, that if there are some Clerics who do wrong, there are straightway a thousand newspapers to haul up those unfortunates, and cry, "Fie upon them, fie upon them!" while, though the press is always ready to yell and bellow excommunication against these stray delinquent parsons, it somehow takes very little count of the many good ones—of the tens of thousands of honest men, who lead Christian lives, who give to the poor generously, who deny themselves rigidly, and live and die in their duty, without ever a newspaper paragraph in their favour. My beloved friend and reader, I wish you and I could do the same: and let me whisper my belief, *entre nous*, that of those eminent philosophers who cry out against parsons the loudest, there are not many who have got their knowledge of the church by going thither often.

But you who have ever listened to village bells, or have walked to church as children on sunny Sabbath mornings; you who have ever seen the parson's wife tending the poor man's bedside; or the town clergyman threading the dirty stairs of noxious alleys upon his sacred business;—do not raise a shout when one of these falls away, or yell with the mob that howls after him.

Every man can do that. When old Father Noah was overtaken in his cups, there was only one of his sons that dared to make merry at his disaster, and he was not the most virtuous of the family. Let us too turn away silently, nor huzzah like a parcel of school-boys, because some big young rebel suddenly starts up and whops the schoolmaster.

I confess, though, if I had by me the names of those seven or eight Irish bishops, the probates of whose wills were mentioned in last year's journals, and who died leaving behind them some two hundred thousand pounds a-piece—I would like to put *them* up as patrons of my Clerical Snobs, and operate upon them as successfully as I see from the newspapers Mr. Eisenberg, Chiropodist, has lately done upon "His Grace the Right Reverend Lord Bishop of Tapioca."

And I confess that when those Right Reverend Prelates come up to the gates of Paradise with their probates of wills in their hands, I think that their chance is ... But the gates of Paradise is a far way to follow their Lordships; so let us trip down again, lest awkward questions be asked there about our own favourite vices too.

And don't let us give way to the vulgar prejudice, that clergymen are an overpaid and luxurious body of men. When that eminent ascetic, the late Sydney Smith—(by the way, by what law of nature is it that so many Smiths in this world are called Sydney Smith?)—lauded the system of great prizes in the Church,—without which he said gentlemen would not be induced to follow the clerical profession, he admitted most pathetically that the clergy in general were by no means to be envied for their worldly prosperity. From reading the works of some modern writers of repute, you would fancy that a parson's life was passed in gorging himself with plum-pudding and port-wine; and that his Reverence's fat chaps were always greasy with the crackling of tithe-pigs. Caricaturists delight to represent him so: round, short-necked, pimple-faced, apo-plectic, bursting out of waist-coat, like a black-pudding—a shovel-hatted, fuzz-wigged Silenus. Whereas, if you take the real man, the poor fellow's flesh-pots are very scantily furnished with meat. He labours commonly for a wage that a tailor's foreman would despise: he has, too, such claims upon his dismal income as most philosophers would rather grumble to meet; many tithes are levied upon *his* pocket, let it be remembered, by those who grudge him his means of livelihood. He has to dine with the Squire: and his wife must dress neatly; and he must "look like a gentleman," as they call it, and bring up his six great hungry sons as such. Add to this, if he does his duty, he has such temptations to spend his money as no mortal man could withstand. Yes; you who can't resist purchasing a chest of cigars, because they are so good; or an ormolu clock at Howell and James's, because it is such a bargain; or a box at the Opera, because Lablache and Grisi are divine in the *Puritani*; fancy how difficult it is for a parson to resist spending a half-crown when John Breakstone's family are without a loaf; or "standing" a bottle of port for poor old Polly Rabbits, who has her thirteenth child; or treating himself to a suit of corduroys for little Bob Scarecrow, whose breeches are sadly out at elbows. Think of these temptations brother moralists and philosophers, and don't be too hard on the parson.

But what is this? Instead of "showing up" the parsons, are we indulging in maudlin praises of that monstrous black-coated race? O saintly Francis, lying at rest under the turf; O Jimmy, and Johnny, and Willy, friends of my youth! O noble and dear old Elias! how should he who knows you not respect you and your calling? May this pen never write a pennyworth again, if it ever casts ridicule upon either!

CHAPTER XII

On Clerical Snobs and Snobbishness

"Dear Mr. Snob," an amiable young correspondent writes, who signs himself Snobling, "ought the clergyman who, at the request of a noble Duke, lately interrupted a marriage ceremony between two persons perfectly authorised to marry, to be ranked or not among the Clerical Snobs?"

This, my dear young friend, is not a fair question. One of the illustrated weekly papers has already seized hold of the clergyman, and blackened him most unmercifully, by representing him in his cassock performing the marriage service. Let that be sufficient punishment; and, if you please, do not press the query.

It is very likely that if Miss Smith had come with a licence to marry Jones, the parson in question, not seeing old Smith present, would have sent off the beadle in a cab to let the old gentleman know what was going on; and would have delayed the service until the arrival of Smith senior. He very likely thinks it his duty to ask *all* marriageable young ladies, who come without their papa, why their parent is absent; and, no doubt, *always* sends off the beadle for that missing governor.

Or, it is very possible that the Duke of Cœurdelion was Mr. What-d'ye-call'im's most intimate friend, and has often said to him, "What-d'ye-call'im, my boy, my daughter must never marry the Capting. If ever they try at your church, I beseech you, considering the terms of intimacy on which we are, to send off Rattan in a hack-cab to fetch me."

In either of which cases, you see, dear Snobling, that though the parson would not have been authorised, yet he might have been excused for interfering. He has no more right to stop my marriage than to stop my dinner, to both of which, as a free-born Briton, I am entitled by law, if I can pay for them. But, consider pastoral solicitude, a deep sense of the duties of his office, and pardon this inconvenient, but genuine zeal.

But if the clergyman did in the Duke's case what he would *not* do in Smith's; if he has no more acquaintance with the Cœurdelion family than I have with the Royal and Serene House of Saxe-Coburg Gotha,—*then*, I confess, my dear Snobling, your question might elicit a disagreeable reply, and one which I respectfully decline to give. I wonder what Sir George Tufto would say, if a sentry left his post because a noble lord (not in the least connected with the service) begged the sentinel not to do his duty!

Alas! that the beadle who canes little boys and drives them out, cannot drive worldliness out too: and what is worldliness but snobbishness? When, for instance, I read in the newspapers that the Right Reverend the Lord Charles James administered the rite of confirmation to *a party of the juvenile nobility* at the Chapel Royal,—as if the Chapel Royal were a sort of ecclesiastical Almack's, and young people were to get ready for the next world in little exclusive genteel knots of the aristocracy, who were not to be disturbed in their journey thither by the company of the vulgar:—when I read such a paragraph as that (and one or two such generally appear during the present fashionable season), it seems to me to be the most odious, mean, and disgusting part of that odious, mean, and disgusting publication the *Court Circular*; and that snobbishness is therein carried to quite an awful pitch. What, gentlemen, can't we even in the Church acknowledge a republic? There, at least, the Heralds' College itself might allow that we all of us have the same pedigree, and are direct descendants of Eve and Adam, whose inheritance is divided amongst us.

I hereby call upon all Dukes, Earls, Baronets, and other potentates, not to lend themselves to this shameful scandal and error, and beseech all bishops who read this publication to take the matter into consideration, and to protest against the continuance of the practice, and to declare, "We *won't* confirm or christen Lord Tomnoddy, or Sir Carnaby Jenks, to the exclusion of any other young Christian;" the which declaration if their Lordships are induced to make, a great *lapis offensionis* will be removed, and the Snob Papers will not have been written in vain.

A story is current of a celebrated *nouveau-riche*, who, having had occasion to oblige that excellent prelate the Bishop of Bullocksmithy, asked his Lordship, in return, to confirm his children privately in his Lordship's own chapel; which ceremony the grateful prelate accordingly performed. Can satire go farther than this? Is there, even in this most amusing of prints, any more *naïve* absurdity? It is as if a man wouldn't go to heaven unless he went in a special train, or as if he thought (as some people think about vaccination) Confirmation more effectual when administered at first hand. When that eminent person, the Begum Sumroo, died, it is said she left ten thousand pounds to the Pope, and ten thousand to the Archbishop of Canterbury,—so that there should be no mistake,—so as to make sure of having the ecclesiastical authorities on her side. This is only a little more openly and undisguisedly snobbish than the cases before alluded to. A well-bred Snob is just as secretly proud of his riches and honours as a *parvenu* Snob who makes the most ludicrous exhibition of them; and a high-born Marchioness or Duchess just as vain of herself and her diamonds, as Queen Quashyboo, who sews a pair of epaulets on to her skirt, and turns out in state in a cocked hat and feathers.

It is not out of disrespect to my "Peerage," which I love and honour (indeed, have I not said before, that I should be ready to jump out of my skin if two Dukes would walk down Pall Mall with me?)—it is not out of disrespect for the individuals, that I wish these titles had never been invented; but, consider, if there were no tree, there would be no shadow; and how much more honest society would be, and how much more serviceable the clergy would be (which is our present consideration), if these temptations of rank and continual baits of worldliness were not in existence, and perpetually thrown out to lead them astray.

65

I have seen many examples of their falling away. When, for instance, Tom Sniffle first went into the country as Curate for Mr. Fuddleston (Sir Huddleston Fuddleston's brother), who resided on some other living, there could not be a more kind, hard-working, and excellent creature than Tom. He had his aunt to live with him. His conduct to his poor was admirable. He wrote annually reams of the best-intentioned and most vapid sermons. When Lord Brandyball's family first came down into the country, and invited him to dine at Brandyball Park, Sniffle was so agitated that he almost forgot how to say grace, and upset a bowl of currant-jelly sauce in Lady Fanny Toffy's lap.

What was the consequence of his intimacy with that noble family? He quarrelled with his aunt for dining out every night. The wretch forgot his poor altogether, and killed his old nag by always riding over to Brandyball; where he revelled in the maddest passion for Lady Fanny. He ordered the neatest new clothes and ecclesiastical waist-coats from London; he appeared with corazza-shirts, lackered boots, and perfumery; he bought a blood-horse from Bob Toffy: was seen at archery meetings, public breakfasts,—actually at cover; and, I blush to say, that I saw him in a stall at the Opera; and afterwards riding by Lady Fanny's side in Rotten Row. He *double-barrelled* his name (as many poor Snobs do), and instead of T. Sniffle, as formerly, came out, in a porcelain card, as Rev. T. D'Arcy Sniffle, Burlington Hotel.

The end of all this may be imagined: when the Earl of Brandyball was made acquainted with the curate's love for Lady Fanny, he had that fit of the gout which so nearly carried him off (to the inexpressible grief of his son, Lord Alicompayne), and uttered that remarkable speech to Sniffle, which disposed of the claims of the latter:—"If I didn't respect the Church, Sir," his Lordship said, "by Jove, I'd kick you downstairs:" his Lordship then fell back into the fit aforesaid; and Lady Fanny, as we all know, married General Podager.

As for poor Tom, he was over head and ears in debt as well

as in love: his creditors came down upon him. Mr. Hemp, of Portugal Street, proclaimed his name lately as a reverend outlaw; and he has been seen at various foreign watering-places; sometimes doing duty; sometimes "coaching" a stray gentleman's son at Carlsruhe or Kissingen; sometimes—must we say it?—lurking about the roulette-tables with a tuft to his chin.

If temptation had not come upon this unhappy fellow in the shape of a Lord Brandyball, he might still have been following his profession, humbly and worthily. He might have married his cousin with four thousand pounds, the wine-merchant's daughter (the old gentleman quarrelled with his nephew for not soliciting wine-orders from Lord B. for him): he might have had seven children, and taken private pupils, and eked out his income, and lived and died a country parson.

Could he have done better? You who want to know how great, and good, and noble such a character may be, read Stanley's "Life of Doctor Arnold."

CHAPTER XIII

On Clerical Snobs

Among the varieties of the Snob Clerical, the University Snob and the Scholastic Snob ought never to be forgotten; they form a very strong battalion in the black-coated army.

The wisdom of our ancestors (which I admire more and more every day) seemed to have determined that the education of youth was so paltry and unimportant a matter, that almost any man, armed with a birch and a regulation cassock and degree, might undertake the charge: and many an honest country gentleman may be found to the present day, who takes very good care to have a character with his butler when he engages him, and will not purchase a horse without the strongest warranty and the closest inspection; but sends off his son, young John Thomas, to school without asking any questions about the Schoolmaster, and places the lad at Switchester College, under Doctor Block, because he (the good old English gentleman) had been at Switchester, under Doctor Buzwig, forty years ago.

We have a love for all little boys at school; for many scores of thousands of them read and love *Punch*:—may he never write a word that shall not be honest and fit for them to read! He will not have his young friends to be Snobs in the future, or to be bullied by Snobs, or given over to such to be educated. Our connexion with the youth at the Universities is very close and affectionate. The candid undergraduate is our friend. The pompous old College Don trembles in his common room, lest we should attack him and show him up as a Snob.

When railroads were threatening to invade the land which they have since conquered, it may be recollected what a shrieking and outcry the authorities of Oxford and Eton made, lest the iron abominations should come near those seats of pure learning, and tempt the British youth astray. The supplications were in vain; the railroad is in upon them, and the old-world institutions are doomed. I felt charmed to read in the papers the other day a most veracious puffing advertisement headed, "To College and back for Five Shillings." "The College Gardens (it said) will be thrown open on this occasion: the College youths will perform a regatta; the Chapel of King's College will have its celebrated music;"—and all for five shillings! The Goths have got into Rome; Napoleon Stephenson draws his republican lines round the sacred old cities; and the ecclesiastical big-wigs who garrison them must prepare to lay down key and crosier before the iron conqueror.

If you consider, dear reader, what profound snobbishness the University System produced, you will allow that it is time to attack some of those feudal middle-age superstitions. If you go down for five shillings to look at the "College Youths," you may see one sneaking down the court without a tassel to his cap; another with a gold or silver fringe to his velvet trencher; a third lad with a master's gown and hat, walking at ease over the sacred College grass-plats, which common men must not tread on.

He may do it because he is a nobleman. Because a lad is a lord, the University gives him a degree at the end of two years which another is seven in acquiring. Because he is a lord, he has no call to go through an examination. Any man who has not been to College and back for five shillings, would not believe in such distinctions in a place of education, so absurd and monstrous do they seem to be.

The lads with gold and silver lace are sons of rich gentlemen, and called Fellow Commoners; they are privileged to feed better than the pensioners, and to have wine with their victuals, which the latter can only get in their rooms.

The unlucky boys who have no tassels to their caps, are called sizars—*servitors* at Oxford—(a very pretty and gentle-manlike title). A distinction is made in their clothes because they are poor; for which reason they wear a badge of poverty, and are not allowed to take their meals with their fellow-students.

When this wicked and shameful distinction was set up, it was of a piece with all the rest—a part of the brutal, unchristian, blundering feudal system. Distinctions of rank were then so strongly insisted upon, that it would have been thought blasphemy to doubt them, as blasphemous as it is in parts of the United States now for a nigger to set up as the equal of a white man. A ruffian like Henry VIII. talked as gravely about the divine powers vested in him, as if he had been an inspired prophet. A wretch like James I. not only believed that there was in himself a particular sanctity, but other people believed him. Government regulated the length of a merchant's shoes as well as meddled with his trade, prices, exports, machinery. It thought itself justified in roasting a man for his religion, or pulling a Jew's teeth out if he did not pay a contribution, or ordered him to dress in a yellow gabardine, and locked him in a particular quarter.

Now a merchant may wear what boots he pleases, and has pretty nearly acquired the privilege of buying and selling without the Government laying its paws upon the bargain. The stake for heretics is gone; the pillory is taken down; Bishops are even found lifting up their voices against the remains of persecution, and ready to do away with the last Catholic Disabilities. Sir Robert Peel, though he wished it ever so much, has no power over Mr. Benjamin Disraeli's grinders, or any means of violently handling that gentleman's jaw. Jews are not called upon to wear badges: on the contrary, they may live in Piccadilly, or the Minories, according to fancy; they may dress like Christians, and do sometimes in a most elegant and fashionable manner.

Why is the poor College servitor to wear that name and that badge still? Because Universities are the last places into which Reform penetrates. But now that she can go to College and back for five shillings, let her travel down thither.

CHAPTER XIV

On University Snobs

All the men of Saint Boniface will remember Hugby and
Crump. They were tutors in our time, and Crump is since
advanced to be President of the College. He was formerly, and
is now, a rich specimen of a University Snob.

At five-and-twenty, Crump invented three new metres, and
published an edition of an exceedingly improper Greek
Comedy, with no less than twenty emendations upon the
German text of Schnupfenius and Schnapsius. These services
to religion instantly pointed him out for advancement in the
Church, and he is now President of Saint Boniface, and very
narrowly escaped the bench.

Crump thinks Saint Boniface the centre of the world, and his
position as President the highest in England. He expects the
fellows and tutors to pay him the same sort of service that
Cardinals pay to the Pope. I am sure Crawler would have no
objection to carry his trencher, or Page to hold up the skirts of
his gown as he stalks into chapel. He roars out the responses
there as if it were an honour to heaven that the President of
Saint Boniface should take a part in the service, and in his own
lodge and college acknowledges the Sovereign only as his
superior.

When the allied monarchs came down, and were made
Doctors of the University, a breakfast was given at Saint
Boniface; on which occasion Crump allowed the Emperor
Alexander to walk before him, but took the *pas* himself of the
King of Prussia and Prince Blucher. He was going to put the
Hetman Platoff to breakfast at a side-table with the under
college tutors; but he was induced to relent, and merely
entertained that distinguished Cossack with a discourse on his
own language, in which he showed that the Hetman knew
nothing about it.

As for us undergraduates, we scarcely knew more about

Crump than about the Grand Lama. A few favoured youths are asked occasionally to tea at the lodge; but they do not speak unless first addressed by the Doctor; and if they venture to sit down, Crump's follower, Mr. Toady, whispers, "Gentlemen, will you have the kindness to get up?—The President is passing;" or "Gentlemen, the President prefers that undergraduates should not sit down;" or words to a similar effect.

To do Crump justice, he does not cringe now to great people. He rather patronizes them than otherwise; and, in London, speaks quite affably to a Duke who has been brought up at his college, or holds out a finger to a Marquis. He does not disguise his own origin, but brags of it with considerable self-gratulation:—"I was a Charity-boy," says he; "see what I am now; the greatest Greek scholar of the greatest College of the greatest University of the greatest Empire in the world." The argument being, that this is a capital world for beggars, because he, being a beggar, has managed to get on horseback.

Hugby owes his eminence to patient merit and agreeable perseverance. He is a meek, mild, inoffensive creature, with just enough of scholarship to fit him to hold a lecture, or set an examination paper. He rose by kindness to the aristocracy. It was wonderful to see the way in which that poor creature grovelled before a nobleman or a lord's nephew, or even some noisy and disreputable commoner, the friend of a lord. He used to give the young noblemen the most painful and elaborate breakfasts, and adopt a jaunty genteel air, and talk with them (although he was decidedly serious) about the opera, or the last run with the hounds. It was good to watch him in the midst of a circle of young tufts, with his mean, smiling, eager, uneasy familiarity. He used to write home confidential letters to their parents, and made it his duty to call upon them when in town, to condole or rejoice with them when a death, birth, or marriage took place in their family; and to feast them whenever they came to the University. I recollect a letter lying on a desk in his lecture-room for a whole term, beginning, "My Lord Duke." It was to show us that he corresponded with such dignities.

When the late lamented Lord Glenlivat, who broke his neck at a hurdle-race, at the premature age of twenty-four, was at the University, the amiable young fellow, passing to his rooms in the early morning, and seeing Hugby's boots at his door, on the same staircase, playfully wadded the insides of the boots with cobbler's wax, which caused excruciating pains to the Rev. Mr. Hugby, when he came to take them off the same evening, before dining with the Master of St. Crispin's.

Everybody gave the credit of this admirable piece of fun to Lord Glenlivat's friend, Bob Tizzy, who was famous for such feats, and who had already made away with the college pump-handle; filed St. Boniface's nose smooth with his face; carried off four images of nigger-boys from the tobacconists; painted the senior proctor's horse pea-green, &c. &c.; and Bob (who was of the party certainly, and would not peach,) was just on the point of incurring expulsion, and so losing the family living which was in store for him, when Glenlivat nobly stepped forward, owned himself to be the author of the delightful *jeu-d'esprit*, apologized to the tutor, and accepted the rustication.

Hugby cried when Glenlivat apologized; if the young nobleman had kicked him round the court, I believe the tutor would have been happy, so that an apology and a re-conciliation might subsequently ensue. "My lord," said he, " in your conduct on this and all other occasions, you have acted as becomes a gentleman; you have been an honour to the University, as you will be to the peerage, I am sure, when the amiable vivacity of youth is calmed down, and you are called upon to take your proper share in the government of the nation." And when his lordship took leave of the University, Hugby presented him with a copy of his "Sermons to a Nobleman's Family" (Hugby was once private tutor to the sons of the Earl of Muffborough), which Glenlivat presented in return to Mr. William Ramm, known to the fancy as the Tutbury

Pet, and the sermons now figure on the boudoirtable of Mrs. Ramm, behind the bar of her house of entertainment, "The Game Cock and Spurs," near Woodstock, Oxon.

At the beginning of the long vacation, Hugby comes to town, and puts up in handsome lodgings near St. James's Square; rides in the Park in the afternoon; and is delighted to read his name in the morning papers among the list of persons present at Muffborough House and the Marquis of Farintosh's evening-parties. He is a member of Sydney Scraper's Club, where, however, he drinks his pint of claret.

Sometimes you may see him on Sundays, at the hour when tavern doors open, whence issue little girls with great jugs of porter; when charity-boys walk the streets, bearing brown dishes of smoking shoulders of mutton and baked 'taturs; when Sheeny and Moses are seen smoking their pipes before their lazy shutters in Seven Dials; when a crowd of smiling persons in clean outlandish dresses, in monstrous bonnets and flaring printed gowns, or in crumpled glossy coats and silks that bear the creases of the drawers where they have lain all the week, file down High Street,—sometimes, I say, you may see Hugby coming out of the Church of St. Giles-in-the-Fields, with a stout gentlewoman leaning on his arm, whose old face bears an expression of supreme pride and happiness as she glances round at all the neighbours, and who faces the curate himself, and marches into Holborn, where she pulls the bell of a house over which is inscribed, "Hugby, Haberdasher." It is the mother of the Rev. F. Hugby, as proud of her son in his white choker as Cornelia of her jewels at Rome. That is old Hugby bringing up the rear with the Prayer-books, and Betsy Hugby the old maid, his daughter,—old Hugby, Haberdasher and Churchwarden.

In the front room upstairs, where the dinner is laid out, there is a picture of Muffborough Castle; of the Earl of Muffborough, K.X., Lord-Lieutenant for Diddlesex; an engraving, from an almanac, of Saint Boniface College, Oxon; and a sticking-plaster portrait of Hugby when young, in a cap and gown. A copy of his "Sermons to a Nobleman's Family" is on the bookshelf, by the "Whole Duty of Man," the Reports of the Missionary Societies, and the "Oxford University Calendar." Old Hugby knows part of this by heart; every living belonging to Saint Boniface, and the name of every tutor, fellow, nobleman, and undergraduate.

He used to go to meeting and preach himself, until his son took orders; but of late the old gentleman has been accused of Puseyism, and is quite pitiless against the Dissenters.

CHAPTER XV

On University Snobs

I Should like to fill several volumes with accounts of various University Snobs; so fond are my reminiscences of them and so numerous are they. I should like to speak, above all, of the wives and daughters of some of the Professor-Snobs; their amusements, habits, jealousies; their innocent artifices to entrap young men; their picnics, concerts, and evening-parties. I wonder what has become of Emily Blades, daughter of Blades, the Professor of the Mandingo language? I remember her shoulders to this day, as she sat in the midst of a crowd of about seventy young gentlemen, from Corpus and Catherine Hall, entertaining them with ogles and French songs on the guitar. Are you married, fair Emily of the shoulders? What beautiful ringlets those were that used to dribble over them!– what a waist!–what a killing sea-green shot-silk gown!–what a cameo, the size of a muffin! There were thirty-six young men of the University in love at one time with Emily Blades; and no words are sufficient to describe the pity, the sorrow, the deep, deep commiseration–the rage, fury, and uncharitableness, in other words–with which the Miss Trumps (daughter of Trumps, the Professor of Phlebotomy) regarded her, because she *didn't* squint, and because she *wasn't* marked with the small-pox.

As for the young University Snobs, I am getting too old, now, to speak of such very familiarly. My recollections of them lie in the far, far past–almost as far back as Pelham's time.

We *then* used to consider Snobs raw-looking lads, who never missed chapel; who wore high-lows and no straps; who walked two hours on the Trumpington road every day of their lives; who carried off the college scholarships, and who overrated themselves in hall. We were premature in pronouncing our verdict of youthful Snobbishness. The man without straps fulfilled his destiny and duty. He eased his old governor, the curate in Westmoreland, or helped his sister to set up the Ladies' School. He wrote a "Dictionary," or a "Treatise on Conic Sections," as his nature and genius prompted. He got a fellowship, and then took to himself a wife, and a living. He presides over a parish now, and thinks it rather a dashing thing to belong to the "Oxford and Cambridge Club;" and his parishioners love him, and snore under his sermons. No, no, *he* is not a Snob. It is not straps that make the gentleman, or high-lows that unmake him, be they ever so thick. My son, it is you who are the Snob if you lightly despise a man for doing his duty, and refuse to shake an honest man's hand because it wears a Berlin glove.

We then used to consider it not the least vulgar for a parcel of lads who had been whipped three months previous, and were not allowed more than three glasses of port at home, to sit down to pineapples and ices at each other's rooms, and fuddle themselves with champagne and claret.

One looks back to what was called "a wine-party" with a sort of wonder. Thirty lads round a table covered with bad sweetmeats, drinking bad wines, telling bad stories, singing bad songs over and over again. Milk punch—smoking—ghastly headache—frightful spectacle of dessert-table next morning, and smell of tobacco—your guardian, the clergyman, dropping in, in the midst of this—expecting to find you deep in Algebra, and discovering the Gyp administering soda-water.

There were young men who despised the lads who indulged in the coarse hospitalities of wine-parties, who prided themselves in giving *récherché* little French dinners. Both wine-party-givers and dinner-givers were Snobs.

There were what used to be called "dressy" Snobs:—Jimmy, who might be seen at five o'clock elaborately rigged out, with a camellia in his button-hole, glazed boots, and fresh kid-gloves twice a-day;—Jessamy, who was conspicuous for his "jewell-ery,"—a young donkey, glittering all over with chains, rings, and shirt-studs;—Jacky, who rode every day solemnly on the Blenheim Road, in pumps and white silk stockings, with his hair curled,—all three of whom flattered themselves they gave laws to the University about dress—all three most odious varieties of Snobs.

Sporting Snobs of course there were, and are always—those happy beings in whom Nature has implanted a love of slang: who loitered about the horsekeeper's stables, and drove the London coaches—a stage in and out—and might be seen swaggering through the courts in pink of early mornings, and indulged in dice and blind-hookey at nights, and never missed a race or a boxing-match; and road flat races, and kept bull-terriers. Worse Snobs even than these were poor miserable wretches who did not like hunting at all, and could not afford it, and were in mortal fear at a two-foot ditch; but who hunted because Glenlivat and Cinqbars hunted. The Billiard Snob and the Boating Snob were varieties of these, and are to be found elsewhere than in universities.

Then there were Philosophical Snobs, who used to ape statesmen at the spouting-clubs, and who believed as a fact that Government always had an eye on the Unviersity for the selection of orators for the House of Commons. There were audacious young free-thinkers, who adored nobody or nothing, except perhaps Robespierre and the Koran, and panted for the day when the pale name of priest should shrink and dwindle away before the indignation of an enlightened world.

But the worst of all University Snobs are those unfortunates who go to rack and ruin from their desire to ape their betters. Smith becomes acquainted with great people at college, and is ashamed of his father the tradesman. Jones has fine acquaintances, and lives after their fashion like a gay free-hearted fellow as he is, and ruins his father, and robs his sister's portion, and cripples his younger brother's outset in life, for the pleasure of entertaining my lord, and riding by the side of Sir John. And though it may be very good fun for Robinson to fuddle himself at home as he does at College, and to be brought home by the policeman he has just been trying to knock down—think what fun it is for the poor old soul his mother!—the half-pay captain's widow, who has been pinching herself all her life long, in order that that jolly young fellow might have a University education.

CHAPTER XVI

On Literary Snobs

What will he say about Literary Snobs? has been a question, I make no doubt, often asked by the public. How can he let off his own profession? Will that truculent and unsparing monster who attacks the nobility, the clergy, the army, and the ladies, indiscriminately, hesitate when the turn comes to *égorger* his own flesh and blood?

My dear and excellent querist, whom does the schoolmaster flog so resolutely as his own son? Didn't Brutus chop his offspring's head off? You have a very bad opinion indeed of the present state of literature and of literary men, if you fancy that any one of us would hesitate to stick a knife into his neighbour penman, if the latter's death could do the State any service.

But the fact is, that in the literary profession THERE ARE NO SNOBS. Look round at the whole body of British men of letters, and I defy you to point out among them a single instance of vulgarity, or envy, or assumption.

Men and women, as far as I have known them, they are all modest in their demeanour, elegant in their manners, spotless in their lives, and honourable in their conduct to the world and to each other. You *may*, occasionally, it is true, hear one literary man abusing his brother; but why? Not in the least out of malice; not at all from envy; merely from a sense of truth and public duty. Suppose, for instance, I good-naturedly point out a blemish in my friend *Mr. Punch's* person, and say, *Mr. P.* has a hump-back, and his nose and chin are more crooked than those features in the Apollo or Antinous, which we are accustomed to consider as our standards of beauty; does this argue malice on my part towards *Mr. Punch?* Not in the least. It is the critic's duty to point out defects as well as merits, and he invariably does his duty with the utmost gentleness and candour.

An intelligent foreigner's testimony about our manners is always worth having, and I think, in this respect, the work of an eminent American, Mr. N. P. Willis, is eminently valuable and impartial. In his "History of Ernest Clay," a crack magazine-writer, the reader will get an exact account of the life of a popular man of letters in England. He is always the great lion of society.

He takes the *pas* of dukes and earls; all the nobility crowd to see him: I forget how many baronesses and duchesses fall in love with him. But on this subject let us hold our tongues. Modesty forbids that we should reveal the names of the heart-broken countesses and dear marchionesses who are pining for every one of the contributors in *Punch*.

If anybody wants to know how intimately authors are connected with the fashionable world, they have but to read the genteel novels. What refinement and delicacy pervades the works of Mrs. Barnaby! What delightful good company do you meet with in Mrs. Armytage! She seldom introduces you to anybody under a marquis! I don't know anything more delicious than the pictures of genteel life in "Ten Thousand a Year," except perhaps the "Young Duke," and "Coningsby." There's a modest grace about *them*, and an air of easy high fashion, which only belongs to blood, my dear Sir—to true blood.

And what linguists many of our writers are! Lady Bulwer, Lady Londonderry, Sir Edward himself—they write the French language with a luxurious elegance and ease which sets them far above their continental rivals, of whom not one (except Paul de Kock) knows a word of English.

And what Briton can read without enjoyment the works of James, so admirable for terseness; and the playful humour and dazzling offhand lightness of Ainsworth? Among other humourists, one might glance at a Jerrold, the chivalrous advocate of Toryism and Church and State; an à Beckett, with a lightsome pen, but a savage earnestness of purpose; a Jeames, whose pure style, and wit unmingled with buffoonery, was relished by a congenial public.

Speaking of critics, perhaps there never was a review that has done so much for literature as the admirable *Quarterly*. It has its prejudices, to be sure, as which of us have not? It goes out of its way to abuse a great man, or lays mercilessly on to such pretenders as Keats and Tennyson; but, on the other hand, it is the friend of all young authors, and has marked and nurtured all the rising talent of the country. It is loved by everybody. There, again, is *Blackwood's Magazine*—conspicuous for modest elegance and amiable satire; that review never passes the bounds of politeness in a joke. It is the arbiter of manners; and, while gently exposing the foibles of Londoners (for whom the *beaux esprits* of Edinburgh entertain a justifiable contempt), it is never coarse in its fun. The fiery enthusiasm of the *Athenæum* is well known: and the bitter wit of the too difficult *Literary Gazette*. The *Examiner* is perhaps too timid, and the *Spectator* too boisterous in its praise—but who can carp at these minor faults? No, no; the critics of England and the authors of England are unrivalled as a body; and hence it becomes impossible for us to find fault with them.

Above all, I never knew a man of letters *ashamed of his profession*. Those who know us, know what an affectionate and brotherly spirit there is among us all. Sometimes one of us rises in the world: we never attack him or sneer at him under those circumstances, but rejoice to a man at his success. If Jones dines with a lord, Smith never says Jones is a courtier and cringer. Nor, on the other hand, does Jones, who is in the habit of frequenting the society of great people, give himself any airs on account of the company he keeps; but will leave a duke's arm in Pall Mall to come over and speak to poor Brown, the young penny-a-liner.

That sense of equality and fraternity amongst authors has always struck me as one of the most amiable characteristics of the class. It is because we know and respect each other, that the world respects us so much; that we hold such a good position in society, and demean ourselves so irreproachably when there.

Literary persons are held in such esteem by the nation, that about two of them have been absolutely invited to court during the present reign; and it is probable that towards the end of the season, one or two will be asked to dinner by Sir Robert Peel.

They are such favourites with the public, that they are continually obliged to have their pictures taken and published; and one or two could be pointed out, of whom the nation insists upon having a fresh portrait every year. Nothing can be more gratifying than this proof of the affectionate regard which the people has for its instructors.

Literature is held in such honour in England, that there is a sum of near twelve hundred pounds per annum set apart to pension deserving persons following that profession. And a great compliment this is, too, to the professors, and a proof of their generally prosperous and flourishing condition. They are generally so rich and thrifty, that scarcely any money is wanted to help them.

If every word of this is true, how, I should like to know, am I to write about Literary Snobs?

CHAPTER XVII

A Little about Irish Snobs

You do not, to be sure, imagine that there are no other Snobs in Ireland than those of the amiable party who wish to make pikes of iron railroads (it's a fine Irish economy), and to cut the throats of the Saxon invaders. These are of the venomous sort; and had they been invented in his time, St. Patrick would have banished them out of the kingdom along with the other dangerous reptiles.

I think it is the Four Masters, or else it's Olaus Magnus, or else it's certainly O'Neill Daunt, in the "Catechism of Irish History," who relates that when Richard the Second came to Ireland, and the Irish chiefs did homage to him, going down on their knees—the poor simple creatures!—and worshipping and wondering before the English king and the dandies of his court, my lords the English noblemen mocked and jeered at their uncouth Irish admirers, mimicked their talk and gestures, pulled their poor old beards, and laughed at the strange fashion of their garments.

The English Snob rampant always does this to the present day. There is no Snob in existence, perhaps, that has such an indomitable belief in himself: that sneers you down all the rest of the world besides, and has such an insufferable, admirable, stupid contempt for all people but his own—nay, for all sets but his own. "Gwacious Gad!" what stories about "the Iwish" these young dandies accompanying King Richard must have had to tell, when they returned to Pall Mall, and smoked their cigars upon the steps of "White's!"

The Irish snobbishness develops itself not in pride so much as in servility and mean admirations, and trumpery imitations of their neighbours. And I wonder De Tocqueville and De Beaumont, and *The Times'* Commissioner, did not explain the Snobbishness of Ireland as contrasted with our own. Ours is that of Richard's Norman Knights,—haughty, brutal, stupid, and perfectly self-confident;—theirs, of the poor, wondering, kneeling, simple chieftains. They are on their knees still before English fashion—these simple, wild people; and indeed it is hard not to grin at some of their *naive* exhibitions.

Some years since, when a certain great orator was Lord Mayor of Dublin, he used to wear a red gown and a cocked hat, the splendour of which delighted him as much as a new curtain-ring in her nose or a string of glass-beads round her neck charms Queen Quasheeneaboo. He used to pay visits to people in this dress; to appear at meetings hundreds of miles off, in the red velvet gown. And to hear the people crying "Yes, me Lard!" and "No, me Lard!" and to read the prodigious accounts of his Lordship in the papers: it seemed as if the people and he liked to be taken in by this twopenny splendour. Twopenny magnificence, indeed, exists all over Ireland, and may be considered as the great characteristic of the Snobbishness of that country.

When Mrs. Mulholligan, the grocer's lady, retires to Kingstown, she has "Mulholliganville" painted over the gate of her villa; and receives you at a door that won't shut, or gazes at you out of a window that is glazed with an old petticoat.

Be it ever so shabby and dismal, nobody ever owns to keeping a shop. A fellow whose stock in trade is a penny roll or a tumbler of lollipops, calls his cabin the "American Flour Stores," or the "Depository for Colonial Produce," or some such name.

As for Inns, there are none in the country; Hotels abound, as well furnished as Mulholliganville; but again there are no such people as landlords and landladies: the landlord is out with the hounds, and my lady in the parlour talking with the Captain or playing the piano.

If a gentleman has a hundred a year to leave to his family they all become gentlemen, all keep a nag, ride to hounds, and swagger about in the "Phaynix," and grow tufts to their chins like so many real aristocrats.

A friend of mine has taken to be a painter, and lives out of

Ireland, where he is considered to have disgraced the family by choosing such a profession. His father is a wine-merchant; and his elder brother an apothecary.

The number of men one meets in London and on the Continent who have a pretty little property of five-and-twenty hundred a year in Ireland is prodigious: those who *will* have nine thousand a year in land when somebody dies are still more numerous. I myself have met as many descendants from Irish kings as would form a brigade.

And who has not met the Irishman who apes the Englishman, and who forgets his country and tries to forget his accent, or to smother the taste of it, as it were? "Come, dine with me, my boy," says O'Dowd, of O'Dowdstown: "you'll *find us all English there;*" which he tells you with a brogue as broad as from here to Kingstown Pier. And did you never hear Mrs. Captain Macmanus talk about "I-ah-land," and her account of her "fawther's esteet?" Very few men have rubbed through the world without hearing and witnessing some of these Hibernian phenomena—these twopenny splendours.

And what say you to the summit of society—the Castle—with a sham king, and sham lords-in-waiting, and sham loyalty, and a sham Haroun Alraschid, to go about in a sham disguise, making believe to be affable and splendid? That Castle is the pink and pride of Snobbishness. A *Court Circular* is bad enough, with two columns of print about a little baby that's christened—but think of people liking a sham *Court Circular!*

I think the shams of Ireland are more outrageous than those of any country. A fellow shows you a hill and says, "That's the highest mountain in all Ireland;" or a gentleman tells you he is descended from Brian Boroo, and has his five-and-thirty hundred a year; or Mrs. Macmanus describes her fawther's esteet; or ould Dan rises and says the Irish women are the loveliest, the Irish men the bravest, the Irish land the most fertile in the world: and nobody believes anybody—the latter doesn't believe his story nor the hearer: but they make-believe to believe, and solemnly do honour to humbug.

O Ireland! O my country! (for I make little doubt that I am descended from Brian Boroo too) when will you acknowledge that two and two make four, and call a pikestaff a pikestaff!—that is the very best use you can make of the latter. Irish snobs will dwindle away then, and we shall never hear tell of Hereditary Bondsmen.

CHAPTER XVIII

Party-Giving Snobs

❧ Our selection of Snobs has lately been too exclusively of a political character. "Give us private Snobs," cry the dear ladies. (I have before me the letter of one fair correspondent of the fishing village of Brighthelmstone in Sussex, and could her commands ever be disobeyed?) "Tell us more, dear Mr. Snob, about your experience of Snobs in society." Heaven bless the dear souls!–they are accustomed to the word now–the odious, vulgar, horrid, unpronounceable word slips out of their lips with the prettiest glibness possible. I should not wonder if it were used at Court amongst the Maids of Honour. In the very best society I know it is. And why not? Snobbishness is vulgar– the mere words are not: that which we call a Snob, by any other name would still be Snobbish.

Well, then. As the season is drawing to a close: as many hundreds of kind souls, snobbish or otherwise, have quitted London; as many hospitable carpets are taken up; and window-blinds are pitilessly papered with the *Morning Herald;* and mansions once inhabited by cheerful owners are now consigned to the care of the housekeeper's dreary *locum tenens*–some mouldy old woman, who, in reply to the hopeless clanging of the bell, peers at you for a moment from the area, and then slowly unbolting the great hall-door, informs you my lady has left town, or that "the family's in the country," or "gone up the Rind,"–or what not; as the season and parties are over; why not consider Party-giving Snobs for a while, and review the conduct of some of those individuals who have quitted the town for six months?

Some of those worthy Snobs are making-believe to go yachting, and, dressed in telescopes and pea-jackets, are passing their time between Cherbourg and Cowes; some living higgledy-piggledy in dismal little huts in Scotland, provisioned with canisters of portable soup, and fricandeaux hermetically sealed in tin, are passing their days slaughtering grouse on the moors; some are dozing and bathing away the effects of the season at Kissingen, or watching the ingenious game of *Trente et quarante* at Homburg and Ems. We can afford to be very bitter upon them now they are all gone. Now there are no more parties, let us have at the Party-giving Snobs. The dinner-giving, the ball-giving, the *déjeuner*-giving, the *conversazione*-giving Snobs—Lord! Lord! what havoc might have been made amongst them had we attacked them during the plethora of the season! I should have been obliged to have a guard to defend me from fiddlers and pastrycooks, indignant at the abuse of their patrons. Already I'm told that, from some flippant and unguarded expressions considered derogatory to Baker Street and Harley Street, rents have fallen in these respectable quarters; and orders have been issued that at least Mr. Snob shall be asked to parties there no more. Well, them—now they are *all* away, let us frisk at our ease, and have at everything, like the bull in the china-shop. They mayn't hear of what is going on in their absence, and if they do, they can't bear malice for six months. We will begin to make it up with them about next February, and let next year take care of itself. We shall have no more dinners from the dinner-giving Snobs: no more balls from the ball-givers: no more *conversaziones* (thank Mussy! as Jeames says,) from the Conversazione Snob: and what is to prevent us from telling the truth?

The snobbishness of Conversazione Snobs is very soon disposed of: as soon as that cup of washy bohea that is handed to you in the tea-room; or the muddy remnant of ice that you grasp in the suffocating scuffle of the assembly upstairs.

Good heavens! What do people mean by going there? What is done there, that everybody throngs into those three little rooms? Was the Black Hole considered to be an agreeable *réunion*, that Britons in the dog-days here seek to imitate it? After being rammed to a jelly in a doorway (where you feel your feet going through Lady Barbara Macbeth's lace flounces, and get a look from that haggard and painted old harpy, compared to which the gaze of Ugolino is quite cheerful); after withdrawing your elbow out of poor gasping Bob Guttleton's white waistcoat, from which cushion it was impossible to remove it, though you knew you were squeezing poor Bob into an apoplexy—you find yourself at last in the reception-room, and try to catch the eye of Mrs. Botibol, the *conversazione*-giver. When you catch her eye, you are expected to grin, and she smiles too, for the four hundredth time that night; and, if she's *very* glad to see you, waggles her little hand before her face as if to blow you a kiss, as the phrase is.

Why the deuce should Mrs. Botibol blow me a kiss? I wouldn't kiss her for the world. Why do I grin when I see her, as if I was delighted? Am I? I don't care a straw for Mrs. Botibol. I know what she thinks about me. I know what she said about my last volume of poems (I had it from a dear mutual friend). Why, I say in a word, are we going on ogling and telegraphing each other in this insane way?—Because we are both performing the ceremonies demanded by the Great Snob Society; whose dictates we all of us obey.

Well; the recognition is over—my jaws have returned to their usual English expression of subdued agony and intense gloom, and the Botibol is grinning and kissing her fingers to somebody else, who is squeezing through the aperture by which we have just entered. It is Lady Ann Clutterbuck, who has her Friday evenings, as Botibol (Botty, we call her,) has her Wednesdays. That is Miss Clementina Clutterbuck, the cadaverous young woman in green, with florid auburn hair, who has published her volume of poems ("The Death-Shriek;" "Damiens;" "The Faggot of Joan of Arc;" and "Translations from the German"—of course). The conversazione-women salute each other, calling each other "My dear Lady Ann" and "My dear good Eliza," and hating each other, as women hate who give parties on Wednesdays and Fridays. With inexpressible pain dear good Eliza sees Ann go up and coax and wheedle Abou Gosh, who has just arrived from Syria, and beg him to patronize her Fridays.

All this while, amidst the crowd and the scuffle, and a perpetual buzz and chatter, and the flare of the wax-candles, and an intolerable smell of musk—what the poor Snobs who write fashionable romances call "the gleam of gems, the odour of perfumes, the blaze of countless lamps"—a scrubby-looking, yellow-faced foreigner, with cleaned gloves, is warbling, inaudibly in a corner, to the accompaniment of another. "The Great Cacafogo," Mrs. Botibol whispers, as she passes you by. "A great creature, Thumpenstrumpff, is at the instrument—the Hetman Platoff's pianist, you know."

To hear this Cacafogo and Thumpenstrumpff, a hundred people are gathered together—a bevy of dowagers, stout or scraggy; a faint sprinkling of misses; six moody-looking lords, perfectly meek and solemn; wonderful foreign Counts, with bushy whiskers and yellow faces, and a great deal of dubious jewellery; young dandies with slim waists and open necks, and self-satisfied simpers, and flowers in their buttons; the old, stiff, stout, bald-headed *conversazione roués*, whom you meet everywhere—who never miss a night of this delicious enjoyment; the three last-caught lions of the season—Higgs, the traveller, Biggs, the novelist, and Toffey, who has come out so on the sugar question; Captain Flash, who is invited on account of his pretty wife, and Lord Ogleby, who goes wherever she goes. *Que sçais-je?* Who are the owners of all those showy scarfs and white neckcloths?—Ask little Tom Prig, who is there in all his glory, knows everybody, has a story about every one; and, as he trips home to his lodgings in Jermyn Street, with his gibus-hat and his little glazed pumps, thinks he is the fashionablest young fellow in town, and that he really has passed a night of exquisite enjoyment.

You go up (with your usual easy elegance of manner) and talk to Miss Smith in a corner.

"OH, MR. SNOB! I'M AFRAID YOU'RE SADLY SATIRICAL."

That's all she says. If you say it's fine weather, she bursts out laughing; or hint that it's very hot, she vows you are the drollest wretch! Meanwhile Mrs. Botibol is simpering on fresh arrivals; the individual at the door is roaring out their names; poor Cacafogo is quavering away in the music-room, under the impression that he will be *lancé* in the world by singing inaudibly here. And what a blessing it is to squeeze out of the door, and into the street, where a half-hundred of carriages are in waiting; and where the link-boy, with that unnecessary lantern of his, pounces upon all who issue out, and will insist upon getting your noble honour's lordship's cab.

And to think that there are people who, after having been to Botibol on Wednesday, will go to Clutterbuck on Friday!

CHAPTER XIX

Dining-Out Snobs

In England Dinner-giving Snobs occupy a very important place in society, and the task of describing them is tremendous. There was a time in my life when the consciousness of having eaten a man's salt rendered me dumb regarding his demerits, and I thought it a wicked act and a breach of hospitality to speak ill of him.

But why should a saddle-of-mutton blind you, or a turbot and lobster-sauce shut your mouth for ever? With advancing age, men see their duties more clearly. I am not to be hoodwinked any longer by a slice of venison, be it ever so fat; and as for being dumb on account of turbot and lobster-sauce—of course I am; good manners ordain that I should be so, until I have swallowed the compound—but not afterwards; directly the victuals are discussed, and John takes away the plate, my tongue begins to wag. Does not yours, if you have a pleasant neighbour?—a lovely creature, say, of some five-and-thirty, whose daughters have not yet quite come out—they are the best talkers. As for your young misses, they are only put about the table to look at—like the flowers in the centre-piece. Their blushing youth and natural modesty preclude them from that easy, confidential, conversational *abandon* which forms the delight of the intercourse with their dear mothers. It is to these, if he would prosper in his profession, that the Dining-out Snob should address himself. Suppose you sit next to one of these, how pleasant it is, in the intervals of the banquet, actually to abuse the victuals and the giver of the entertainment! It's twice as *piquant* to make fun of a man under his very nose.

"What *is* a Dinner-giving Snob?" some innocent youth, who is not *répandu* in the world, may ask—or some simple reader who has not the benefits of London experience.

My dear sir, I will show you—not all, for that is impossible— but several kinds of Dinner-giving Snobs. For instance, suppose you, in the middle rank of life, accustomed to Mutton, roast on Tuesday, cold on Wednesday, hashed on Thursday, &c., with small means and a small establishment, choose to waste the former and set the latter topsy-turvy by giving entertainments unnaturally costly—you come into the Dinner-giving Snob class at once. Suppose you get in cheap-made dishes from the pastrycook's, and hire a couple of green-grocers, or carpet-beaters, to figure as footmen, dismissing honest Molly, who waits on common days, and bedizening your table (ordinarily ornamented with willow-pattern crockery) with twopenny-halfpenny Birmingham plate. Suppose you pretend to be richer and grander than you ought to be—you are a Dinner-giving Snob. And oh, I tremble to think how many and many a one will read this!

A man who entertains in this way—and, alas, how few do not!—is like a fellow who would borrow his neighbour's coat to make a show in, or a lady who flaunts in the diamonds from next door—a humbug, in a word, and amongst the Snobs he must be set down.

A man who goes out of his natural sphere of society to ask Lords, Generals, Aldermen, and other persons of fashion, but is niggardly of his hospitality towards his own equals, is a Dinner-giving Snob. My dear friend, Jack Tufthunt, for example, knows *one* Lord whom he met at a watering-place: old Lord Mumble, who is as toothless as a three-months-old baby, and as mum as an undertaker, and as dull as—well, we will not particularise. Tufthunt never has a dinner now but you see this solemn old toothless patrician at the right-hand of Mrs. Tufthunt—Tufthunt is a Dinner-giving Snob.

Old Livermore, old Soy, old Chutney, the East Indian Director, old Cutler, the Surgeon, &c.,—that society of old fogies, in fine, who give each other dinners round and round, and dine for the mere purpose of guttling—these, again, are Dinner-giving Snobs.

Again, my friend Lady MacScrew, who has three grenadier flunkeys in lace round the table, and serves up a scrag-of-mutton on silver, and dribbles you out bad sherry and port by thimblefuls, is a Dinner-giving Snob of the other sort; and I confess, for my part, I would rather dine with old Livermore or old Soy than with her Ladyship.

Stinginess is snobbish. Ostentation is snobbish. Too great profusion is snobbish. Tuft-hunting is snobbish. But I own there are people more snobbish than all those whose defects are above mentioned: viz., those individuals who can, and don't give dinners at all. The man without hospitality shall never sit *sub iisdem trabibus* with *me*. Let the sordid wretch go mumble his bone alone!

What, again, is true hospitality? Alas, my dear friends and brother Snobs! how little do we meet of it after all! Are the motives *pure* which induce your friends to ask you to dinner? This has often come across me. Does your entertainer want something from you? For instance, I am not of a suspicious turn; but it *is* a fact that when Hookey is bringing out a new work, he asks the critics all round to dinner; that when Walker has got his picture ready for the Exhibition, he somehow grows exceedingly hospitable, and has his friends of the press to a quiet cutlet and a glass of Sillery. Old Hunks, the miser, who died lately (leaving his money to his housekeeper) lived many years on the fat of the land, by simply taking down, at all his friends', the names and Christian names *of all the children*. But though you may have your own opinion about the hospitality of your acquaintances; and though men who ask you from sordid motives are most decidedly Dinner-giving Snobs, it is best not to inquire into their motives too keenly. Be not too curious about the mouth of a gift-horse. After all, a man does not intend to insult you by asking you to dinner.

Though, for that matter, I know some characters about town who actually consider themselves injured and insulted if the dinner or the company is not to their liking. There is Guttleton, who dines at home off a shilling's-worth of beef from the cookshop, but if he is asked to dine at a house where there are not peas at the end of May, or cucumbers in March along with the turbot, thinks himself insulted by being invited. "Good Ged!" says he, "what the deuce do the Forkers mean by asking *me* to a family dinner? I can get mutton at home;" or "What infernal impertinence it is of the Spooners to get *entrées* from the pastrycook's, and fancy that *I* am to be deceived with their stories about their French cook!" Then, again, there is Jack Puddington—I saw that honest fellow t'other day quite in a rage, because, as chance would have it, Sir John Carver asked him to meet the very same party he had met at Colonel Cramley's the day before, and he had not got up a new set of stories to entertain them. Poor Dinner-giving Snobs! you don't know what small thanks you get for all your pains and money! How we Dining-out Snobs sneer at your cookery, and pooh-pooh your old hock, and are incredulous about your four-and-sixpenny champagne, and know that the side-dishes of today are *réchauffés* from the dinner of yesterday, and mark how certain dishes are whisked off the table untasted, so that they may figure at the banquet tomorrow. Whenever, for my part, I see the head man particularly anxious to *escamoter* a fricandeau or a blanc-mange, I always call out, and insist upon massacring it with a spoon. All this sort of conduct makes one popular with the Dinner-giving Snob. One friend of mine, I know, has made a prodigious sensation in good society, by announcing àpropos of certain dishes when offered to him, that he never eats aspic except at Lord Tittup's, and that Lady Jiminy's *chef* is the only man in London who knows how to dress—*Filet en serpenteau*—or *Suprême de volaille aux truffes*.

CHAPTER XX

Dinner-Giving Snobs Further Considered

If my friends would but follow the present prevailing fashion, I think they ought to give me a testimonial for the paper on Dinner-giving Snobs, which I am now writing. What do you say now to a handsome comfortable dinner-service of plate (*not* including plates, for I hold silver plates to be sheer wantonness, and would almost as soon think of silver tea-cups), a couple of near teapots, a coffeepot, trays, &c., with a little inscription to my wife, Mrs. Snob; and a half-score of silver tankards for the little Snoblings, to glitter on the homely table where they partake of their quotidian mutton?

If I had my way, and my plans could be carried out, dinner-giving would increase as much on the one hand as dinner-giving Snobbishness would diminish:—to my mind the most amiable part of the work lately published by my esteemed friend (if upon a very brief acquaintance he will allow me to call him so), Alexis Soyer, the regenerator—what he (in his noble style) would call the most succulent, savoury, and elegant passages—are those which relate, not to the grand banquets and ceremonial dinners, but to his "dinners at home."

The "dinner at home" ought to be the centre of the whole system of dinner-giving. Your usual style of meal—that is, plenteous, comfortable, and in its perfection—should be that to which you welcome your friends, as it is that of which you partake yourself.

For, towards what woman in the world do I entertain a higher regard than towards the beloved partner of my existence, Mrs. Snob? Who should have a greater place in my affections than her six brothers (three or four of whom we are pretty sure will favour us with their company at seven o'clock), or her angelic mother, my own valued mother-in-law?—for whom, finally, would I wish to cater more generously than for your very humble servant, the present writer? Now, nobody supposes that the Birmingham plate is had out, the disguised carpet-beaters introduced to the exclusion of the neat parlour-maid, the miserable *entrées* from the pastrycook's ordered in, and the children packed off (as it is supposed) to the nursery, but really only to the staircase, down which they slide during the dinner-time, waylaying the dishes as they come out, and fingering the round bumps on the jellies, and the forced-meat balls in the soup—nobody, I say, supposes that a dinner at home is characterized by the horrible ceremony, the foolish makeshifts, the mean pomp and ostentation which distinguish our banquets on grand field-days.

Such a notion is monstrous. I would as soon think of having my dearest Bessy sitting opposite me in a turban and bird of paradise, and showing her jolly mottled arms out of blond sleeves in her famous red satin gown: ay, or of having Mr. Toole every day, in a white waistcoat, at my back, shouting, "Silence *faw* the chair!"

Now, if this be the case; if the Brummagem-plate pomp and the processions of disguised footmen are odious and foolish in everyday life, why not always? Why should Jones and I, who are in the middle rank, alter the modes of our being to assume an *éclat* which does not belong to us—to entertain our friends, who (if we are worth anything, and honest fellows at bottom,) are men of the middle rank too, who are not in the least deceived by our temporary splendour, and who play off exactly the same absurd trick upon us when they ask us to dine?

If it be pleasant to dine with your friends, as all persons with good stomachs and kindly hearts will, I presume, allow it to be, it is better to dine twice than to dine once. It is impossible for men of small means to be continually spending five-and-twenty or thirty shillings on each friend who sits down to their table. People dine for less. I myself have seen at my favourite Club (the Senior United Service), his Grace the Duke of Wellington quite contented with the joint, one-and-three, and half-pint of sherry wine, nine; and if his Grace, why not you and I?

This rule I have made, and found the benefit of. Whenever I

ask a couple of Dukes and a Marquis or so to dine with me, I set them down to a piece of beef, or a leg of mutton and trimmings. The grandees thank you for this simplicity, and appreciate the same. My dear Jones, ask any of those whom you have the honour of knowing, if such be not the case.

I am far from wishing that their Graces should treat me in a similar fashion. Splendour is a part of their station, as decent comfort (let us trust), of yours and mine. Fate has comfortably appointed gold plate for some, and has bidden others contentedly to wear the willow-pattern. And being perfectly contented (indeed humbly thankful—for look around, O Jones, and see the myriads who are not so fortunate,) to wear honest linen, while magnificos of the world are adorned with cambric and point-lace, surely we ought to hold as miserable, envious fools, those wretched Beaux Tibbs's of society, who sport a lace dickey, and nothing besides,—the poor silly jays, who trail a peacock's feather behind them, and think to simulate the gorgeous bird whose nature it is to strut on palace-terraces, and to flaunt his magnificent fan-tail in the sunshine!

The jays with peacocks' feathers are the Snobs of this world: and never, since the days of Æsop, were they more numerous in any land than they are at present in this free country.

How does this most ancient apologue apply to the subject in hand—the Dinner-giving Snob. The imitation of the great is universal in this city, from the palaces of Kensingtonia and Belgravia, even to the remotest corner of Brunswick Square. Peacocks' feathers are stuck in the tails of most families. Scarce one of us domestic birds but imitates the lanky, pavonine strut, and shrill, genteel scream. O you misguided dinner-giving Snobs, think how much pleasure you lose, and how much mischief you do with your absurd grandeurs and hypocrisies! You stuff each other with unnatural forced-meats, and entertain each other to the ruin of friendship (let alone health) and the destruction of hospitality and good-fellowship—you, who but for the peacock's tail might chatter away so much at your ease, and be so jovial and happy!

When a man goes into a great set company of dinner-giving and dinner-receiving Snobs, if he has a philosophical turn of mind, he will consider what a huge humbug the whole affair is: the dishes, and the drink, and the servants, and the plate, and the host and hostess, and the conversation, and the company,— the philosopher included.

The host is smiling, and hob-nobbing, and talking up and down the table; but a prey to secret terrors and anxieties, lest the wines he has brought up from the cellar should prove insufficient; lest a corked bottle should destroy his calculations; or our friend the carpet-beater, by making some *bévue*, should disclose his real quality of greengrocer, and show that he is not the family butler.

The hostess is smiling resolutely through all the courses, smiling through her agony; though her heart is in the kitchen, and she is speculating with terror lest there be any disaster there. If the *soufflé* should collapse, or if Wiggins does not send the ices in time—she feels as if she would commit suicide—that smiling, jolly woman!

The children upstairs are yelling, as their maid is crimping their miserable ringlets with hot tongs, tearing Miss Emmy's hair out by the roots, or scrubbing Miss Polly's dumpy nose with mottled soap till the little wretch screams herself into fits. The young males of the family are employed, as we have stated, in piratical exploits upon the landing-place.

The servants are not servants, but the before-mentioned retail tradesmen.

The plate is not plate, but a mere shiny Birmingham lacquer; and so is the hospitality, and everything else.

The talk is Birmingham talk. The wag of the party, with bitterness in his heart, having just quitted his laundress, who is dunning him for her bill, is firing off good stories; and the opposition wag is furious that he cannot get an innings. Jawkins, the great conversationalist, is scornful and indignant with the pair of them, because he is kept out of court. Young Muscadel, that cheap dandy, is talking Fashion and Almack's out of the *Morning Post*, and disgusting his neighbour, Mrs. Fox, who reflects that she has never been there. The widow is vexed out of patience, because her daughter Maria has got a place beside young Cambric, the penniless curate, and not by Colonel Goldmore, the rich widower from India. The Doctor's wife is sulky, because she has not been led out before the barrister's lady; old Doctor Cork is grumbling at the wine, and Guttleton sneering at the cookery.

And to think that all these people might be so happy, and easy, and friendly, were they brought together in a natural unpretentious way, and but for an unhappy passion for peacocks' feathers in England. Gentle shades of Marat and Robespierre! when I see how all the honesty of society is corrupted among us by the miserable fashion-worship, I feel as angry as Mrs. Fox just mentioned, and ready to order a general *battue* of peacocks.

CHAPTER XXI

Some Continental Snobs

Now that September has come, and all our Parliamentary duties are over, perhaps no class of Snobs are in such high feather as the Continental Snobs. I watch these daily as they commence their migrations from the beach at Folkestone. I see shoals of them depart (not perhaps without an innate longing too to quit the Island along with those happy Snobs). Farewell, dear friends, I say: you little know that the individual who regards you from the beach is your friend and historiographer and brother.

I went today to see our excellent friend Snooks, on board the "Queen of the French;" many scores of Snobs were there, on the deck of that fine ship, marching forth in their pride and bravery. They will be at Ostend in four hours; they will inundate the Continent next week; they will carry into far lands the famous image of the British Snob. I shall not see them—but am with them in spirit: and indeed there is hardly a country in the known and civilized world in which these eyes have not beheld them.

I have seen Snobs, in pink coats and hunting-boots, scouring over the Campagna of Rome; and have heard their oaths and their well-known slang in the galleries of the Vatican, and under the shadowy arches of the Coliseum. I have met a Snob on a dromedary in the desert, and picknicking under the Pyramid of Cheops. I like to think how many gallant British Snobs there are, at this minute of writing, pushing their heads out of every window in the courtyard of "Meurice's" in the Rue de Rivoli; or roaring out, "Garsong, du pang," "Garson, du vang;" or swaggering down the Toledo at Naples, or even how many will be on the look-out for Snooks on Ostend Pier,—for Snooks, and the rest of the Snobs on board the "Queen of the French."

Look at the Marquis of Carabas and his two carriages. My Lady Marchioness comes on board, looks round with that happy air of mingled terror and impertinence which distinguishes her ladyship, and rushes to her carriage, for it is impossible that she should mingle with the other Snobs on deck. There she sits, and will be ill in private. The strawberry-leaves on her chariot-panels are engraved on her ladyship's heart. If she were going to heaven instead of to Ostend, I rather think she would expect to have *des places réservées* for her, and would send to order the best rooms. A courier, with his money-bag of office round his shoulders—a huge scowling footman, whose dark pepper-and-salt livery glistens with the heraldic insignia of the Carabases—a brazen-looking, tawdry French *femme-de-chambre* (none but a female pen can do justice to that wonderful tawdry toilette of the lady's-maid *en voyage*—and a miserable *dame de compagnie*, are ministering to the wants of her ladyship and her King Charles's spaniel. They are rushing to and fro with eau-de-Cologne, pocket-handkerchiefs, which are all fringe and cipher, and popping mysterious cushions behind and before, and in every available corner of the carriage.

The little Marquis, her husband, is walking about the deck in a bewildered manner, with a lean daughter on each arm: the carroty-tufted hope of the family is already smoking on the foredeck in a travelling costume checked all over, and in little lacquer-tipped jean boots, and a shirt embroidered with pink boa-constrictors. What is it that gives travelling Snobs such a marvellous propensity to rush into a costume? Why should a man not travel in a coat, &c.? but think proper to dress himself like a harlequin in mourning? See, even young Aldermanbury, the tallow-merchant, who has just stepped on board, has got a travelling-dress gaping all over with pockets; and little Tom Tapeworm, the lawyer's clerk out of the City, who has but three weeks' leave, turns out in gaiters and a bran new shooting-jacket, and must let the moustaches grow on his little snuffy upper lip, forsooth!

Pompey Hicks is giving elaborate directions to his servant, and asking loudly, "Davis, where's the dwessing-case?" and

"Davis, you'd best take the pistol-case into the cabin." Little Pompey travels with a dressing-case, and without a beard: who he is going to shoot with his pistols, who on earth can tell? and what he is to do with his servant but wait upon him, I am at a loss to conjecture.

Look at honest Nathan Houndsditch and his lady, and their little son. What a noble air of blazing contentment illuminates the features of those Snobs of Eastern race! What a toilette Houndsditch's is! What rings and chains, what gold-headed canes and diamonds, what a tuft the rogue has got to his chin (the rogue! he will never spare himself any cheap enjoyment!) Little Houndsditch has a little cane with a gilt head and little mosaic ornaments—altogether an extra air. As for the lady, she is all the colours of the rainbow! she has a pink parasol, with a white lining, and a yellow bonnet, and an emerald green shawl, and a shot-silk pelisse; and drab boots and rhubarb-coloured gloves; and parti-coloured glass buttons, expanding from the size of a fourpenny-piece to a crown, glitter and twiddle all down the front of her gorgeous costume. I have said before, I like to look at "the Peoples" on their gala days, they are so picturesquely and outrageously splendid and happy.

Yonder comes Captain Bull; spick and span, tight and trim; who travels for four or six months every year of his life; who does not commit himself by luxury of raiment or insolence of demeanour, but I think is as great a Snob as any man on board. Bull passes the season in London, sponging for dinners, and sleeping in a garret near his Club. Abroad, he has been everywhere; he knows the best wine at every inn in every capital in Europe; lives with the best English company there; has seen every palace and picture-gallery from Madrid to Stockholm; speaks an abominable little jargon of half-a-dozen languages—and knows nothing—nothing. Bull hunts tufts on the Continent, and is a sort of amateur courier. He will scrape acquaintance with old Carabas before they make Ostend; and will remind his lordship that he met him at Vienna twenty years ago, or gave him a glass of Schnapps up the Righi. We have said

Bull knows nothing: he knows the birth, arms, and pedigree of all the peerage, has poked his little eyes into every one of the carriages on board—their panels noted and their crests surveyed; he knows all the Continental stories of English scandal—how Count Towrowski ran off with Miss Baggs at Naples—how *very* thick Lady Smigsmag was with young Cornichon of the French Legation at Florence—the exact amount which Jack Deuceace won of Bob Greengoose at Baden—what it is that made the Staggs settle on the Continent: the sum for which the O'Goggarty estates are mortgaged, &c. If he can't catch a lord he will hook on to a baronet, or else the old wretch will catch hold of some beardless young stripling of fashion, and show him "life" in various and amiable and inaccessible quarters. Faugh! the old brute! If he has every one of the vices of the most boisterous youth, at least he is comforted by having no conscience. He is utterly stupid, but of a jovial turn. He believes himself to be quite a respectable member of society: but perhaps the only good action he ever did in his life is the involuntary one of giving an example to be avoided, and showing what an odious thing in the social picture is that figure of the debauched old man who passes through life rather a decorous Silenus, and dies some day in his garret, alone, unrepenting, and unnoted, save by his astonished heirs, who find that the dissolute old miser has left money behind him. See! he is up to old Carabas already! I told you he would.

Yonder you see the old Lady Mary MacScrew, and those middle-aged young women her daughters; they are going to cheapen and haggle in Belgium and up the Rhine until they meet with a boarding-house where they can live upon less board-wages than her ladyship pays her footmen. But she will exact and receive considerable respect from the British Snobs located in the watering-place which she selects for her summer residence, being the daughter of the Earl of Haggistoun. That broad-shouldered buck, with the great whiskers and the cleaned white kid-gloves, is Mr. Phelim Clancy of Poldoodystown: he calls himself Mr. De Clancy; he endeavours to disguise his native brogue with the richest superposition of English; and if you play at billiards or *écarté* with him, the chances are that you will win the first game, and he the seven or eight games ensuing.

That overgrown lady with the four daughters, and the young dandy from the University, her son, is Mrs. Kewsy, the eminent barrister's lady, who would rather die than not be in the fashion. She has the "Peerage" in her carpet-bag, you may be sure; but she is altogether cut out by Mrs. Quod, the attorney's wife, whose carriage, with the apparatus of rumbles, dickeys, and imperials, scarcely yields in splendour to the Marquis of Carabas's own travelling-chariot, and whose courier has even bigger whiskers and a larger morocco money-bag than the Marquis's own travelling gentleman. Remark her well: she is talking to Mr. Spout, the new Member for Jawborough, who is going out to inspect the operations of the Zollverein, and will put some very severe questions to Lord Palmerston next session upon England and her relations with the Prussian-blue trade, the Naples-soap trade, the German-tinder trade, &c. Spout will patronize King Leopold at Brussels; will write letters from abroad to the *Jawborough Independent*; and in his quality of *Member du Parliamong Britannique*, will expect to be invited to a family dinner with every sovereign whose dominions he honours with a visit during his tour.

The next person is—but hark! the bell for shore is ringing, and, shaking Snooks's hand cordially, we rush on to the pier, waving him a farewell as the noble black ship cuts keenly through the sunny azure waters, bearing away that cargo of Snobs outward bound.

CHAPTER XXII

Continental Snobbery Continued

We are accustomed to laugh at the French for their braggadocio propensities, and intolerable vanity about la France, la gloire, l'Empereur, and the like; and yet I think in my heart that the British Snob, for conceit and self-sufficiency and braggartism in his way, is without a parallel. There is always something uneasy in a Frenchman's conceit. He brags with so much fury, shrieking, and gesticulation; yells out so loudly that the Français is at the head of civilization, the centre of thought, &c.; that one can't but see the poor fellow has a lurking doubt in his own mind that he is not the wonder he professes to be.

About the British Snob, on the contrary, there is commonly no noise, no bluster, but the calmness of profound conviction. We are better than all the world; we don't question the opinion at all; it's an axiom. And when a Frenchman bellows out, *"La France, Monsieur, la France est à la tête du monde civilisé!"* we laugh good-naturedly at the frantic poor devil. *We* are the first chop of the world: we know the fact so well in our secret hearts that a claim set up elsewhere is simply ludicrous. My dear brother reader, say, as a man of honour, if you are not of this opinion? Do you think a Frenchman your equal? You don't—you gallant British Snob—you know you don't: no more, perhaps, does the Snob your humble servant, brother.

And I am inclined to think it is this conviction, and the consequent bearing of the Englishman towards the foreigner whom he condescends to visit, this confidence of superiority which holds up the head of the owner of every English hat-box from Sicily to St. Petersburg, that makes us so magnificently hated throughout Europe as we are; this—more than all our little victories, and of which many Frenchmen and Spaniards have never heard—this amazing and indomitable insular pride, which animates my lord in his travelling-carriage as well as John in the rumble.

If you read the old Chronicles of the French wars, you find precisely the same character of the Englishman, and Henry V.'s people behaved with just the cool domineering manner of our gallant veterans of France and the Peninsula. Did you never hear Colonel Cutler and Major Slasher talking over the war after dinner? or Captain Boarder describing his action with the "Indomptable?" "Hang the fellows," says Boarder, "their practice was very good. I was beat off three times before I took her." "Cuss those carabineers of Milhaud's," says Slasher, "what work they made of our light cavalry!" implying a sort of surprise that the Frenchman should stand up against Britons at all: a good-natured wonder that the blind, mad, vain-glorious, brave poor devils should actually have the courage to resist an Englishman. Legions of such Englishmen are patronizing Europe at this moment, being kind to the Pope, or good-natured to the King of Holland, or condescending to inspect the Prussian reviews. When Nicholas came here, who reviews a quarter of a million of pairs of moustaches to his breakfast every morning, we took him off to Windsor and showed him two whole regiments of six or eight hundred Britons a-piece, with an air as much as to say,—"There, my boy, look at *that*. Those are *Englishmen*, those are, and your master whenever you please," as the nursery song says. The British Snob is long, long past scepticism, and can afford to laugh quite good-humouredly at those conceited Yankees, or besotted little Frenchmen, who set up as models of mankind. *They* forsooth?

I have been led into these remarks by listening to an old fellow at the Hôtel du Nord, at Boulogne, and who is evidently of the Slasher sort. He came down and seated himself at the breakfast-table with a surly scowl on his salmon-coloured bloodshot face, strangling in a tight, cross-barred cravat; his linen and his appointments so perfectly stiff and spotless that everybody at once recognized him as a dear countryman. Only our port-wine and other admirable institutions could have produced a figure so insolent, so stupid, so gentlemanlike.

After a while our attention was called to him by his roaring out, in a voice of plethoric fury, "O!"

Everybody turned round at the "O," conceiving the Colonel to be, as his countenance denoted him, in intense pain; but the waiters knew better, and instead of being alarmed, brought the Colonel the kettle. "O," it appears, is the French for hot-water. The Colonel (though he despises it heartily) thinks he speaks the language remarkably well. Whilst he was inhausting his smoking tea, which went rolling and gurgling down his throat, and hissing over the "hot coppers" of that respectable veteran, a friend joined him, with a wizened face and very black wig, evidently a Colonel too.

The two warriors, waggling their old heads at each other, presently joined breakfast, and fell into conversation, and we had the advantage of hearing about the old war, and some pleasant conjectures as to the next, which they considered imminent. They psha'd the French fleet; they pooh-pooh'd the French commercial marine; they showed how, in a war, there would be a cordon ("a cordong, by —") of steamers along our coast, and "by —," ready at a minute to land anywhere on the other shore, to give the French as good a thrashing as they got in the last war, "by —." In fact, a rumbling cannonade of oaths was fired by the two veterans during the whole of their conversation.

There was a Frenchman in the room, but as he had not been above ten years in London, of course he did not speak the language, and lost the benefit of the conversation. "But, O my country!" said I to myself, "it's no wonder that you are so beloved! If I were a Frenchman, how I would hate you!"

That brutal, ignorant, peevish bully of an Englishman is showing himself in every city of Europe. One of the dullest creatures under heaven, he goes trampling Europe under foot, shouldering his way into galleries and cathedrals, and bustling into palaces with his buckram uniform. At church or theatre, gala or picture-gallery, *his* face never varies. A thousand delightful sights pass before his bloodshot eyes, and don't

WIGGINS AT HOME.

WIGGINS AT BOULOGNE.

WIGGINS AT SEA.

affect him. Countless brilliant scenes of life and manners are shown him, but never move him. He goes to church, and calls the practices there degrading and superstitious; as if *his* alter was the only one that was acceptable. He goes to picture-galleries, and is more ignorant about Art than a French shoeblack. Art, Nature pass, and there is no dot of admiration in his stupid eyes: nothing moves him, except when a very great man comes his way, and then the rigid, proud, self-confident, inflexible British Snob can be as humble as a flunkey and as supple as a harlequin.

CHAPTER XXIII

English Snobs on the Continent

"What is the use of Lord Rosse's telescope?" my friend Panwiski exclaimed the other day. "It only enables you to see a few hundred thousands of miles farther. What were thought to be mere nebulæ, turn out to be most perceivable starry systems; and beyond these, you see other nebulæ, which a more powerful glass will show to be stars, again; and so they go on glittering and winking away into eternity." With which my friend Pan, heaving a great sigh, as if confessing his inability to look Infinity in the face, sank back resigned, and swallowed a large bumper of claret.

I (who, like other great men, have but one idea), thought to myself, that as the stars are, so are the Snobs: the more you gaze upon those luminaries, the more you behold—now nebulously congregated—now faintly distinguishable—now brightly defined—until they twinkle off in endless blazes, and fade into the immeasurable darkness. I am but as a child playing on the sea-shore. Some telescopic philosopher will arise one day, some great Snobonomer, to find the laws of the great science which we are now merely playing with, and to define, and settle, and classify that which is at present but vague theory, and loose though elegant assertion.

Yes: a single eye can but trace a very few and simple varieties of the enormous universe of Snobs. I sometimes think of appealing to the public, and calling together a congress of *savans*, such as met at Southampton—each to bring his contributions and read his paper on the Great Subject. For what can a single poor few do, even with the subject at present in hand? English Snobs on the Continent—though they are a hundred thousand times less numerous than on their native island, yet even these few are too many. One can only fix a stray one here and there. The individuals are caught—the thousands escape. I have noted down but three whom I have met with in my walk this morning through this pleasant marine city of Boulogne.

There is the English Raff Snob, that frequents *estaminets* and *cabarets;* who is heard yelling, "We won't go home till morning:" and startling the midnight echoes of quiet Continental towns with shrieks of English slang. The boozy unshorn wretch is seen hovering round quays as packets arrive, and tippling drams in inn bars where he gets credit. He talks French with slang familiarity: he and his like quite people the debt-prisons on the Continent. He plays pool at the billiard-houses, and may be seen engaged at cards and dominoes of forenoons. His signature is to be seen on countless bills of exchange: it belonged to an honourable family once, very likely; for the English Raff most probably began by being a gentleman, and has a father over the water who is ashamed to hear his name. He has cheated the old "governor" repeatedly in better days, and swindled his sisters of their portions, and robbed his younger brothers. Now he is living on his wife's jointure: she is hidden away in some dismal garret, patching shabby finery and cobbling up old clothes for her children—the most miserable and slatternly of women.

Or sometimes the poor woman and her daughters go about timidly, giving lessons in English and music, or do embroidery and work underhand, to purchase the means for the *pot-au-feu;* while Raff is swaggering on the quay, or tossing off glasses of cognac at the *café*. The unfortunate creature has a child still every year, and her constant hypocrisy is to try and make her girls believe that their father is a respectable man, and to huddle him out of the way when the brute comes home drunk.

Those poor ruined souls get together and have a society of their own, the which it is very affecting to watch—those tawdry pretences at gentility, those flimsy attempts at gaiety: those woful sallies: that jingling old piano; oh, it makes the heart sick to see and hear them. As Mrs. Raff, with her company of pale daughters, gives a penny tea to Mrs. Diddler, they talk about bygone times and the fine society they kept; and they sing

113

feeble songs out of tattered old music-books; and while engaged in this sort of entertainment, in comes Captain Raff with his greasy hat on one side, and straightway the whole of the dismal room reeks with a mingled odour of smoke and spirits.

Has not everybody who has lived abroad met Captain Raff? His name is proclaimed, every now and then, by Mr. Sheriff's Officer Hemp; and about Boulogne, and Paris, and Brussels, there are so many of his sort that I will lay a wager that I shall be accused of gross personality for showing him up. Many a less irreclaimable villain is transported; many a more honourable man is at present at the treadmill; and although we are the noblest, greatest, most religious, and most moral people in the world, I would still like to know where, except in the United Kingdom, debts are a matter of joke, and making tradesmen "suffer" a sport that gentlemen own to? It is dishonourable to owe money in France. You never hear people in other parts of Europe brag of their swindling; or see a prison in a large Continental town which is not more or less peopled with English rogues.

A still more loathsome and dangerous Snob than the above transparent and passive scamp, is frequent on the continent of Europe, and my young Snob friends who are travelling thither should be especially warned against him. Captain Legg is a gentleman, like Raff, though perhaps of a better degree. He has robbed his family too, but of a great deal more, and has boldly dishonoured bills for thousands, where Raff has been boggling over the clumsy conveyance of a ten-pound note. Legg is always at the best inn, with the finest waistcoats and moustaches, or tearing about in the flashest of britzkas, while poor Raff is tipsifying himself with spirits, and smoking cheap tobacco. It is amazing to think that Legg, so often shown up, and known everywhere, is flourishing yet. He would sink into utter ruin, but for the constant and ardent love of gentility that distinguishes the English Snob. There is many a young fellow of the middle classes who must know Legg to be a rogue and a cheat; and yet from his desire to be in the fashion, and his admiration of tip-top swells, and from his ambition to air himself by the side of a Lord's son, will let Legg make an income out of him; content to pay, so long as he can enjoy that society. Many a worthy father of a family, when he hears that his son is riding about with Captain Legg, Lord Levant's son, is rather pleased that young Hopeful should be in such good company.

Legg and his friend, Major Macer, make professional tours through Europe, and are to be found at the right places at the right time. Last year I heard how my young acquaintance, Mr. Muff, from Oxford, going to see a little life at a Carnival ball at Paris, was accosted by an Englishman who did not know a word of the d— language, and hearing Muff speak it so admirably, begged him to interpret to a waiter with whom there was a dispute about refreshments. It was quite a comfort, the stranger said, to see an honest English face; and did Muff know where there was a good place for supper? So those two went to supper, and who should come in, of all men in the world, but Major Macer? And so Legg introduced Macer, and so there came on a little intimacy, and three-card loo, &c. &c. Year after year scores of Muffs, in various places in the world, are victimised by Legg and Macer. The story is so stale, the trick of seduction so entirely old and clumsy, that it is only a wonder people can be taken in any more: but the temptations of vice and gentility together are too much for young English Snobs, and those simple young victims are caught fresh every day. Though it is only to be kicked and cheated by men of fashion, your true British Snob will present himself for the honour.

I need not allude here to that very common British Snob, who makes desperate efforts at becoming intimate with the great Continental aristocracy, such as old Rolls, the baker, who has set up his quarters in the Faubourg St. Germain, and will receive none but Carlists, and no French gentleman under the rank of a Marquis. We can all of us laugh at *that* fellow's pretensions well enough—we who tremble before a great man of our own nation. But, as you say, my brave and honest John Bull of a Snob, a French Marquis of twenty descents is very different from an English Peer; and a pack of beggarly German and Italian Fürsten and Principi awaken the scorn of an honest-minded Briton. But our aristocracy!—that's a very different matter. They are the real leaders of the world—the real old original and-no-mistake nobility. Off with your cap, Snob; down on your knees, Snob, and truckle.

CHAPTER XXIV

On Some Country Snobs

Tired of the town, where the sight of the closed shutters of the nobility, my friends, makes my heart sick in my walks; afraid almost to sit in those vast Pall Mall solitudes, the Clubs, and of annoying the Club waiters, who might, I thought, be going to shoot in the country, but for me, I determined on a brief tour in the provinces, and paying some visits in the country which were long due.

My first visit was to my friend Major Ponto (H.P. of the Horse Marines), in Mangelwurzelshire. The Major, in his little phaeton, was in waiting to take me up at the station. The vehicle was not certainly splendid, but such a carriage as would accommodate a plain man (as Ponto said he was) and a numerous family. We drove by beautiful fresh fields and green hedges, through a cheerful English landscape; the high-road, as smooth and trim as the way in a nobleman's park, was charmingly chequered with cool shade and golden sunshine. Rustics in snowy smock-frocks jerked their hats off smiling as we passed. Children, with cheeks as red as the apples in the orchards, bobbed curtsies to us at the cottage-doors. Blue church spires rose here and there in the distance: and as the buxom gardener's wife opened the white gate at the Major's little ivy-covered lodge, and we drove through the neat plantations of firs and evergreens, up to the house, my bosom felt a joy and elation which I thought it was impossible to experience in the smoky atmosphere of a town. "Here," I mentally exclaimed, "is all peace, plenty, happiness. Here, I shall be rid of Snobs. There can be none in this charming Arcadian spot."

Stripes, the Major's man (formerly corporal in his gallant corps), received my portmanteau, and an elegant little present, which I had brought from town as a peace-offering to Mrs. Ponto; viz., a cod and oysters from Grove's, in a hamper about the size of a coffin.

Ponto's house ("The Evergreens" Mrs. P. has christened it) is a perfect Paradise of a place. It is all over creepers, and bow-windows, and verandahs. A wavy lawn tumbles up and down all round it, with flower-beds of wonderful shapes, and zigzag gravel walks, and beautiful but damp shrubberies of myrtles and glistening laurestines, which have procured it its change of name. It was called Little Bullock's Pound in old Doctor Ponto's time. I had a view of the pretty grounds and the stable, and the adjoining village and church, and a great park beyond, from the windows of the bedroom whither Ponto conducted me. It was the yellow bedroom, the freshest and pleasantest of bed-chambers; the air was fragrant with a large bouquet that was placed on the writing-table; the linen was fragrant with the lavender in which it had been laid; the chintz hangings of the bed and the big sofa were, if not fragrant with flowers, at least painted all over with them; the pen-wiper on the table was the imitation of a double dahlia; and there was accommodation for my watch in a sunflower on the mantelpiece. A scarlet-leafed creeper came curling over the windows, through which the setting sun was pouring a flood of golden light. It was all flowers and freshness. Oh, how unlike those black chimney-pots in St. Alban's Place, London, on which these weary eyes are accustomed to look.

"It must be all happiness here, Ponto," said I, flinging myself down into the snug *bergère*, and inhaling such a delicious draught of country air as all the *millefleurs* of Mr. Atkinson's shop cannot impart to any the most expensive pocket-handkerchief.

"Nice place, isn't it?" said Ponto. "Quiet and unpretending. I like everything quiet. You've not brought your valet with you? Stripes will arrange your dressing things;" and that functionary, entering at the same time, proceeded to gut my portmanteau, and to lay out the black kerseymeres, "the rich cut velvet Genoa waistcoat," the white choker, and other polite articles of evening costume, with great gravity and despatch. "A great dinner-party," thinks I to myself, seeing these preparations

118

(and not, perhaps, displeased at the idea that some of the best people in the neighbourhood were coming to see me). "Hark, there's the first bell ringing!" said Ponto, moving away: and, in fact, a clamorous harbinger of victuals began clanging from the stable turret, and announced the agreeable fact that dinner would appear in half-an-hour. "If the dinner is as grand as the dinner-bell," thought I, "faith, I'm in good quarters!" and had leisure, during the half-hour's interval, not only to advance my own person to the utmost polish of elegance which it is capable of receiving, to admire the pedigree of the Pontos hanging over the chimney, and the Ponto crest and arms emblazoned on the wash-hand basin and jug, but to make a thousand reflections on the happiness of a country life—upon the innocent friendliness and cordiality of rustic intercourse; and to sigh for an opportunity of retiring, like Ponto, to my own fields, to my own vine and fig-tree, with a placens uxor in my domus, and a half-score of sweet young pledges of affection sporting round my paternal knee.

Clang! At the end of the thirty minutes, dinner-bell number two pealed from the adjacent turret. I hastened downstairs, expecting to find a score of healthy country folks in the drawing-room. There was only one person there; a tall and Roman-nosed lady, glistening over with bugles, in deep mourning. She rose, advanced two steps, made a majestic curtsey, during which all the bugles in her awful head-dress began to twiddle and quiver—and then said, "Mr. Snob, we are very happy to see you at the Evergreens," and heaved a great sigh.

This, then, was Mrs. Major Ponto; to whom, making my very best bow, I replied, that I was very proud to make her acquaintance, as also that of so charming a place as the Evergreens.

Another sigh. "We are distantly related, Mr. Snob," said she, shaking her melancholy head. "Poor dear Lord Rubadub!"

"Oh!" said I, not knowing what the deuce Mrs. Major Ponto meant.

"Major Ponto told me that you were of the Leicestershire Snobs: a very old family, and related to Lord Snobbington, who married Laura Rubadub, who is a cousin of mine, as was her poor dear father, for whom we are mourning. What a seizure! only sixty-three, and apoplexy quite unknown until now in our family! In life we are in death, Mr. Snob. Does Lady Snobbington bear the deprivation well?"

"Why, really, ma'am, I—I don't know," I replied, more and more confused.

As she was speaking I heard a sort of *cloop*, by which well-known sound I was aware that somebody was opening a bottle of wine, and Ponto entered, in a huge white neckcloth, and a rather shabby black suit.

"My love," Mrs. Major Ponto said to her husband, "we were talking of our cousin—poor dear Lord Rubadub. His death has placed some of the first families in England in mourning. Does Lady Rubadub keep the house in Hill Street, do you know?"

I didn't know, but I said, "I believe she does," at a venture; and, looking down to the drawing-room table, saw the inevitable, abominable, maniacal, absurd, disgusting "Peerage" open on the table, interleaved with annotations, and open at the article "Snobbington."

"Dinner is served," says Stripes, flinging open the door; and I gave Mrs. Major Ponto my arm.

CHAPTER XXV

A Visit to Some Country Snobs

Of the dinner to which we now sat down, I am not going to be a severe critic. The mahogany I hold to be inviolable; but this I will say, that I prefer sherry to marsala when I can get it, and the latter was the wine of which I have no doubt I heard the "cloop" just before dinner. Nor was it particularly good of its kind; however, Mrs. Major Ponto did not evidently know the difference, for she called the liquor Amontillado during the whole of the repast, and drank but half a glass of it, leaving the rest for the Major and his guest.

Stripes was in the livery of the Ponto family—a thought shabby, but gorgeous in the extreme—lots of magnificent worsted lace, and livery buttons of a very notable size. The honest fellow's hands, I remarked, were very large and black; and a fine odour of the stable was wafted about the room as he moved to and fro in his ministration. I should have preferred a clean maidservant, but the sensations of Londoners are too acute perhaps on these subjects; and a faithful John, after all, *is* more genteel.

From the circumstance of the dinner being composed of pig's-head mock-turtle soup, of pig's-fry and roast ribs of pork, I am led to imagine that one of Ponto's black Hampshires had been sacrificed a short time previous to my visit. It was an excellent and comfortable repast; only there *was* rather a sameness in it, certainly. I made a similar remark the next day.

During the dinner Mrs. Ponto asked me many questions regarding the nobility, my relatives. "When Lady Angelina Skeggs would come out; and if the countess her mamma" (this was said with much archness and he-he-ing) "still wore that extraordinary purple hair-dye?" "Whether my Lord Guttlebury kept, besides his French chef, and an English cordon-bleu for the roasts, an Italian for the confectionery?" "Who attended at Lady Clapperclaw's conversazioni?" and "whether Sir John Champignon's 'Thursday mornings' were pleasant?" "Was it true that Lady Carabas, wanting to pawn her diamonds, found that they were paste, and that the Marquis had disposed of them beforehand?" "How was it that Snuffin, the great tobacco-merchant, broke off the marriage which was on the tapis between him and their second daughter; and was it true that a mulatto lady came over from the Havanna and forbade the match?"

"Upon my word, Madam," I had begun, and was going on to say that I didn't know one word about all these matters which seemed so to interest Mrs. Major Ponto, when the Major, giving me a tread or stamp with his large foot under the table, said—

"Come, come, Snob my boy, we are all tiled, you know. We *know* you're one of the fashionable people about town: *we* saw your name at Lady Clapperclaw's *soirées*, and the Champignon breakfasts; and as for the Rubadubs, of course, as relations——"

"Oh, of course, I dine there twice a week," I said; and then I remembered that my cousin, Humphry Snob, of the Middle Temple, *is* a great frequenter of genteel societies, and to have seen his name in the *Morning Post* at the tag-end of several party lists. So, taking the hint, I am ashamed to say I indulged Mrs. Major Ponto with a deal of information about the first families in England, such as would astonish those great personages if they knew it. I described to her most accurately the three reigning beauties of last season at Almack's: told her in confidence that his Grace the D—— of W—— was going to be married the day after his Statue was put up; that his Grace the D—— of D—— was also about to lead the fourth daughter of the Archduke Stephen to the hymeneal altar:—and talked to her, in a word, just in the style of Mrs. Gore's last fashionable novel.

Mrs. Major was quite fascinated by this brilliant conversation. She began to trot out scraps of French, just for all the world as they do in the novels; and kissed her hand to me quite graciously, telling me to come soon to caffy, *ung pu de Musick o salong*—with which she tripped off like an elderly fairy.

"Shall I open a bottle of port, or do you ever drink such a

thing as Hollands and water?" says Ponto, looking ruefully at me. This was a very different style of thing to what I had been led to expect from him at our smoking-room at the Club: where he swaggers about his horses and his cellar: and slapping me on the shoulder used to say, "Come down to Mangel-wurzelshire, Snob my boy, and I'll give you as good a day's shooting and as good a glass of claret as any in the county."—"Well," I said, "I liked Hollands much better than port, and gin even better than Hollands." This was lucky: it *was* gin; and Stripes brought in hot water on a splendid plated tray.

The jingling of a harp and piano soon announced that Mrs. Ponto's *ung pu de Musick* had commenced, and the smell of the stable again entering the dining-room, in the person of Stripes, summoned us to *caffy* and the little concert. She beckoned me with a winning smile to the sofa, on which she made room for me, and where we could command a fine view of the backs of the young ladies who were performing the musical entertainment. Very broad backs they were too, strictly according to the present mode, for crinoline or its substitutes is not an expensive luxury, and young people in the country can afford to be in the fashion at very trifling charges. Miss Emily Ponto at the piano, and her sister Maria at that somewhat exploded instrument, the harp, were in light blue dresses that looked all flounce, and spread out like Mr. Green's balloon when inflated.

"Brilliant touch Emily has—what a fine arm Maria's is," Mrs. Ponto remarked good-naturedly, pointing out the merits of her daughters, and waving her own arm in such a way as to show that she was not a little satisfied with the beauty of that member. I observed she had about nine bracelets and bangles, consisting of chains and padlocks, the Major's miniature, and a variety of brass serpents, with fiery ruby or tender turquoise eyes, writhing up to her elbow almost, in the most profuse contortions.

"You recognize those polkas? They were played at Devonshire House on the 23rd of July, the day of the grand fête." So I said yes—I knew 'em quite intimately; and began wagging my head as if in acknowledgment of those old friends.

When the performance was concluded, I had the felicity of a presentation and conversation with the two tall and scraggy Miss Pontos; and Miss Wirt, the governess, sat down to entertain us with variations on "Sich a gettin' up Stairs." They were determined to be in the fashion.

For the performance of the "Gettin' up Stairs," I have no other name but that it was a *stunner*. First Miss Wirt, with great deliberation, played the original and beautiful melody, cutting it, as it were, out of the instrument, and firing off each note so loud, clear, and sharp, that I am sure Stripes must have heard it in the stable.

"What a finger!" says Mrs. Ponto; and indeed it *was* a finger, as knotted as a turkey's drumstick, and splaying all over the piano. When she had banged out the tune slowly, she began a different manner of "Gettin' up Stairs," and did so with a fury and swiftness quite incredible. She spun upstairs; she whirled upstairs: she galloped upstairs; she rattled upstairs; and then having got the tune to the top landing, as it were, she hurled it down again shrieking to the bottom floor, where it sank in a crash as if exhausted by the breathless rapidity of the descent. Then Miss Wirt played the "Gettin' up Stairs" with the most pathetic and ravishing solemnity: plaintive moans and sobs issued from the keys—you wept and trembled as you were gettin' upstairs. Miss Wirt's hands seemed to faint and wail and die in variations: again, and she went up with a savage clang and rush of trumpets, as if Miss Wirt was storming a breach; and although I knew nothing of music, as I sat and listened with my mouth open to this wonderful display, my *caffy* grew cold, and I wondered the windows did not crack and the chandelier start out of the beam at the sound of this earthquake of a piece of music.

"Glorious creature! Isn't she?" said Mrs. Ponto. "Squirtz's favourite pupil—inestimable to have such a creature. Lady Carabas would give her eyes for her! A prodigy of accomplishments! Thank you, Miss Wirt!"—and the young ladies gave a heave and a gasp of admiration—a deep-breathing gushing sound, such as you hear at church when the sermon comes to a full stop.

Miss Wirt put her two great double-knuckled hands round a waist of her two pupils, and said, "My dear children, I hope you will be able to play it soon as well as your poor little governess. When I lived with the Dunsinanes, it was the dear Duchess's favourite, and Lady Barbara and Lady Jane Macbeth learned it. It was while hearing Jane play that, I remember, that dear Lord Castletoddy first fell in love with her? and though he is but an Irish Peer, with not more than fifteen thousand a year, I persuaded Jane to have him. Do you know Castletoddy, Mr. Snob?—round towers—sweet place—County Mayo. Old Lord Castletoddy (the present Lord was then Lord Inishowan) was a most eccentric old man—they say he was mad. I heard his Royal Highness the poor dear Duke of Sussex—(*such* a man, my dears, but alas! addicted to smoking!)—I heard his Royal Highness say to the Marquis of Anglesea, 'I am sure Castletoddy is mad!' but Inishowan wasn't in marrying my sweet Jane, though the dear child had but her ten thousand pounds *pour tout potage!*"

"Most invaluable person," whispered Mrs. Major Ponto to me. "Has lived in the very highest society;" and I, who have been accustomed to see governesses bullied in the world, was delighted to find this one ruling the roast, and to think that even the majestic Mrs. Ponto bent before her.

As for *my* pipe, so to speak, it went out at once. I hadn't a word to say against a woman who was intimate with every Duchess in the Red Book. She wasn't the rosebud, but she had been near it. She had rubbed shoulders with the great, and about these we talked all the evening incessantly, and about the fashions, and about the Court, until bed-time came.

"And are there Snobs in this Elysium?" I exclaimed, jumping into the lavender-perfumed bed. Ponto's snoring boomed from the neighbouring bed-room in reply.

CHAPTER XXVI

On Some Country Snobs

Something like a journal of the proceedings of the Evergreens may be interesting to those foreign readers of *Punch* who want to know the customs of an English gentleman's family and household. There's plenty of time to keep the Journal. Piano-strumming begins at six o'clock in the morning; it lasts till breakfast, with but a minute's intermission, when the instrument changes hands, and Miss Emily practises in place of her sister Miss Maria.

In fact, the confounded instrument never stops: when the young ladies are at their lessons, Miss Wirt hammers away at those stunning variations, and keeps her magnificent finger in exercise.

I asked this great creature in what other branches of education she instructed her pupils? "The modern languages," says she modestly: "French, German, Spanish, and Italian, Latin and the rudiments of Greek if desired. English of course; the practice of Elocution, Geography, and Astronomy, and the Use of the Globes, Algebra (but only as far as quadratic equations); for a poor ignorant female, you know, Mr. Snob, cannot be expected to know everything. Ancient and Modern History no young woman can be without; and of these I make my beloved pupils *perfect mistresses*. Botany, Geology, and Mineralogy, I consider as amusements. And with these I assure you we manage to pass the days at the Evergreens not unpleasantly."

Only these, thought I—what an education! But I looked in one of Miss Ponto's manuscript song-books and found five faults of French in four words: and in a waggish mood asking Miss Wirt whether Dante Algiery was so called because he was born at Algiers, received a smiling answer in the affirmative, which made me rather doubt about the accuracy of Miss Wirt's knowledge.

When the above little morning occupations are concluded,

these unfortunate young women perform what they call Calisthenic Exercises in the garden. I saw them today, without any crinoline, pulling the garden-roller.

Dear Mrs. Ponto was in the garden too, and as limp as her daughters; in a faded bandeau of hair, in a battered bonnet, in a holland pinafore, in pattens, on a broken chair, snipping leaves off a vine. Mrs. Ponto measures many yards about in an evening. Ye heavens! what a guy she is in that skeleton morning-costume!

Besides Stripes, they keep a boy called Thomas or Tummus. Tummus works in the garden or about the pigsty and stable; Thomas wears a page's costume of eruptive buttons.

When anybody calls, and Stripes is out of the way, Tummus flings himself like mad into Thomas's clothes, and comes out metamorphosed like Harlequin in the pantomime. Today, as Mrs. P. was cutting the grape-vine, as the young ladies were at the roller, down comes Tummus like a roaring whirlwind, with "Missus, Missus, there's company coomin'!" Away skurry the young ladies from the roller, down comes Mrs. P. from the old chair, off flies Tummus to change his clothes, and in an incredibly short space of time Sir John Hawbuck, my Lady Hawbuck, and Master Hugh Hawbuck are introduced into the garden with brazen effrontery by Thomas, who says, "Please Sir Jan and my Lady to walk this year way: *I know* Missus is in the rose-garden."

And there, sure enough, she was!

In a pretty little garden bonnet, with beautiful curling ringlets, with the smartest of aprons and the freshest of pearl-coloured gloves, this amazing woman was in the arms of her dearest Lady Hawbuck. "Dearest Lady Hawbuck, how good of you! Always among my flowers! can't live away from them!"

"Sweets to the sweet! hum—a-ha—haw!" says Sir John Hawbuck, who piques himself on his gallantry, and says nothing without "a-hum—a-ha—a-haw!"

"Whereth yaw pinnafaw?" cries Master Hugh. "*We* thaw you in it, over the wall, didn't we, Pa?"

"Hum—a-ha—a-haw!" burst out Sir John, dreadfully alarmed. "Where's Ponto? Why wasn't he at Quarter Sessions? How are his birds this year, Mrs. Ponto—have those Carabas pheasants done any harm to your wheat? a-hum—a-ha—a-haw!" and all this while he was making the most ferocious and desperate signals to his youthful heir.

"Well, she *wath* in her pinnafaw, wathn't she, Ma?" says Hugh, quite unabashed; which question Lady Hawbuck turned away with a sudden query regarding her dear darling daughters, and the *enfant terrible* was removed by his father.

"I hope you weren't disturbed by the music?" Ponto says. "My girls, you know, practise four hours a day, you know—must do it, you know—absolutely necessary. As for me, you know I'm an early man, and in my farm every morning at five—no, no laziness for *me*."

The facts are these. Ponto goes to sleep directly after dinner on entering the drawing-room, and wakes up when the ladies leave off practice at ten. From seven till ten, and from ten till five, is a very fair allowance of slumber for a man who says he's *not* a lazy man. It is my private opinion that when Ponto retires to what is called his "Study," he sleeps too. He locks himself up there daily two hours with the newspaper.

I saw the *Hawbuck* scene out of the Study, which commands the garden. It's a curious object, that Study. Ponto's library mostly consists of boots. He and Stripes have important interviews here of mornings, when the potatoes are discussed, or the fate of the calf ordained, or sentence passed on the pig, &c. All the Major's bills are docketed on the Study table and displayed like a lawyer's briefs. Here, too, lie displayed his hooks, knives, and other gardening irons, his whistles, and strings of spare buttons. He has a drawer of endless brown paper for parcels, and another containing a prodigious and never-failing supply of string. What a man can want with so many gig-whips I can never conceive. These, and fishing-rods, and landing-nets, and spurs, and boot-trees, and balls for horses, and surgical implements for the same, and favourite pots of shiny blacking, with which he paints his own shoes in the most elegant manner, and buckskin gloves stretched out on their trees, and his gorget, sash, and sabre of the Horse Marines, with his boot-hooks underneath in a trophy; and the family medicine-chest, and in a corner the very rod with which he used to whip his son, Wellesley Ponto, when a boy (Wellesley never entered the "Study" but for that awful purpose)—all these, with "Mogg's Road Book," the *Gardeners' Chronicle*, and a backgammon board, form the Major's library. Under the trophy there's a picture of Mrs. Ponto, in a light blue dress and train, and no waist, when she was first married; a fox's brush lies over the frame, and serves to keep the dust off that work of art.

"My library's small," says Ponto, with the most amazing impudence, "but well selected, my boy—well selected. I have been reading the 'History of England' all the morning."

CHAPTER XXVII

A Visit to Some Country Snobs

We had the fish, which, as the kind reader may remember, I had brought down in a delicate attention to Mrs. Ponto, to variegate the repast of next day; and cod and oyster-sauce, twice laid, salt cod and scolloped oysters, formed parts of the bill of fare, until I began to fancy that the Ponto family, like our late revered monarch George II., had a fancy for stale fish. And about this time, the pig being consumed, we began upon a sheep.

But how shall I forget the solemn splendour of a second course, which was served up in great state by Stripes in a silver dish and cover, a napkin twisted round his dirty thumbs; and consisted of a landrail, not much bigger than a corpulent sparrow.

"MY LOVE, WILL YOU TAKE ANY GAME?"

"My love, will you take any game?" says Ponto, with prodigious gravity; and stuck his fork into that little mouthful of an island in the silver sea. Stripes, too, at intervals, dribbled out the Marsala with a solemnity which would have done honour to a Duke's butler. The Barmecide's dinner to Shacabac was only one degree removed from these solemn banquets.

As there were plenty of pretty country places close by; a comfortable country town, with good houses of gentlefolks; a beautiful old parsonage, close to the church whither we went (and where the Carabas family have their ancestral carved and monumented Gothic pew), and every appearance of good society in the neighbourhood, I rather wondered we were not enlivened by the appearance of some of the neighbours at the Evergreens, and asked about them.

"We can't in our position of life—we can't well associate with the attorney's family, as I leave you to suppose," said Mrs. Ponto, confidentially. "Of course not," I answered, though I didn't know why. "And the Doctor?" said I.

"A most excellent worthy creature," says Mrs. P.; "saved Maria's life—really a learned man; but what can one do in one's position? One may ask one's medical man to one's table certainly: but his family, my dear Mr. Snob!"

"Half-a-dozen little gallipots," interposed Miss Wirt, the governess; "he, he, he!" and the young ladies laughed in chorus.

"We only live with the county families," Miss Wirt[1] continued, tossing up her head. "The Duke is abroad: we are at feud with the Carabases; the Ringwoods don't come down till Christmas: in fact, nobody's here till the hunting-season—positively nobody."

---

1 I have since heard that this aristocratic lady's father was a livery-button maker in St. Martin's Lane: where he met with misfortunes, and his daughter acquired her taste for heraldry. But it may be told to her credit, that out of her earnings she has kept the bed-ridden old bankrupt in great comfort and secrecy at Pentoville; and furnished her brother's outfit for the Cadetship which her patron, Lord Swigglebiggle, gave her when he was at the Board of Control. I have this information from a friend. To hear Miss Wirt herself, you would fancy that her Papa was a Rothschild, and that the markets of Europe were convulsed when he went into the *Gazette*.

"Whose is the large red house just outside of the town?"

"What! the *château-calicot*? he, he, he! That purse-proud ex-linen-draper, Mr. Yardley, with the yellow liveries, and the wife in red velvet? How *can* you, my dear Mr. Snob, be so satirical? The impertinence of those people is really something quite overwhelming."

"Well, then, there is the parson, Doctor Chrysostom. He's a gentleman, at any rate."

At this Mrs. Ponto looked at Miss Wirt. After their eyes had met and they had wagged their heads at each other, they looked up to the ceiling. So did the young ladies. They thrilled. It was evident I had said something very terrible. Another black sheep in the Church? thought I, with a little sorrow; for I don't care to own that I have a respect for the cloth. "I—I hope there's nothing wrong?"

"Wrong?" says Mrs. P., clasping her hands with a tragic air.

"Oh!" says Miss Wirt, and the two girls, gasping in chorus.

"Well," says I, "I'm very sorry for it. I never saw a nicer-looking old gentleman, or a better school, or heard a better sermon."

"He used to preach those sermons in a surplice," hissed out Mrs. Ponto. "He's a Puseyite, Mr. Snob."

"Heavenly powers!" says I, admiring the pure ardour of these female theologians; and Stripes came in with the tea. It's so weak that no wonder Ponto's sleep isn't disturbed by it.

Of mornings we used to go out shooting. We had Ponto's own fields to sport over (where we got the fieldfare), and the non-preserved part of the Hawbuck property: and one evening in a stubble of Ponto's skirting the Carabas woods, we got among some pheasants, and had some real sport. I shot a hen, I know, greatly to my delight. "Bag it," says Ponto, in rather a hurried manner: "here's somebody coming." So I pocketed the bird.

"You infernal poaching thieves!" roars out a man from the hedge in the garb of a gamekeeper. "I wish I could catch you on this side of the hedge. I'd put a brace of barrels into you, that I would."

"Curse that Snapper," says Ponto, moving off; "he's always watching me like a spy."

"Carry off the birds, you sneaks, and sell 'em in London," roars the individual, who it appears was a keeper of Lord Carabas. "You'll get six shillings a brace for 'em."

"*You* know the price of 'em well enough, and so does your master too, you scoundrel," says Ponto, still retreating.

"We kills 'em on our ground," cries Mr. Snapper. "*We* don't set traps for other people's birds. We're no decoy ducks. We're no sneaking poachers. We don't shoot 'ens, like that 'ere Cockney, who's got the tail of one a-sticking out of his pocket. Only just come across the hedge, that's all."

"I tell you what," says Stripes, who was out with us as keeper this day (in fact he's keeper, coachman, gardener, valet, and bailiff, with Tummus under him), "if *you'll* come across, John Snapper, and take your coat off, I'll give you such a whopping as you've never had since the last time I did it at Guttlebury Fair."

"Whop one of your own weight," Mr. Snapper said, whistling his dogs, and disappearing into the wood. And so we came out of this controversy rather victoriously; but I began to alter my preconceived ideas of rural felicity.

CHAPTER XXVIII

On Some Country Snobs

"Be hanged to your aristocrats!" Ponto said, in some conversation we had regarding the family at Carabas, between whom and the Evergreens there was a feud. "When I first came into the county—it was the year before Sir John Buff contested in the Blue interest—the Marquis, then Lord St. Michaels, who, of course, was Orange to the core, paid me and Mrs. Ponto such attentions, that I fairly confess I was taken in by the old humbug, and thought that I'd met with a rare neighbour. 'Gad, Sir, we used to get pines from Carabas, and pheasants from Carabas, and it was—'Ponto, when will you come over and shoot?'—and—'Ponto, our pheasants want thinning,'—and my Lady would insist upon her dear Mrs. Ponto coming over to Carabas to sleep, and put me I don't know to what expense for turbans and velvet gowns for my wife's toilette. Well, Sir, the election takes place, and though I was always a Liberal, personal friendship of course induces me to plump for St. Michaels, who comes in at the head of the poll. Next year, Mrs. P. insists upon going to town—with lodgings in Clarges Street at ten pounds a week, with a hired brougham, and new dresses for herself and the girls, and the deuce and all to pay. Our first cards were to Carabas House; my Lady's are returned by a great big flunkey: and I leave you to fancy my poor Betsy's discomfiture as the lodging-house maid took in the cards, and Lady St. Michaels drives away, though she actually saw us at the drawing-room window. Would you believe it, Sir, that though we called four times afterwards, those infernal aristocrats never returned our visit; that though Lady St. Michaels gave nine dinner-parties and four *déjeûners* that season, she never asked us to one; and that she cut us dead at the Opera, though Betsy was nodding to her the whole night? We wrote to her for tickets for Almack's; she writes to say that all hers were promised; and said, in the presence of Wiggins, her lady's-maid, who told it to

Diggs, my wife's woman, that she couldn't conceive how people in our station of life could so far forget themselves as to wish to appear in any such place! Go to Castle Carabas! I'd sooner die than set my foot in the house of that impertinent, insolvent, insolent jackanapes—and I hold him in scorn!" After this, Ponto gave me some private information regarding Lord Carabas's pecuniary affairs; how he owed money all over the county; how Jukes the carpenter was utterly ruined and couldn't get a shilling of his bill; how Biggs the butcher hanged himself for the same reason; how the six big footmen never received a guinea of wages, and Snaffle, the state coachman, actually took off his blown-glass wig of ceremony and flung it at Lady Carabas's feet on the terrace before the Castle; all which stories, as they are private, I do not think proper to divulge. But these details did not stifle my desire to see the famous mansion of Castle Carabas, nay, possibly excited my interest to know more about that lordly house and its owners.

At the entrance of the park there are a pair of great gaunt mildewed lodges—mouldy Doric temples with black chimney-pots, in the finest classic taste, and the gates of course are surmounted by the *chats bottés*, the well-known supporters of the Carabas family. "Give the lodge-keeper a shilling," says Ponto, (who drove me near to it in his four-wheeled cruelty-chaise). "I warrant it's the first piece of ready money she has received for some time." I don't know whether there was any foundation for this sneer, but the gratuity was received with a curtsey, and the gate opened for me to enter. "Poor old porteress!" says I, inwardly. "You little know that it is the Historian of Snobs whom you let in!" The gates were passed. A damp green stretch of park spread right and left immeasurably, confined by a chilly gray wall, and a damp long straight road between two huge rows of moist, dismal lime-trees, leads up to the Castle. In the midst of the park is a great black tank or lake, bristling over with rushes, and here and there covered over with patches of pea-soup. A shabby temple rises on an island in this delectable lake, which is approached by a rotten barge that lies at roost in a dilapidated boat-house. Clumps of elms and oaks dot over the huge green flat. Every one of them would have been down long since, but that the Marquis is not allowed to cut the timber.

Up that long avenue the Snobographer walked in solitude. At the seventy-ninth tree on the left-hand side, the insolvent butcher hanged himself. I scarcely wondered at the dismal deed, so woful and sad were the impressions connected with the place. So, for a mile and a half I walked—alone and thinking of death.

I forgot to say the house is in full view all the way—except when intercepted by the trees on the miserable island in the lake—an enormous red-brick mansion, square, vast, and dingy. It is flanked by four stone towers with weathercocks. In the midst of the grand façade is a huge Ionic portico, approached by a vast, lonely, ghastly staircase. Rows of black windows, framed in stone, stretch on either side, right and left—three storeys and eighteen windows of a row. You may see a picture of the palace and staircase, in the "Views of England and Wales," with four carved and gilt carriages waiting at the gravel walk, and several parties of ladies and gentlemen in wigs and hoops, dotting the fatiguing lines of the stairs.

But these stairs are made in great houses for people *not* to ascend. The first Lady Carabas (they are but eighty years in the peerage), if she got out of her gilt coach in a shower, would be wet to the skin before she got half-way to the carved Ionic portico, where four dreary statues of Peace, Plenty, Piety and Patriotism, are the only sentinels. You enter these palaces by back-doors. "That was the way the Carabases got their peerage," the misanthropic Ponto said after dinner.

Well—I rang the bell at a little low side-door; it clanged and jingled and echoed for a long, long while, till at length a face, as of a housekeeper, peered through the door, and, as she saw my hand in my waistcoat pocket, opened it. Unhappy, lonely housekeeper, I thought. Is Miss Crusoe in her island more solitary? The door clapped to, and I was in Castle Carabas.

"The side entrance and 'All," says the housekeeper. "The halligator hover the mantelpiece was brought home by Hadmiral St. Michaels, when a Capting with Lord Hanson. The harms on the cheers is the harms of the Carabas family." The hall was rather comfortable. We went clapping up a clean stone backstair, and then into a back passage cheerfully decorated with ragged light-green Kidderminster, and issued upon

"THE GREAT 'ALL.

"The great 'all is seventy-two feet in lenth, fifty-six in breath, and thirty-eight feet 'igh. The carvings of the chimlies, representing the buth of Venus, and Ercules, and Eyelash, is by Van Chislum, the most famous sculpture of his hage and country. The ceiling, by Calimanco, represents Painting, Harchitecture and Music (the naked female figure with the barrel horgan) introducing George, fust Lord Carabas, to the Temple of the Muses. The winder ornaments is by Vanderputty. The floor is Patagonian marble; and the chandelier in the centre was presented to Lionel, second Marquis, by Lewy the Sixteenth, whose 'ead was cut hoff in the French Revelation. We now henter

"THE SOUTH GALLERY.

"One 'undred and forty-eight in lenth by thirty-two in breath; it is profusely hornaminted by the choicest works of Hart. Sir Andrew Katz, founder of the Carabas family and banker of the Prince of Horange, Kneller. Her present Ladyship, by Lawrence. Lord St. Michaels, by the same—he is represented sittin' on a rock in velvit pantaloons. Moses in the bullrushes— the bull very fine, by Paul Potter. The toilet of Venus, Fantaski. Flemish Bores drinking, Van Ginnums. Jupiter and Europia, de Horn. The Grandjunction Canal, Venis, by Candleetty; and Italian Bandix, by Slavata Rosa."

—And so this worthy woman went on, from one room into another, from the blue room to the green, and the green to the grand saloon, and the grand saloon to the tapestry closet, cackling her list of pictures and wonders: and furtively turning up a corner of brown holland to show the colour of the old, faded, seedy, mouldy, dismal hangings.

At last we came to her Ladyship's bed-room. In the centre of this dreary apartment there is a bed about the size of one of those whizgig temples in which the Genius appears in a pantomime. The huge gilt edifice is approached by steps, and so tall, that it might be let off in floors, for sleeping-rooms for all the Carabas family. An awful bed! A murder might be done at one end of that bed, and people sleeping at the other end be ignorant of it! Gracious powers! fancy Little Lord Carabas in a nightcap ascending those steps after putting out the candle!

The sight of that seedy and solitary splendour was too much for me. I should go mad were I that lonely housekeeper—in those enormous galleries—in that lonely library, filled up with ghastly folios that nobody dares read, with an inkstand on the centre table like the coffin of a baby, and sad portraits staring at you from the bleak walls with their solemn mouldy eyes. No wonder that Carabas does not come down here often. It would require two thousand footmen to make the place cheerful. No wonder the coachman resigned his wig, that the masters are insolvent, and the servants perish in this huge dreary out-at-elbow place.

A single family has no more right to build itself a temple of that sort than to erect a tower of Babel. Such a habitation is not decent for a mere mortal man. But, after all, I suppose poor Carabas had no choice. Fate put him there as it sent Napoleon to St. Helena. Suppose it had been decreed by Nature that you and I should be Marquises? We wouldn't refuse, I suppose, but take Castle Carabas and all, with debts, duns, and mean makeshifts, and shabby pride, and swindling magnificence.

Next season, when I read of Lady Carabas's splendid entertainments in the *Morning Post*, and see the poor old insolvent cantering through the Park—I shall have a much tenderer interest in these great people than I have had heretofore. Poor old shabby Snob! Ride on and fancy the world is still on its knees before the house of Carabas! Give yourself airs, poor old bankrupt Magnifico, who are under money-obligations to your flunkeys; and must stoop so as to swindle poor tradesmen! And for us, O my brother Snobs, oughtn't we to feel happy if our walk through life is more even, and that we are out of the reach of that surprising arrogance and that astounding meanness to which this wretched old victim is obliged to mount and descend.

CHAPTER XXIX

A Visit to Some Country Snobs

Notable as my reception had been (under that unfortunate mistake of Mrs. Ponto that I was related to Lord Snobbington, which I was not permitted to correct), it was nothing compared to the bowing and kotooing, the raptures and flurry which preceded and welcomed the visit of a real live lord and lord's son, a brother officer of Cornet Wellesley Ponto, in the 120th Hussars, who came over with the young Cornet from Guttlebury, where their distinguished regiment was quartered. This was my Lord Gules, Lord Saltire's grandson and heir: a very young, short, sandy-haired and tobacco-smoking nobleman, who cannot have left the nursery very long, and who, though he accepted the honest Major's invitation to the Evergreens in a letter written in a school-boy handwriting, with a number of faults of spelling, may yet be a very fine classical scholar for what I know: having had his education at Eton, where he and young Ponto were inseparable.

At any rate, if he can't write, he has mastered a number of other accomplishments wonderful for one of his age and size. He is one of the best shots and riders in England. He rode his horse Abracadabra, and won the famous Guttlebury steeple-chase. He has horses entered at half the races in the country (under other people's names; for the old lord is a strict hand, and will not hear of betting or gambling). He has lost and won such sums of money as my Lord George himself might be proud of. He knows all the stables, and all the jockeys, and has all the "information," and is a match for the best Leg at Newmarket. Nobody was ever known to be "too much" for him: at play or in the stable.

Although his grandfather makes him a moderate allowance, by the aid of *post-obits* and convenient friends he can live in a splendour becoming his rank. He has not distinguished himself in the knocking down of policemen much; he is not big enough for that. But, as a light-weight, his skill is of the very highest order. At billiards he is said to be first-rate. He drinks and smokes as much as any two of the biggest officers in his regiment. With such high talents, who can say how far he may not go? He may take to politics as a *délassement*, and be Prime Minister after Lord George Bentinck.

My young friend Wellesley Ponto is a gaunt and bony youth, with a pale face profusely blotched. From his continually pulling something on his chin, I am led to fancy that he believes he has what is called an Imperial growing there. That is not the only tuft that is hunted in the family, by the way. He can't, of course, indulge in those expensive amusements which render his aristocratic comrade so respected: he bets pretty freely when he is in cash, and rides when somebody mounts him (for he can't afford more than his regulation chargers). At drinking he is by no means inferior; and why do you think he brought his noble friend, Lord Gules, to the Evergreens?—Why? because he intended to ask his mother to order his father to pay his debts, which she couldn't refuse before such an exalted presence. Young Ponto gave me all this information with the most engaging frankness. We are old friends. I used to tip him when he was at school.

"Gad!" says he, "our wedgment's so *doothid* exthpenthif. Must hunt, you know. A man couldn't live in the wedgment if he didn't. Mess expenses enawmuth. Must dine at mess. Must drink champagne and claret. Ours ain't a port and sherry light-infantry mess. Uniforms awful. Fitzstultz, our colonel, will have 'em so. Must be a distinction, you know. At his own expense Fitzstultz altered the plumes in the men's caps (you called them shaving-brushes, Snob, my boy: most absurd and unjust that attack of yours by the way); that altewation alone cotht him five hundred pound. The year befaw latht he holthed the wegiment at an immenthe expenthe, and we're called the Queen'th Own Pyebalds from that day. Ever theen uth on pawade? The Empewar Nicolath burtht into tearth of envy when he thaw uth at Windthor. And you see," continued my young friend, "I brought Gules down with me, as the Governor is very sulky about shelling out, just to talk my mother over, who can do anything with him. Gules told her that I was Fitzstultz's favourite of the whole regiment; and, Gad! she thinks the Horse Guards will give me my troop for nothing, and he humbugged the Governor that I was the greatest screw in the army. Ain't it a good dodge?"

With this Wellesley left me to go and smoke a cigar in the stables with Lord Gules, and make merry over the cattle there, under Stripes's superintendence. Young Ponto laughed with his friend, at the venerable four-wheeled cruelty-chaise; but seemed amazed that the latter should ridicule still more an ancient chariot of the build of 1824, emblazoned immensely with the arms of the Pontos and the Snaileys, from which latter distinguished family Mrs. Ponto issued.

I found poor Pon in his study among his boots, in such a rueful attitude of despondency, that I could not but remark it. "Look at that!" says the poor fellow, handing me over a document. "It's the second change in uniform since he's been in the army, and yet there's no extravagance about the lad. Lord Gules tells me he is the most careful youngster in the regiment. God bless him! But look at that! by heaven, Snob, look at that and say how can a man of nine hundred keep out of the Bench? He gave a sob as he handed me the paper across the table; and his old face, and his old corduroys, and his shrunk shooting-jacket, and his lean shanks, looked, as he spoke, more miserably haggard, bankrupt, and threadbare.

Lieut. Wellesley Ponto, 120th Queen's Own Pyebald Hussars,
To Knopf and Stecknadel,
Conduit Street, London.

	£	s.	d.
Dress Jacket, richly laced with gold	35	0	0
Ditto Pelisse ditto, and trimmed with sable	60	0	0
Undress Jacket, trimmed with gold	15	15	0
Ditto Pelisse	30	0	0

Dress Pantaloons	12	0	0
Ditto Overalls, gold lace on sides	6	6	0
Undress ditto ditto	5	5	0
Blue Braided Frock	14	14	0
Forage Cap	3	3	0
Dress Cap, gold lines, plume and chain	25	0	0
Gold Barrelled Sash	11	18	0
Sword	11	11	0
Ditto Belt and Sabretache	16	16	0
Pouch and Belt	15	15	0
Sword Knot	1	4	0
Cloak	13	13	0
Valise	3	13	6
Regulation Saddle	7	17	6
Ditto Bridle, complete	10	10	0
A Dress Housing, complete	30	0	0
A pair of Pistols	10	10	0
A Black Sheepskin, edged	6	18	0
	£347	9	0

That evening Mrs. Ponto and her family made their darling Wellesley give a full, true, and particular account of everything that had taken place at Lord Fitzstultz's? how many servants waited at dinner; and how the ladies Schneider dressed; and what his Royal Highness said when he came down to shoot; and who was there? "What a blessing that boy is to me!" said she, as my pimple-faced young friend moved off to resume smoking operations with Gules in the now vacant kitchen:— and poor Ponto's dreary and desperate look, shall I ever forget that?

O you parents and guardians! O you men and women of sense in England! O you legislators about to assemble in Parliament! read over that tailor's bill above printed—read over that absurd catalogue of insane gimcracks and madman's tomfoolery—and say how are you ever to get rid of Snobbishness when society does so much for its education?

Three hundred and forty pounds for a young chap's saddle and breeches! Before George, I would rather be a Hottentot or a Highlander. We laugh at poor Jocko, the monkey, dancing in uniform; or at poor Jeames, the flunkey, with his quivering calves and plush tights; or at the nigger Marquis of Marmalade, dressed out with sabre and epaulets, and giving himself the airs of a field-marshal. Lo! is not one of the Queen's Pyebalds, in full fig, as great and foolish a monster?

CHAPTER XXX

On Some Country Snobs

At last came that fortunate day at the Evergreens, when I was to be made acquainted with some of the "county families" with whom only people of Ponto's rank condescended to associate. And now, although poor Ponto had just been so cruelly made to bleed on occasion of his son's new uniform, and though he was in the direst and most cut-throat spirits with an overdrawn account at the banker's, and other pressing evils of poverty; although a tenpenny bottle of Marsala and an awful parsimony presided generally at his table, yet the poor fellow was obliged to assume the most frank and jovial air of cordiality; and all the covers being removed from the hangings, and new dresses being procured for the young ladies, and the family plate being unlocked and displayed, the house and all within assumed a benevolent and festive appearance. The kitchen fires began to blaze, the good wine ascended from the cellar, a professed cook actually came over from Guttlebury to compile culinary abominations. Stripes was in a new coat, and so was Ponto, for a wonder, and Tummus's button-suit was worn *en permanence*.[1]

And all this to show off the little lord, thinks I. All this in honour of a stupid little cigarrified Cornet of dragoons, who can barely write his name,—while an eminent and profound moralist like—somebody—is fobbed off with cold mutton and relays of pig. Well, well: a martyrdom of cold mutton is just bearable. I pardon Mrs. Ponto, from my heart I do, especially as I wouldn't turn out of the best bedroom, in spite of all her hints; but held my ground in the chintz tester, vowing that Lord Gules, as a young man, was quite small and hardy enough to make himself comfortable elsewhere.

---

1 I caught him in this costume, trying the flavour of the sauce of a tipsycake, which was made by Mrs. Ponto's own hands for her guests' delectation.

The great Ponto party was a very august one. The Hawbucks came in their family coach, with the blood-red hand emblazoned all over it: and their man in yellow livery waited in country fashion at table, only to be exceeded in splendour by the Hipsleys, the opposition baronet, in light blue. The old Ladies Fitzague drove over in their little old chariot with the fat black horses, the fat coachman, the fat footman—(why are dowagers' horses and footmen always fat?) And soon after these personages had arrived, with their auburn fronts and red beaks and turbans, came the Honourable and Reverend Lionel Pettipois, who with General and Mrs. Sago formed the rest of the party. "Lord and Lady Frederick Howlet were asked, but they have friends at Ivybush," Mrs. Ponto told me; and that very morning, the Castlehaggards sent an excuse, as her ladyship had a return of the quinsy. Between ourselves, Lady Castlehaggard's quinsy always comes on when there is dinner at the Evergreens.

If the keeping of polite company could make a woman happy, surely my kind hostess Mrs. Ponto was on that day a happy woman. Every person present (except the unlucky impostor who pretended to a connexion with the Snobbington Family, and General Sago, who had brought home I don't know how many lacs of rupees from India) was related to the Peerage or the Baronetage. Mrs. P. had her heart's desire. If she had been an Earl's daughter herself could she have expected better company?—and her family were in the oil-trade at Bristol, as all her friends very well know.

What I complained of in my heart was not the dining—which, for this once, was plentiful and comfortable enough—but the prodigious dulness of the talking part of the entertainment. O my beloved brother Snobs of the City, if we love each other no better than our country brethren, at least we amuse each other more; if we bore ourselves, we are not called upon to go ten miles to do it!

For instance, the Hipsleys came ten miles from the south, and the Hawbucks ten miles from the north, of the Evergreens;

and were magnates in two different divisions of the county of Mangelwurzelshire. Hipsley, who is an old baronet, with a bothered estate, did not care to show his contempt for Hawbuck, who is a new creation, and rich. Hawbuck, on his part, gives himself patronizing airs to General Sago, who looks upon the Pontos as little better than paupers. "Old Lady Blanche," says Ponto, "I hope will leave something to her goddaughter—my second girl—we've all of us half-poisoned ourselves with taking her physic."

Lady Blanche and Lady Rose Fitzague have, the first, a medical, and the second a literary turn. I am inclined to believe the former had a wet *compresse* around her body, on the occasion when I had the happiness of meeting her. She doctors everybody in the neighbourhood, of which she is the ornament; and has tried everything on her own person. She went into Court, and testified publicly her faith in St. John Long: she swore by Doctor Buchan, she took quantities of Gambouge's Universal Medicine, and whole boxfuls of Parr's Life Pills. She has cured a multiplicity of headaches by Squinstone's Eyesnuff; she wears a picture of Hahnemann in her bracelet and a lock of Priessnitz's hair in a brooch. She talked about her own complaints and those of her *confidante* for the time being, to every lady in the room successively, from our hostess down to Miss Wirt, taking them into corners, and whispering about bronchitis, hepatitis, St. Vitus, neuralgia, cephalalgia, and so forth. I observed poor fat Lady Hawbuck in a dreadful alarm after some communication regarding the state of her daughter Miss Lucy Hawbuck's health, and Mrs. Sago turn quite yellow, and put down her third glass of Madeira, at a warning glance from Lady Blanche.

Lady Rose talked literature, and about the book-club at Guttlebury, and is very strong in voyages and travels. She has a prodigious interest in Borneo, and displayed a knowledge of the history of the Punjaub and Kaffirland that does credit to her memory. Old General Sago, who sat perfectly silent and plethoric, roused up as from a lethargy when the former

147

country was mentioned, and gave the company his story about a hog-hunt at Ramjugger. I observed her ladyship treated with something like contempt her neighbour the Reverend Lionel Pettipois, a young divine whom you may track through the country by little "awakening" books at half-a-crown a hundred, which dribble out of his pockets wherever he goes. I saw him give Miss Wirt a sheaf of "The Little Washerwoman on Putney Common," and to Miss Hawbuck a couple of dozen of "Meat in the Tray; or the Young Butcher-boy Rescued;" and on paying a visit to Guttlebury gaol, I saw two notorious fellows waiting their trial there (and temporarily occupied with a game of cribbage), to whom his Reverence offered a tract as he was walking over Crackshins Common, and who robbed him of his purse, umbrella, and cambric handkerchief, leaving him the tracts to distribute elsewhere.

CHAPTER XXXI

A Visit to Some Country Snobs

"Why, dear Mr. Snob," said a young lady of rank and fashion (to whom I present my best compliments), "if you found everything so *snobbish* at the Evergreens, if the pig bored you and the mutton was not to your liking, and Mrs. Ponto was a humbug, and Miss Wirt a nuisance, with her abominable piano practice,—why did you stay so long?"

Ah, Miss, what a question! Have you never heard of gallant British soldiers storming batteries, of doctors passing nights in plague wards of lazarettos, and other instances of martyrdom? What do you suppose induced gentlemen to walk two miles up to the batteries of Sobraon, with a hundred and fifty thundering guns bowling them down by hundreds?—not pleasure, surely. What causes your respected father to quit his comfortable home for his chambers, after dinner, and pore over the most dreary law papers until long past midnight? Duty, Mademoiselle; duty, which must be done alike by military, or legal, or literary gents. There's a power of martyrdom in our profession.

You won't believe it? Your rosy lips assume a smile of incredulity—a most naughty and odious expression in a young lady's face. Well, then, the fact is, that my chambers, No. 24, Pump Court, Temple, were being painted by the Honourable Society, and Mrs. Slamkin, my laundress, having occasion to go into Durham to see her daughter, who is married, and has presented her with the sweetest little grandson—a few weeks could not be better spent than in rusticating. But ah, how delightful Pump Court looked when I revisited its well-known chimney-pots! *Cari luoghi.* Welcome, welcome, O fog and smut!

But if you think there is no moral in the foregoing account of the Pontine family, you are, Madam, most painfully mistaken. In this very chapter we are going to have the moral—why, the whole of the papers are nothing *but* the moral, setting forth as they do the folly of being a Snob.

You will remark that in the Country Snobography my poor friend Ponto has been held up almost exclusively for the public gaze—and why? Because we went to no other house? Because other families did not welcome us to their mahogany? No, no. Sir John Hawbuck of the Haws, Sir John Hipsley of Briary Hall, don't shut the gates of hospitality: of General Sago's mulligatawny I could speak from experience. And the two old ladies at Guttlebury, were they nothing? Do you suppose that an agreeable young dog, who shall be nameless, would not be made welcome? Don't you know that people are too glad to see *anybody* in the country?

But those dignified personages do not enter into the scheme of the present work, and are but minor characters of our Snob drama; just as, in the play, kings and emperors are not half so important as many humble persons. The *Doge of Venice*, for instance, gives way to *Othello*, who is but a nigger; and the *King of France* to *Falconbridge*, who is a gentleman of positively no birth at all. So with the exalted characters above mentioned. I perfectly well recollect that the claret at Hawbuck's was not by any means so good as that of Hipsley's, while, on the contrary, some white hermitage at the Haws (by the way, the butler only gave me half a glass each time) was supernacular. And I remember the conversations. O Madam, Madam, how stupid they were! The subsoil ploughing; the pheasants and poaching; the row about the representation of the county; the Earl of Mangelwurzelshire being at variance with his relative and nominee, the Honourable Marmaduke Tomnoddy; all these I could put down, had I a mind to violate the confidence of private life; and a great deal of conversation about the weather, the Mangelwurzelshire Hunt, new manures, and eating and drinking, of course.

But *cui bono*? In these perfectly stupid and honourable families there is not that Snobbishness which it is our purpose to expose. An ox is an ox—a great hulking, fat-sided, bellowing, munching Beef. He ruminates according to his nature, and consumes his destined portion of turnips or oilcake, until the time comes for his disappearance from the pastures, to be succeeded by other deep-lunged and fat-ribbed animals. Perhaps we do not respect an ox. We rather acquiesce in him. The Snob, my dear Madam, is the Frog that tries to swell himself to ox size. Let us pelt the silly brute out of his folly.

Look, I pray you, at the case of my unfortunate friend Ponto, a good-natured, kindly English gentleman—not over-wise, but quite passable—fond of port-wine, of his family, of country sports and agriculture, hospitably minded, with as pretty a little patrimonial country-house as heart can desire, and a thousand pounds a year. It is not much; but, *entre nous*, people can live for less, and not uncomfortably.

For instance, there is the doctor, whom Mrs. P. does not condescend to visit: that man educates a mirific family, and is loved by the poor for miles round: and gives them port-wine for physic and medicine, gratis. And how these people can get on with their pittance, as Mrs. Ponto says, is a wonder to *her*.

Again, there is the clergyman, Doctor Chrysostom,—Mrs. P. says they quarrelled about Puseyism, but I am given to understand it was because Mrs. C. had the *pas* of her at the Haws—you may see what the value of his living is any day in the "Clerical Guide;" but you don't know what he gives away.

Even Pettipois allows that, in whose eyes the Doctor's surplice is a scarlet abomination; and so does Pettipois do his duty in his way, and administer not only his tracts and his talk, but his money and his means to his people. As a lord's son, by the way, Mrs. Ponto is uncommonly anxious that he should marry *either* of the girls whom Lord Gules does not intend to choose.

Well, although Pon's income would make up almost as much as that of these three worthies put together—oh, my dear Madam, see in what hopeless penury the poor fellow lives! What tenant can look to *his* forbearance? What poor man can hope for *his* charity? "Master's the best of men," honest Stripes says, "and when we was in the ridgment a more free-handed chap didn't live. But the way in which Missus *du* scryou, I wonder the young ladies is alive, that I du!"

They live upon a fine governess and fine masters, and have clothes made by Lady Carabas's own milliner; and their brother rides with earls to cover; and only the best people in the county visit at the Evergreens, and Mrs. Ponto thinks herself a paragon of wives and mothers, and a wonder of the world, for doing all this misery and humbug, and snobbishness, on a thousand a year.

What an inexpressible comfort it was, my dear Madam, when Stripes put my portmanteau in the four-wheeled chaise, and (poor Pon being touched with sciatica) drove me over to the "Carabas Arms" at Guttlebury, where we took leave. There were some bagmen there, in the Commercial Room, and one talked about the house he represented; and another about his dinner, and a third about the Inns on the road, and so forth—a talk, not very wise, but honest and to the purpose—about as good as that of the country gentlemen: and oh, how much pleasanter than listening to Miss Wirt's show-pieces on the piano, and Mrs. Ponto's genteel cackle about the fashion and the county families!

CHAPTER XXXII

Snobbium Gatherum

When I see the great effect which these papers are producing on an intelligent public, I have a strong hope that before long we shall have a regular Snob-department in the newspapers, just as we have the Police Courts and the Court News at present. When a flagrant case of bone-crushing or Poor-law abuse occurs in the world, who so eloquent as *The Times* to point it out? When a gross instance of Snobbishness happens, why should not the indignant journalist call the public attention to that delinquency too?

How, for instance, could that wonderful case of the Earl of Mangelwurzel and his brother be examined in the Snobbish point of view? Let alone the hectoring, the bullying, the vapouring, the bad grammar, the mutual recriminations, lie-givings, challenges, retractions, which abound in the fraternal dispute—put out of the question these points as concerning the individual nobleman and his relative, with whose personal affairs we have nothing to do—and consider how intimately corrupt, how habitually grovelling and mean, how entirely Snobbish, in a word, a whole county must be which can find no better chiefs or leaders than these two gentlemen. "We don't want," the great county of Mangelwurzelshire seems to say, "that a man should be able to write good grammar; or that he should keep a Christian tongue in his head; or that he should have the commonest decency of temper, or even a fair share of good sense, in order to represent us in Parliament. All we require is, that a man should be recommended to us by the Earl of Mangelwurzelshire. And all that we require of the Earl of Mangelwurzelshire is that he should have fifty thousand a year and hunt the country." O you pride of all Snobland! O you crawling, truckling, self-confessed lacqueys and parasites!

But this is growing too savage: don't let us forget our usual amenity, and that tone of playfulness and sentiment with which the beloved reader and writer have pursued their mutual reflections hitherto. Well, Snobbishness pervades the little Social Farce as well as the great State Comedy; and the self-same moral is tacked to either.

There was, for instance, an account in the papers of a young lady who, misled by a fortune-teller, actually went part of the way to India (as far as Bagnigge Wells, I think,) in search of a husband who was promised her there. Do you suppose this poor deluded little soul would have left her shop for a man below her in rank, or for anything but a darling of a Captain in epaulets and a red coat? It was her Snobbish sentiment that misled her, and made her vanities a prey to the swindling fortune-teller.

Case 2 was that of Mademoiselle de Saugrenue, "the interesting young Frenchwoman with a profusion of jetty ringlets," who lived for nothing at a boarding-house at Gosport, was then conveyed to Fareham gratis: and being there, and lying on the bed of the good old lady her entertainer, the dear girl took occasion to rip open the mattress, and steal a cash-box, with which she fled to London. How would you account for the prodigious benevolence exercised towards the interesting young French lady? Was it her jetty ringlets on her charming face?—Bah! Do ladies love others for having pretty faces and black hair?—she said *she was a relation of* Lord de Saugrenue: talked of her ladyship her aunt, and of herself as a De Saugrenue. The honest boarding-house people were at her feet at once. Good, honest, simple, lord-loving children of Snobland.

Finally, there was the case of "the Right Honourable Mr. Vernon," at York. The Right Honourable was the son of a nobleman, and practised on an old lady. He procured from her dinners, money, wearing-apparel, spoons, implicit credence, and an entire refit of linen. Then he casts his net over a family of father, mother, and daughters, one of whom he proposed to marry. The father lent him money, the mother made jams and pickles for him, the daughters vied with each other in cooking

154

dinners for the Right Honourable—and what was the end? One day the traitor fled, with a teapot and a basketful of cold victuals. It was the "Right Honourable" which baited the hook which gorged all these greedy, simple Snobs. Would they have been taken in by a commoner? What old lady is there, my dear sir, who would take in you and me, were we ever so ill to do, and comfort us, and clothe us, and give us her money, and her silver forks? Alas and alas! what mortal man that speaks the truth can hope for such a landlady? And yet, all these instances of fond and credulous Snobbishness have occurred in the same week's paper with who knows how many score more?

Just as we had concluded the above remarks comes a pretty little note sealed with a pretty little butterfly—bearing a northern postmark—and to the following effect:—

"19*th November*.

"MR. PUNCH,—TAKING great interest in your Snob Papers, we are very anxious to know under what class of that respectable fraternity you would designate us.

"We are three sisters, from seventeen to twenty-two. Our father is *honestly and truly* of a very good family (you will say it is Snobbish to mention that, but I wish to state the plain fact); our maternal grandfather was an Earl.[1]

"We *can* afford to take in a stamped edition of *you*, and all Dickens' works as fast as they come out, but we do *not* keep such a thing as a *Peerage* or even a *Baronetage* in the house.

"We live with every comfort, excellent cellar, &c. &c.; but as we cannot well afford a butler, we have a neat table-maid (though our father was a military man, has travelled much, been in the best society, &c.) We *have* a coachman and helper, but we don't put the latter into buttons, nor make them wait at table, like Stripes and Tummus.[2]

"We are just the same to persons with a handle to their name as to those without it. We wear a moderate modicum of

1 The introduction of Grandpapa is, I fear, Snobbish.
2 That is, as you like. I don't object to buttons in moderation.

crinoline,[1] and are never *limp*[2] in the morning. We have good and abundant dinners on *china* (though we have plate[3]), and just as good when alone as with company.

"Now, my dear *Mr. Punch*, will you *please* give us a short answer in your next number, and I will be *so* much obliged to you. Nobody knows we are writing to you, not even our father; nor will we ever tease you[4] again if you will only give us an answer—just for fun, now do!

"If you get as far as this, which is doubtful, you will probably fling it into the fire. If you do, I cannot help it; but I am of a sanguine disposition, and entertain a lingering hope. At all events, I shall be impatient for next Sunday, for you reach us on that day, and I am ashamed to confess, we *cannot* resist opening you in the carriage driving home from church.[5]

"I remain, &c. &c., for myself and sisters.

"Excuse this scrawl, but I always write *headlong*."[6]

"P.S.—You were rather stupid last week, don't you think?[7] We keep no gamekeeper, and yet have always abundant game for friends to shoot, in spite of the poachers. We never write on perfumed paper—in short, I can't help thinking that if you knew us you would not think us Snobs."

To this I reply in the following manner:—"My dear young ladies, I know your post-town: and shall be at church there the Sunday *after* next; when, will you please to wear a tulip or some little trifle in your bonnets, so that I may know you? You will recognize me and my dress—a quiet-looking young fellow, in a white top-coat, a crimson satin neckcloth, light blue trousers, with glossy tipped boots, and an emerald breast-pin. I shall have a black crape round my white hat: and my usual

1 Quite right.
2 Bless you!
3 Snobbish; and I doubt whether you ought to dine as well when alone as with company. You will be getting too good dinners.
4 We like to be teased; but tell Papa.
5 O garters and stars! what will Captain Gordon and Exeter Hall say to this?
6 Dear little enthusiast!
7 You were never more mistaken, Miss, in your life.

156

bamboo cane with the richly-gilt knob. I am sorry there will be no time to get up moustaches between now and next week.

"From seventeen to two-and-twenty! Ye Gods! what ages! Dear young creatures, I can see you all three. Seventeen suits me, as nearest my own time of life; but mind, I don't say two-and-twenty is too old. No, no. And that pretty, roguish, demure middle one. Peace, peace, thou silly little fluttering heart!

"*You* Snobs, dear young ladies! I will pull any man's nose who says so. There is no harm in being of a good family. You can't help it, poor dears. What's in a name? What is in a handle to it? I confess openly that I should not object to being a Duke myself; and between ourselves you might see a worse leg for a garter.

"*You* Snobs, dear little good-natured things, no!—that is, I hope not—I think not—I won't be too confident—none of us should be—that we are not Snobs. That very confidence savours of arrogance, and to be arrogant is to be a Snob. In all the social gradations from sneak to tyrant, nature has placed a most wondrous and various progeny of Snobs. But are there no kindly natures, no tender hearts, no souls humble, simple, and truth-loving? Ponder well on this question, sweet young ladies. And if you can answer it, as no doubt you can—lucky are you—and lucky the respected Herr Papa, and lucky the three handsome young gentlemen who are about to become each others' brothers-in-law."

CHAPTER XXXIII

Snobs and Marriage

Everybody of the middle rank who walks through this life with a sympathy for his companions on the same journey—at any rate, every man who has been jostling in the world for some three or four lustres—must make no end of melancholy reflections upon the fate of those victims whom Society, that is, Snobbishness, is immolating every day. With love and simplicity and natural kindness Snobbishness is perpetually at war. People dare not be happy for fear of Snobs. People dare not love for fear of Snobs. People pine away lonely under the tyranny of Snobs. Honest kindly hearts dry up and die. Gallant generous lads, blooming with hearty youth, swell into bloated old-bachelorhood, and burst and tumble over. Tender girls wither into shrunken decay, and perish solitary, from whom Snobbishness has cut off the common claim to happiness and affection with which Nature endowed us all. My heart grows sad as I see the blundering tyrant's handiwork. As I behold it I swell with cheap rage, and glow with fury against the Snob. Come down, I say, thou skulking dulness! Come down, thou stupid bully, and give up thy brutal ghost! And I arm myself with the sword and spear, and taking leave of my family, go forth to do battle with that hideous ogre and giant, that brutal despot in Snob Castle, who holds so many gentle hearts in torture and thrall.

When *Punch* is king, I declare there shall be no such thing as old maids and old bachelors. The Rev. Mr. Malthus shall be burned annually, instead of Guy Fawkes. Those who don't marry shall go into the workhouse. It shall be a sin for the poorest not to have a pretty girl to love him.

The above reflections came to mind after taking a walk with an old comrade, Jack Spiggot by name, who is just passing into the state of old-bachelorhood, after the manly and blooming youth in which I remember him. Jack was one of the handsomest fellows in England when we entered together in the Highland Buffs; but I quitted the Cuttykilts early, and lost sight of him for many years.

Ah! how changed he is from those days! He wears a waistband now, and has begun to dye his whiskers. His cheeks, which were red, are now mottled; his eyes, once so bright and steadfast, are the colour of peeled plovers' eggs.

"Are you married, Jack?" says I, remembering how consumedly in love he was with his cousin Letty Lovelace, when the Cuttykilts were quartered at Strathbungo some twenty years ago.

"Married? no," says he. "Not money enough. Hard enough to keep myself, much more a family, on five hundred a year. Come to Dickinson's; there's some of the best Madeira in London, there, my boy." So we went and talked over old times.

The bill for dinner and wine consumed was prodigious, and the quantity of brandy-and-water that Jack took showed what a regular boozer he was. "A guinea or two guineas. What the devil do I care what I spend for my dinner?" says he.

"And Letty Lovelace?" says I.

Jack's countenance fell. However, he burst into a loud laugh presently. "Letty Lovelace!" says he. "She's Letty Lovelace still; but Gad, such a wizened old woman! She's as thin as a thread-paper; (you remember what a figure she had:) her nose has got red, and her teeth blue. She's always ill; always quarrelling with the rest of the family; always psalm-singing, and always taking pills. Gad, I had a rare escape *there*. Push round the grog, old boy."

Straightway memory went back to the days when Letty was the loveliest of blooming young creatures: when to hear her sing was to make the heart jump into your throat: when to see her dance, was better than Montessu or Noblet (they were the Ballet Queens of those days); when Jack used to wear a locket of her hair, with a little gold chain round his neck, and, exhilarated with toddy, after a sederunt of the Cuttykilt mess, used to pull out this token, and kiss it, and howl about it, to the great amusement of the bottle-nosed old Major and the rest of the table.

"My father and hers couldn't put their horses together," Jack said. "The General wouldn't come down with more than six thousand. My governor said it shouldn't be done under eight. Lovelace told him to go and be hanged, and so we parted company. They said she was in a decline. Gammon! She's forty, and as tough and as sour as this bit of lemon-peel. Don't put much into your punch, Snob my boy. No man *can* stand punch after wine."

"And what are your pursuits, Jack?" says I.

"Sold out when the governor died. Mother lives at Bath. Go down there once a year for a week. Dreadful slow. Shilling whist. Four sisters—all unmarried except the youngest—awful work. Scotland in August. Italy in the winter. Cursed rheumatism. Come to London in March, and toddle about at

160

the Club, old boy; and we won't go home till maw-aw-rning till daylight does appear."

"And here's the wreck of two lives!" mused the present Snobographer, after taking leave of Jack Spiggot. "Pretty merry Letty Lovelace's rudder lost and she cast away, and handsome Jack Spiggot stranded on the shore like a drunken Trinculo."

What was it that insulted Nature (to use no higher name), and perverted her kindly intentions towards them? What cursed frost was it that nipped the love that both were bearing, and condemned the girl to sour sterility and the lad to selfish old bachelorhood? It was the infernal Snob tyrant who governs us all, who says, "Thou shalt not love without a lady's-maid; thou shalt not marry without a carriage and horses; thou shalt have no wife in thy heart, and no children on thy knee, without a page in buttons and a French *bonne*; thou shalt go to the devil unless thou hast a brougham; marry poor, and society shall forsake thee; thy kinsmen shall avoid thee as a criminal; thy aunts and uncles shall turn up their eyes and bemoan the sad, sad manner in which Tom or Harry has thrown himself away." You, young woman, may sell yourself without shame, and marry old Crœsus; you, young man, may lie away your heart and your life for a jointure. But if you are poor, woe be to you! Society, the brutal Snob autocrat, cosingns you to solitary perdition. Wither, poor girl, in your garret; rot, poor bachelor, in your Club.

When I see those graceless recluses—those unnatural monks and nuns of the order of St. Beelzebub,[1] my hatred for Snobs, and their worship, and their idols, passes all continence. Let us hew down that man-eating Juggernaut, I say, that hideous Dagon; and I glow with the heroic courage of Tom Thumb, and join battle with the giant Snob.

1 This, of course, is understood to apply only to those unmarried persons whom a mean and Snobbish fear about money has kept from fulfilling their natural destiny. Many persons there are devoted to celibacy because they cannot help it. Of these a man would be a brute who spoke roughly. Indeed, after Miss O'Toole's conduct to the writer, he would be the last to condemn. But never mind, these are personal matter.

CHAPTER XXXIV

Snobs and Marriage

In that noble romance called "Ten Thousand a Year," I remember a profoundly pathetic description of the Christian manner in which the hero, Mr. Aubrey, bore his misfortunes. After making a display of the most florid and grandiloquent resignation, and quitting his country mansion, the writer supposes Aubrey to come to town in a post-chaise and pair, sitting bodkin probably between his wife and sister. It is about seven o'clock, carriages are rattling about, knockers are thundering, and tears bedim the fine eyes of Kate and Mrs. Aubrey as they think that in happier times at this hour—their Aubrey used formerly to go out to dinner to the houses of the aristocracy his friends. This is the gist of the passage—the elegant words I forget. But the noble, noble sentiment I shall always cherish and remember. What can be more sublime than the notion of a great man's relatives in tears about his dinner? With a few touches, what author ever more happily described A Snob?

We were reading the passage lately at the house of my friend, Raymond Gray, Esquire, Barrister-at-Law, an ingenuous youth without the least practice, but who has luckily a great share of good spirits, which enables him to bide his time, and bear laughingly his humble position in the world. Meanwhile, until it is altered, the stern laws of necessity and the expenses of the Northern Circuit oblige Mr. Gray to live in a very tiny mansion in a very queer small square in the airy neighbourhood of Gray's Inn Lane.

What is the more remarkable is, that Gray has a wife there. Mrs. Gray was a Miss Harley Baker: and I suppose I need not say *that* is a respectable family. Allied to the Cavendishes, the Oxfords, the Marrybones, they still, though rather *déchus* from their original splendour, hold their heads as high as any. Mrs. Harley Baker, I know, never goes to church without John behind to carry her prayer-book; nor will Miss Welbeck, her sister, walk twenty yards a-shopping without the protection of Figby, her sugar-loaf page; though the old lady is as ugly as any woman in the parish and as tall and whiskery as a grenadier. The astonishment is, how Emily Harley Baker could have stooped to marry Raymond Gray. She, who was the prettiest and proudest of the family; she, who refused Sir Cockle Byles, of the Bengal Service; she, who turned up her little nose at Essex Temple, Q.C., and connected with the noble house of Albyn; she, who had but £4,000 pour tout potage, to marry a man who had scarcely as much more. A scream of wrath and indignation was uttered by the whole family when they heard of this *mésalliance*. Mrs. Harley Baker never speaks of her daughter now but with tears in her eyes, and as a ruined creature. Miss Welbeck says, "I consider that man a villain;" and has denounced poor good-natured Mrs. Perkins as a swindler, at whose ball the young people met for the first time.

Mr. and Mrs. Gray, meanwhile, live in Gray's Inn Lane aforesaid, with a maid-servant and a nurse, whose hands are very full, and in a most provoking and unnatural state of happiness. They have never once thought of crying about their dinner, like the wretchedly puling and Snobbish womankind of my favourite Snob Aubrey, of "Ten Thousand a Year;" but, on the contrary, accept such humble victuals as fate awards them with a most perfect and thankful good grace—nay, actually have a portion for a hungry friend at times—as the present writer can gratefully testify.

I was mentioning these dinners, and some admirable lemon puddings which Mrs. Gray makes, to our mutual friend the great Mr. Goldmore, the East India Director, when that gentleman's face assumed an expression of almost apoplectic terror, and he gasped out, "What! Do they give dinners?" He seemed to think it a crime and a wonder that such people should dine at all, and that it was their custom to huddle round their kitchen-fire over a bone and a crust. Whenever he meets them in society, it is a matter of wonder to him (and he always

163

expresses his surprise very loud) how the lady can appear decently dressed, and the man have an unpatched coat to his back. I have heard him enlarge upon this poverty before the whole room at the "Conflagrative Club," to which he and I and Gray have the honour to belong.

We meet at the Club on most days. At half-past four, Goldmore arrives in St. James's Street, from the City, and you may see him reading the evening papers in the bow-window of the Club, which enfilades Pall Mall—a large plethoric man, with a bunch of seals in a large bow-windowed light waistcoat. He has large coat-tails, stuffed with agents' letters and papers about companies of which he is a Director. His seals jingle as he walks. I wish I had such a man for an uncle, and that he himself were childless. I would love and cherish him, and be kind to him.

At six o'clock in the full season, when all the world is in St. James's Street, and the carriages are cutting in and out among the cabs on the stand, and the tufted dandies are showing their listless faces out of "White's," and you see respectable gray-headed gentlemen waggling their heads to each other through the plate-glass windows of "Arthur's:" and the red-coats wish to be Briareian, so as to hold all the gentlemen's horses; and that wonderful red-coated royal porter is sunning himself before Marlborough House;—at the noon of London time, you see a light-yellow carriage with black horses, and a coachman in a tight floss-silk wig, and two footmen in powder and white and yellow liveries, and a large woman inside in shot-silk, a poodle, and a pink parasol, which drives up to the gate of the "Conflagrative," and the page goes and says to Mr. Goldmore (who is perfectly aware of the fact, as he is looking out of the windows with about forty other "Conflagrative" bucks), "Your carriage, Sir." G. wags his head. "Remember, eight o'clock precisely," says he to Mulligatawney, the other East India Director; and, ascending the carriage, plumps down by the side of Mrs. Goldmore for a drive in the Park, and then home to Portland Place. As the carriage whirls off, all the young bucks in the Club feel a secret elation. It is a part of their establishment, as it were. That carriage belongs to their Club, and their Club belongs to them. They follow the equipage with interest; they eye it knowingly as they see it in the Park. But halt! we are not come to the Club Snobs yet. O my brave Snobs, what a flurry there will be among you when those papers appear!

Well, you may judge, from the above description, what sort of a man Goldmore is. A dull and pompous Leadenhall Street Crœsus, good-natured withal, and affable—cruelly affable. "Mr. Goldmore can never forget," his lady used to say, "that it was Mrs. Gray's grandfather who sent him to India; and though that young woman has made the most imprudent marriage in the world, and has left her station in society, her husband seems an ingenious and laborious young man, and we shall do everything in our power to be of use to him." So they used to ask the Grays to dinner twice or thrice in a season, when, by way of increasing the kindness, Buff, the butler, is ordered to hire a fly to convey them to and from Portland Place.

Of course I am much too good-natured a friend of both parties not to tell Gray of Goldmore's opinion regarding him, and the nabob's astonishment at the idea of the briefless barrister having any dinner at all. Indeed, Goldmore's saying became a joke against Gray amongst us wags at the Club, and we used to ask him when he tasted meat last? whether we should bring him home something from dinner? and cut a thousand other mad pranks with him in our facetious way.

One day, then, coming home from the Club, Mr. Gray conveyed to his wife the astounding information that he had asked Goldmore to dinner.

"My love," says Mrs. Gray, in a tremor, "how could you be so cruel? Why, the dining-room won't hold Mrs. Goldmore."

"Make your mind easy, Mrs. Gray; her ladyship is in Paris. It is only Crœsus that's coming, and we are going to the play afterwards—to Sadler's Wells. Goldmore said at the Club that he thought Shakspeare was a great dramatic poet, and ought to be patronized; whereupon, fired with enthusiasm, I invited him to our banquet."

"Goodness gracious! what *can* we give him for dinner? He has two French cooks; you know Mrs. Goldmore is always telling us about them; and he dines with Aldermen every day."

> "'A plain leg of mutton, my Lucy,
>   I prithee get ready at three;
> Have it tender, and smoking, and juicy,
>   And what better meat can there be?'"

says Gray, quoting my favourite poet.

"But the cook is ill; and you know that horrible Pattypan the pastrycook's——"

"Silence, Frau!" says Gray, in a deep tragedy voice. "*I* will have the ordering of this repast. Do all things as I bid thee. Invite our friend Snob here to partake of the feast. Be mine the task of procuring it."

"Don't be expensive, Raymond," says his wife.

"Peace, thou timid partner of the briefless one. Goldmore's dinner shall be suited to our narrow means. Only do thou in all things my commands." And seeing by the peculiar expression of the rogue's countenance that some mad waggery was in preparation, I awaited the morrow with anxiety.

CHAPTER XXXV

Snobs and Marriage

Punctual to the hour—(by the way, I cannot omit here to mark down my hatred, scorn, and indignation towards those miserable Snobs who come to dinner at nine, when they are asked at eight, in order to make a sensation in the company. May the loathing of honest folks, the backbiting of others, the curses of cooks, pursue these wretches, and avenge the society on which they trample!)—Punctual, I say, to the hour of five, which Mr. and Mrs. Raymond Gray had appointed, a youth of an elegant appearance, in a neat evening-dress, whose trim whiskers indicated neatness, whose light step denoted activity (for in sooth he was hungry, and always is at the dinner-hour, whatsoever that hour may be), and whose rich golden hair, curling down his shoulders, was set off by a perfectly new four-and-ninepenny silk hat, was seen wending his way down Bittlestone Street, Bittlestone Square, Gray's Inn. The person in question, I need not say, was Mr. Snob. *He* is never late when invited to dine. But to proceed with my narrative:—

Although Mr. Snob may have flattered himself that he made a sensation as he strutted down Bittlestone Street with his richly gilt knobbed cane (and indeed I vow I saw heads looking at me from Miss Squilsby's, the brass-plated milliner opposite Raymond Gray's, who has three silver-paper bonnets, and two fly-blown French prints of fashion in the window), yet what was the emotion produced by my arrival, compared to that with which the little street thrilled, when at five minutes past five the floss-wigged coachman, the yellow hammer-cloth and flunkeys, the black horses and blazing silver harness of Mr. Goldmore whirled down the street! It is a very little street, of very little houses, most of them with very large brass plates like Miss Squilsby's. Coal-merchants, architects and surveyors, two surgeons, a solicitor, a dancing-master, and of course several house-agents, occupy the houses—little two-storeyed edifices with little stucco porticoes. Goldmore's carriage overtopped the roofs almost; the first floors might shake hands with Crœsus as he lolled inside; all the windows of those first floors thronged with children and women in a twinkling. There was Mrs. Hammerly in curl-papers; Mrs. Saxby with her front awry; Mr. Wriggles peering through the gauze curtains, holding the while his hot glass of rum-and-water—in fine, a tremendous commotion in Bittlestone Street, as the Goldmore carriage drove up to Mr. Raymond Gray's door.

"How kind it is of him to come with *both* the footmen!" says little Mrs. Gray, peeping at the vehicle too. The huge domestic, descending from his perch, gave a rap at the door which almost drove in the building. All the heads were out; the sun was shining; the very organ-boy paused; the footmen, the coach, and Goldmore's red face and white waistcoat were blazing in splendour. The herculean plushed one went back to open the carriage-door.

Raymond Gray opened his—in his shirt-sleeves.

He ran up to the carriage. "Come in, Goldmore," says he; "just in time, my boy. Open the door, What-d'ye-call'im, and let your master out,"—and What-d'ye-call'im obeyed mechanically, with a face of wonder and horror, only to be equalled by the look of stupefied astonishment which ornamented the purple countenance of his master.

"Wawt taim will you please have the *cage*, sir?" says What-d'ye-call'im, in that peculiar, unspellable, inimitable, flunkefied pronunciation which forms one of the chief charms of existence.

"Best have it to the theatre at night," Gray exclaims; "it is but a step from here to the Wells, and we can walk there. I've got tickets for all. Be at Sadler's Wells at eleven."

"Yes, at eleven," exclaims Goldmore, perturbedly, and walks with a flurried step into the house, as if he were going to execution (as indeed he was, with that wicked Gray as a Jack

168

Ketch over him). The carriage drove away, followed by numberless eyes from doorsteps and balconies; its appearance is still a wonder in Bittlestone Street.

"Go in there, and amuse yourself with Snob," says Gray, opening the little drawing-room door. "I'll call out as soon as the chops are ready. Fanny's below, seeing to the pudding."

"Gracious mercy!" says Goldmore to me, quite confidentially, "how could he ask us? I really had no idea of this—this utter destitution."

"Dinner, dinner!" roars out Gray, from the dining-room, whence issued a great smoking and frying; and entering that apartment we find Mrs. Gray ready to receive us, and looking perfectly like a Princess who, by some accident, had a bowl of potatoes in her hand, which vegetables she placed on the table. Her husband was meanwhile cooking mutton-chops on a gridiron over the fire.

"Fanny has made the roly-poly pudding," says he; "the chops are my part. Here's a fine one; try this, Goldmore." And he popped a fizzing cutlet on that gentleman's plate. What words, what notes of exclamation can describe the nabob's astonishment?

The tablecloth was a very old one, darned in a score of places. There was mustard in a teacup, a silver fork for Goldmore—all ours were iron.

"I wasn't born with a silver spoon in my mouth," says Gray, gravely. "That fork is the only one we have. Fanny has it generally."

"Raymond!" cries Mrs. Gray, with an imploring face.

"She was used to better things, you know: and I hope one day to get her a dinner-service. I'm told the electro-plate is uncommonly good. Where the deuce *is* that boy with the beer? And now," said he, springing up, "I'll be a gentleman." And so he put on his coat, and sat down quite gravely, with four fresh mutton-chops which he had by this time broiled.

"We don't have meat every day, Mr. Goldmore," he continued, "and it's a treat to me to get a dinner like this. You

169

little know, you gentlemen of England, who live at home at ease, what hardships briefless barristers endure."

"Gracious mercy!" says Mr. Goldmore.

"Where's the half-and-half? Fanny, go over to the 'Keys' and get the beer. Here's sixpence." And what was our astonishment when Fanny got up as if to go!

"Gracious mercy! let *me*," cries Goldmore.

"Not for worlds, my dear sir. She's used to it. They wouldn't serve you as well as they serve her. Leave her alone. Law bless you!" Raymond said, with astounding composure. And Mrs. Gray left the room, and actually came back with a tray on which there was a pewter flagon of beer. Little Polly (to whom, at her christening, I had the honour of presenting a silver mug *ex officio*) followed with a couple of tobacco-pipes, and the queerest roguish look in her round little chubby face.

"Did you speak to Tapling about the gin, Fanny, my dear?" Gray asked, after bidding Polly put the pipes on the chimney-piece, which that little person had some difficulty in reaching. "The last was turpentine, and even your brewing didn't make good punch of it."

"You would hardly suspect, Goldmore, that my wife, a Harley Baker, would ever make gin-punch? I think my mother-in-law would commit suicide if she saw her."

"Don't be always laughing at mamma, Raymond," says Mrs. Gray.

"Well, well she wouldn't die, and I *don't* wish she would. And you don't make gin-punch, and you don't like it either—and—Goldmore, do you drink your beer out of the glass, or out of the perter?"

"Gracious mercy!" ejaculates Crœsus once more, as little Polly, taking the pot with both her little bunches of hands, offers it, smiling, to that astonished Director.

And so, in a word, the dinner commenced, and was presently ended in a similar fashion. Gray pursued his unfortunate guest with the most queer and outrageous description of his struggles, misery, and poverty. He described how he cleaned

the knives when they were first married; and how he used to drag the children in a little cart; how his wife could toss pancakes; and what parts of his dress she made. He told Tibbits, his clerk (who was in fact the functionary who had brought the beer from the public-house, which Mrs. Fanny had fetched from the neighbouring apartment)—to fetch "the bottle of port-wine," when the dinner was over; and told Goldmore as wonderful a history about the way in which that bottle of wine had come into his hands as any of his former stories had been. When the repast was all over, and it was near time to move to the play, and Mrs. Gray had retired, and we were sitting ruminating rather silently over the last glasses of the port, Gray suddenly breaks the silence by slapping Goldmore on the shoulder, and saying, "Now, Goldmore, tell me something."

"What?" asks Crœsus.

"Haven't you had a good dinner?"

Goldmore started, as if a sudden truth had just dawned upon him. He *had* had a good dinner; and didn't know it until then. The three mutton-chops consumed by him were best of the mutton kind; the potatoes were perfect of their order; as for the roly-poly, it was too good. The porter was frothy and cool, and the port-wine was worthy of the gills of a bishop. I speak with ulterior views; for there is more in Gray's cellar.

"Well," says Goldmore, after a pause, during which he took time to consider the momentous question Gray put to him—"'Pon my word—now you say so—I—I have—I really have had a monsous good dinnah—monsous good, upon my ward! Here's your health, Gray, my boy, and your amiable lady; and when Mrs. Goldmore comes back, I hope we shall see you more in Portland Place." And with this the time came for the play, and we went to see Mr. Phelps at Sadler's Walls.

The best of this story (for the truth of every word of which I pledge my honour) is, that after this banquet, which Goldmore enjoyed so, the honest fellow felt a prodigious compassion and regard for the starving and miserable giver of the feast, and determined to help him in his profession. And being a Director of the newly-established Antibilious Life Assurance Company, he has had Gray appointed Standing Counsel, with a pretty annual fee; and only yesterday, in an appeal from Bombay (Buckmuckjee Bobbachee *v.* Ramchowder-Bahawder) in the Privy Council, Lord Brougham complimented Mr. Gray, who was in the case, on his curious and exact knowledge of the Sanscrit language.

Whether he knows Sanscrit or not, I can't say; but Goldmore got him the business; and so I cannot help having a lurking regard for that pompous old Bigwig.

CHAPTER XXXVI

Snobs and Marriage

"We Bachelors in Clubs are very much obliged to you," says my old school and college companion, Essex Temple, "for the opinion which you hold of us. You call us selfish, purple-faced, bloated, and other pretty names. You state, in the simplest possible terms, that we shall go to the deuce. You bid us rot in loneliness, and deny us all claims to honesty, conduct, decent Christian life. Who are you, Mr. Snob, to judge us so? Who are you, with your infernal benevolent smirk and grin, that laugh at all our generation?

"I will tell you my case," says Essex Temple; "mine and my sister Polly's, and you may make what you like of it; and sneer at old maids, and bully old bachelors, if you will.

"I will whisper to you confidentially that my sister Polly was engaged to Serjeant Shirker—a fellow whose talents one cannot deny and be hanged to them, but whom I have always known to be mean, selfish, and a prig. However, women don't see these faults in the men whom Love throws in their way. Shirker, who has about as much warmth as an eel, made up to Polly years and years ago, and was no bad match for a briefless barrister, as he was then.

"Have you ever read Lord Eldon's Life? Do you remember how the sordid old Snob narrates his going out to purchase twopenceworth of sprats, which he and Mrs. Scott fried between them? And how he parades his humility, and exhibits his miserable poverty—he who, at that time, must have been making a thousand pounds a year? Well, Shirker was just as proud of his prudence—just as thankful for his own meanness, and of course would not marry without a competency. Who so honourable? Polly waited, and waited faintly, from year to year. *He* wasn't sick at heart; *his* passion never disturbed his six hours' sleep, or kept his ambition out of mind. He would rather have hugged an attorney any day than have kissed Polly,

173

though she was one of the prettiest creatures in the world; and while she was pining alone upstairs, reading over the stock of half-a-dozen frigid letters that the confounded prig had condescended to write to her, *he*, be sure, was never busy with anything but his briefs in chambers—always frigid, rigid, self-satisfied, and at his duty. The marriage trailed on year after year, while Mr. Serjeant Shirker grew to be the famous lawyer he is.

"Meanwhile, my younger brother, Pump Temple, who was in the 120th Hussars, and had the same little patrimony which fell to the lot of myself and Polly, must fall in love with our cousin, Fanny Figtree, and marry her out of hand. You should have seen the wedding! Six bridesmaids in pink, to hold the fan, bouquet, gloves, scent-bottle, and pocket-handkerchief of the bride; basketfuls of white favours in the vestry, to be pinned on to the footmen and horses; a genteel congregation of curious acquaintance in the pews, a shabby one of poor on the steps; all the carriages of all our acquaintance, whom Aunt Figtree had levied for the occasion; and of course four horses for Mr. Pump's bridal vehicle.

"Then comes the breakfast, or *déjeûner*, if you please, with a brass band in the street, and policemen to keep order. The happy bridegroom spends about a year's income in dresses for the bridesmaids and pretty presents; and the bride must have a *trousseau* of laces, satins, jewel-boxes and tomfoolery, to make her fit to be a lieutenant's wife. There was no hesitation about Pump. He flung about his money as if it had been dross; and Mrs. P. Temple, on the horse Tom Tiddler, which her husband gave her, was the most dashing of military women at Brighton or Dublin. How old Mrs. Figtree used to bore me and Polly with stories of Pump's grandeur and the noble company he kept! Polly lives with the Figtrees, as I am not rich enough to keep a home for her.

"Pump and I have always been rather distant. Not having the slightest notions about horseflesh, he has a natural contempt for me; and in our mother's lifetime, when the good old lady was always paying his debts and petting him, I'm not sure there was not a little jealousy. It used to be Polly that kept the peace between us.

"She went to Dublin to visit Pump, and brought back grand accounts of his doings—gayest man about town—Aide-de-Camp to the Lord Lieutenant—Fanny admired everywhere—Her Excellency godmother to the second boy: the eldest with a string of aristocratic Christian names that made the grandmother wild with delight. Presently Fanny and Pump obligingly came over to London, where the third was born.

"Polly was godmother to this, and who so loving as she and Pump now? 'Oh, Essex,' says she to me, 'he is so good, so generous, so fond of his family: so handsome; who can help loving him, and pardoning his little errors?' One day, while Mrs. Pump was yet in the upper regions, and Doctor Fingerfee's brougham at her door every day, having business at Guildhall, whom should I meet in Cheapside but Pump and Polly? The poor girl looked more happy and rosy than I have seen her these twelve years. Pump, on the contrary, was rather blushing and embarrassed.

"I couldn't be mistaken in her face and its look of mischief and triumph. She had been committing some act of sacrifice. I went to the family stockbroker. She had sold out two thousand pounds that morning and given them to Pump. Quarrelling was useless—Pump had the money; he was off to Dublin by the time I reached his mother's, and Polly radiant still. He was going to make his fortune; he was going to embark the money in the Bog of Allen—I don't know what. The fact is, he was going to pay his losses upon the last Manchester steeple-chase, and I leave you to imagine how much principal or interest poor Polly ever saw back again.

"It was more than half her fortune, and he has had another thousand since from her. Then came efforts to stave off ruin and prevent exposure; struggles on all our parts, and sacrifices, that" (here Mr. Essex Temple began to hesitate)—"that needn't be talked of; but they are of no more use than such sacrifices ever are. Pump and his wife are abroad—I don't like to ask where; Polly has the three children, and Mr. Serjeant Shirker has formally written to break off an engagement, on the conclusion of which Miss Temple must herself have speculated, when she alienated the greater part of her fortune.

"And here's your famous theory of poor marriages!" Essex Temple cries, concluding the above history. "How do you know that I don't want to marry myself? How do you dare sneer at my poor sister? What are we but martyrs of the reckless marriage system which Mr. Snob, forsooth, chooses to advocate?" And he thought he had the better of the argument, which, strange to say, is not my opinion.

But for the infernal Snob-worship, might not every one of these people be happy? If poor Polly's happiness lay in linking her tender arms round such a heartless prig as the sneak who has deceived her, she might have been happy now—as happy as Raymond Raymond in the ballad, with the stone statue by his side. She is wretched because Mr. Serjeant Shirker worships money and ambition, and is a Snob and a coward.

If the unfortunate Pump Temple and his giddy hussy of a wife have ruined themselves, and dragged down others into their calamity, it is because they loved rank, and horses, and plate, and carriages, and *Court Guides*, and millinery, and would sacrifice all to attain those objects.

And who misguides them? If the world were more simple, would not those foolish people follow the fashion? Does not the world love *Court Guides*, and millinery, and plate, and carriages? Mercy on us! Read the fashionable intelligence; read the *Court Circular*; read the genteel novels; survey mankind, from Pimlico to Red Lion Square, and see how the Poor Snob is aping the Rich Snob; how the Mean Snob is grovelling at the feet of the Proud Snob; and the Great Snob is lording it over his humble brother. Does the idea of equality ever enter Dives' head? Will it ever? Will the Duchess of Fitzbattleaxe (I like a good name) ever believe that Lady Crœsus, her next-door neighbour in Belgrave Square, is as good a lady as her Grace?

Will Lady Crœsus ever leave off pining for the Duchess's parties, and cease patronizing Mrs. Broadcloth, whose husband has not got his Baronetcy yet? Will Mrs. Broadcloth ever heartily shake hands with Mrs. Seedy, and give up those odious calculations about poor dear Mrs. Seedy's income? Will Mrs. Seedy, who is starving in her great house, go and live comfortably in a little one, or in lodgings? Will her landlady, Miss Letsam, ever stop wondering at the familiarity of tradespeople, or rebuking the insolence of Suky, the maid, who wears flowers under her bonnet, like a lady?

But why hope, why wish for such times? Do I wish all Snobs to perish? Do I wish these Snob papers to determine? Suicidal fool, art not thou, too, a Snob and a brother?

CHAPTER XXXVII

Club Snobs

As I wish to be particularly agreeable to the ladies (to whom I make my most humble obeisance), we will now, if you please, commence maligning a class of Snobs against whom, I believe, most female minds are embittered,—I mean Club Snobs. I have very seldom heard even the most gentle and placable woman speak without a little feeling of bitterness against those social institutions, those palaces swaggering in St. James's, which are open to the men; while the ladies have but their dingy three-windowed brick boxes in Belgravia or in Paddingtonia, or in the region between the road of Edgeware and that of Gray's Inn.

In my grandfather's time it used to be Freemasonry that roused their anger. It was my grand-aunt (whose portrait we still have in the family) who got into the clock-case at the Royal Rosicrucian Lodge at Bungay, Suffolk, to spy the proceedings of the Society, of which her husband was a member, and being frightened by the sudden whirring and striking eleven of the clock (just as the Deputy-Grand-Master was bringing in the mystic gridiron for the reception of a neophyte), rushed out into the midst of the lodge assembled; and was elected, by a desperate unanimity, Deputy-Grand-Mistress for life. Though that admirable and courageous female never subsequently breathed a word with regard to the secrets of the initiation, yet she inspired all our family with such a terror regarding the mysteries of Jachin and Boaz, that none of our family have ever since joined the Society, or worn the dreadful Masonic insignia.

It is known that Orpheus was torn to pieces by some justly indignant Thracian ladies for belonging to an Harmonic Lodge. "Let him go back to Eurydice," they said, "whom he is pretending to regret so." But the history is given in Dr. Lemprière's elegant dictionary in a manner much more

178

forcible than any which this feeble pen can attempt. At once, then, and without verbiage, let us take up this subject-matter of Clubs.

Clubs ought not, in my mind, to be permitted to bachelors. If my friend of the Cuttykilts had not our Club, the "Union Jack," to go to (I belong to the "U. J." and nine other similar institutions), who knows but he never would be a bachelor at this present moment? Instead of being made comfortable, and cockered up with every luxury, as they are at Clubs, bachelors ought to be rendered profoundly miserable, in my opinion. Every encouragement should be given to the rendering their spare time disagreeable. There can be no more odious object, according to my sentiments, than young Smith, in the pride of health, commanding his dinner of three courses; than middle-aged Jones wallowing (as I may say) in an easy padded arm-chair, over the last delicious novel or brilliant magazine; or than old Brown, that selfish old reprobate for whom mere literature has no charms, stretched on the best sofa, sitting on the second edition of *The Times*, having the *Morning Chronicle* between his knees, the *Herald* pushed in between his coat and waistcoat, the *Standard* under his left arm, the *Globe* under the other pinion, and the *Daily News* in perusal. "I'll trouble you for *Punch*, Mr. Wiggins," says the unconscionable old gormandiser, interrupting our friend, who is laughing over the periodical in question.

This kind of selfishness ought not to be. No, no. Young Smith, instead of his dinner and his wine, ought to be, where?—at the festive tea-table, to be sure, by the side of Miss Higgs, sipping the bohea, or tasting the harmless muffin; which old Mrs. Higgs looks on, pleased at their innocent dalliance, and my friend Miss Wirt, the governess, is performing Thalberg's last sonata in treble X., totally unheeded, at the piano.

Where should the middle-aged Jones be? At his time of life, he ought to be the father of a family. At such an hour—say, at nine o'clock at night—the nursery-bell should have just rung the children to bed. He and Mrs. J. ought to be, by rights, seated on each side of the fire by the dining-room table, a bottle of port-wine between them, not so full as it was an hour since. Mrs. J. has had two glasses; Mrs. Grumble (Jones's mother-in-law) has had three: Jones himself has finished the rest, and dozes comfortably until bed-time.

And Brown, that old newspaper-devouring miscreant, what right has *he* at a club at a decent hour of night? He ought to be playing his rubber with Miss MacWhirter, his wife, and the family apothecary. His candle ought to be brought to him at ten o'clock, and he should retire to rest just as the young people were thinking of a dance. How much finer, simpler, nobler are the several employments I have sketched out for these gentlemen than their present nightly orgies at the horrid Club!

And, ladies, think of men who do not merely frequent the dining-room and library, but who use other apartments of those horrible dens which it is my purpose to batter down; think of Cannon, the wretch, which his coat off, at his age and size, clattering the balls over the billiard-table all night, and making bets with that odious Captain Spot!—think of Pam in a dark room with Bob Trumper, Jack Deuceace, and Charley Vole, playing, the poor dear misguided wretch, guinea points and five pounds on the rubber!—above all, think—oh, think of that den of abomination, which I am told has been established in *some* clubs, called *the Smoking-Room,*—think of the debauchees who congregate there, the quantities of reeking whisky-punch or more dangerous sherry-cobbler which they consume;—think of them coming home at cock-crow and letting themselves into the quiet house with the Chubb key;—think of them, the hypocrites, taking off their insidious boots before they slink upstairs, the children sleeping overhead, the wife of their bosom alone with the waning rushlight in the two-pair front—that chamber so soon to be rendered hateful by the smell of their stale cigars! I am not an advocate of violence; I am not, by nature, of an incendiary turn of mind; but if, my dear ladies, you are for assassinating Mr. Chubb and burning down the Clubhouses in St. James's, there is *one* Snob at least who will not think the worse of you.

The only men who, as I opine, ought to be allowed the use of Clubs, are married men without a profession. The continual presence of these in a house cannot be thought, even by the most uxorious of wives, desirable. Say the girls are beginning to practise their music, which, in an honourable English family, ought to occupy every young gentlewoman three hours; it would be rather hard to call upon poor papa to sit in the drawing-room all that time, and listen to the interminable discords and shrieks which are elicited from the miserable piano during the above necessary operation. A man with a good ear, especially, would go mad, if compelled daily to submit to this horror.

Or suppose you have a fancy to go to the milliner's, or to Howell and James's, it is manifest, my dear Madam, that your husband is much better at the Club during these operations than by your side in the carriage, or perched in wonder upon one of the stools at Shawl and Gimcrack's, whilst young counter-dandies are displaying their wares.

This sort of husbands should be sent out after breakfast, and if not Members of Parliament, or Directors of a Railroad, or an Insurance Company, should be put into their Clubs, and told to remain there until dinner-time. No sight is more agreeable to my truly well-regulated mind than to see the noble characters so worthily employed. Whenever I pass by St. James's Street, having the privilege, like the rest of the world, of looking in at the windows of "Blight's," or "Foodle's," or "Snook's," or the great bay at the "Contemplative Club," I behold with respectful appreciation the figures within—the honest rosy old fogies, the mouldy old dandies, the waist-belts and glossy wigs and tight cravats of those most vacuous and respectable men. Such men are best there during the day-time surely. When you part with them, dear ladies, think of the rapture consequent on their return. You have transacted your household affairs; you have made your purchases; you have paid you visits; you have aired your poodle in the Park; your French maid has completed the toilette which renders you so ravishingly beautiful by candlelight, and you are fit to make home pleasant to him who has been absent all day.

Such men surely ought to have their Clubs, and we will not class them among Club Snobs therefore:—on whom let us reserve our attack for the next chapter.

CHAPTER XXXVIII

Club Snobs

Such a sensation has been created in the Clubs by the appearance of the last paper on Club Snobs, as can't but be complimentary to me who am one of their number.

I belong to many Clubs. The "Union Jack," the "Sash and Marlin-spike"—Military Clubs. "The True Blue," the "No Surrender," the "Blue and Buff," the "Guy Fawkes," and the "Cato Street"—Political Clubs. The "Brummell" and the "Regent"—Dandy Clubs. The "Acropolis," the "Palladium," the "Areopagus," the "Pnyx," the "Pentelicus," the "Ilissus," and the "Poluphloisboio Thalasses"—Literary Clubs. I never could make out how the latter set of Clubs got their names; *I* don't know Greek for one, and I wonder how many other members of those institutions do?

Ever since the Club Snobs have been announced, I observe a sensation created on my entrance into any one of these places. Members get up and hustle together; they nod, they scowl, as they glance towards the present Snob. "Infernal impudent jackanapes! If he shows me up," says Colonel Bludyer, "I'll break every bone in his skin." "I told you what would come of admitting literary men into the Club," says Ranville Ranville to his colleague, Spooney, of the Tape and Sealing-Wax Office. "These people are very well in their proper places, and as a public man, I make a point of shaking hands with them, and that sort of thing; but to have one's privacy obtruded upon by such people is really too much. Come along, Spooney," and the pair of prigs retire superciliously.

As I came into the coffee-room at the "No Surrender," old Jawkins was holding out to a knot of men, who were yawning, as usual. There he stood, waving the *Standard*, and swaggering before the fire. "What," says he, "did I tell Peel last year? If you touch the Corn Laws, you touch the Sugar Question; if you touch the Sugar, you touch the Tea. I am no monopolist. I am a liberal man, but I cannot forget that I stand on the brink of a precipice; and if we are to have Free Trade, give me reciprocity. And what was Sir Robert Peel's answer to me? 'Mr. Jawkins,' he said—"

Here Jawkins's eye suddenly turning on your humble servant, he stopped his sentence, with a guilty look—his stale old stupid sentence, which every one of us at the Club has heard over and over again.

Jawkins is a most pertinacious Club Snob. Every day he is at that fireplace, holding that *Standard*, of which he reads up the leading-article, and pours it out *ore rotundo*, with the most astonishing composure, in the face of his neighbour, who has just read every word of it in the paper. Jawkins has money, as you may see by the tie of his neckcloth. He passes the morning swaggering about the City, in bankers' and brokers' parlours, and says:—"I spoke with Peel yesterday, and his intentions are so and so. Graham and I were talking over the matter, and I pledge you my word of honour, his opinion coincides with mine; and that What-d'ye-call'um is the only measure Government will venture on trying." By evening-paper time he is at the Club: "I can tell you the opinion of the City, my lord," says he, "and the way in which Jones Loyd looks at it is briefly this: Rothschilds told me so themselves. In Mark Lane, people's minds are *quite* made up." He is considered rather a well-informed man.

He lives in Belgravia, of course; in a drab-coloured genteel house, and has everything about him that is properly grave, dismal, and comfortable. His dinners are in the *Morning Herald*, among the parties for the week; and his wife and daughters make a very handsome appearance at the Drawing-Room, once a year, when he comes down to the Club in his Deputy-Lieutenant's uniform.

He is fond of beginning a speech to you by saying, "When I was in the House, I &c."—in fact he sat for Skittlebury for three weeks in the first Reformed Parliament, and was unseated for bribery; since which he has three times unsuccessfully contested that honourable borough.

Another sort of Political Snob I have seen at most Clubs, and that is the man who does not care so much for home politics, but is great upon foreign affairs. I think this sort of man is scarcely found anywhere *but* in Clubs. It is for him the papers provide their foreign articles, at the expense of some ten thousand a year each. He is the man who is really seriously uncomfortable about the designs of Russia, and the atrocious treachery of Louis Philippe. He it is who expects a French fleet in the Thames, and has a constant eye upon the American President, every word of whose speech (goodness help him!) he reads. He knows the names of the contending leaders in Portugal, and what they are fighting about: and it is he who says that Lord Aberdeen ought to be impeached, and Lord Palmerston hanged, or *vice versa*.

Lord Palmerston's being sold to Russia, the exact number of roubles paid, by what House in the City, is a favourite theme with this kind of Snob. I once overheard him—it was Captain Spitfire, R.N. (who had been refused a ship by the Whigs, by the way)—indulging in the following conversation with Mr. Minns after dinner:

"Why wasn't the Princess Scragamoffsky at Lady Palmerston's party, Minns? Because *she can't show*—and why can't she show? Shall I tell you, Minns, why she can't show? The Princess Scragamoffsky's back is flayed alive, Minns—I tell you it's raw, sir? On Tuesday last, at twelve o'clock, three drummers of the Preobajinski Regiment arrived at Ashburnham House, and at half-past twelve, in the yellow drawing-room at the Russian Embassy, before the ambassadress and four ladies'-maids, the Greek Papa, and the Secretary of Embassy, Madame de Scragamoffsky received thirteen dozen. She was knouted, sir, knouted in the midst of England—in Berkeley Square, for having said that the Grand Duchess Olga's hair was red. And now, sir, will you tell me Lord Palmerston ought to continue Minister?"

Minns: "Good Ged!"

Minnis follows Spitfire about, and thinks him the greatest and wisest of human beings.

CHAPTER XXXIX

Club Snobs

Why does not some great author write "The Mysteries of the Club-houses: or St. James's Street unveiled." It would be a fine subject for an imaginative writer. We must all as boys, remember when we went to the fair, and had spent all our money—the sort of awe and anxiety with which we loitered round the outside of the show, speculating upon the nature of the entertainment going on within.

Man is a Drama—of Wonder and Passion, and Mystery and Meanness, and Beauty and Truthfulness, and Etcetera. Each Bosom is a Booth in Vanity Fair. But let us stop this capital style, I should die if I kept it up for a column (a pretty thing a column all capitals would be, by the way). In a Club, though there mayn't be a soul of your acquaintance in the room, you have always the chance of watching strangers, and speculating on what is going on within those tents and curtains of their souls, their coats and waistcoats. This is a never-failing sport. Indeed I am told there are some Clubs in the town where nobody ever speaks to anybody. They sit in the coffee-room, quite silent, and watching each other.

Yet how little you can tell from a man's outward demeanour! There's a man at our Club—large, heavy, middle-aged—gorgeously dressed—rather bald—with lacquered boots—and a boa when he goes out; quiet in demeanour, always ordering and consuming a *recherché* little dinner: whom I have mistaken for Sir John Pocklington any time these five years, and respected as a man with five hundred pounds *per diem*; and I find he is but a clerk in an office in the City, with not two hundred pounds income, and his name is Jubber. Sir John Pocklington was, on the contrary, the dirty little snuffy man who cried out so about the bad quality of the beer, and grumbled at being overcharged three-halfpence for a herring, seated at the next table to Jubber on the day when some one pointed the Baronet out to me.

Take a different sort of mystery. I see, for instance, old Fawney stealing round the rooms of the Club with glassy meaningless eyes and an endless greasy simper—he fawns on everybody he meets, and shakes hands with you, and blesses you, and betrays the most tender and astonishing interest in your welfare. You know him to be a quack and a rogue, and he knows you know it. But he wriggles on his way, and leaves a track of slimy flattery after him wherever he goes. Who can penetrate that man's mystery? What earthly good can he get from you or me? You don't know what is working under that leering tranquil mask. You have only the dim instinctive repulsion that warns you, you are in the presence of a knave—beyond which fact all Fawney's soul is a secret to you.

I think I like to speculate on the young men best. Their play is opener. You know the cards in their hand, as it were. Take, for example, Messrs. Spavin and Cockspur.

A specimen or two of this sort of young fellows may be found, I believe, at most Clubs. They know nobody. They bring a fine smell of cigars into the room with them, and they growl together, in a corner, about sporting matters. They recollect the history of that short period in which they have been ornaments of the world by the names of winning horses. As political men talk about "the Reform year," "the year the Whigs went out," and so forth, these young sporting bucks speak of *Tarnation's* year, or *Opodeldoc's* year, or the year when *Catawampus* ran second for the Chester Cup. They play at billiards in the morning, they absorb pale ale for breakfast, and "top up" with glasses of strong waters. They read *Bell's Life* (and a very pleasant paper too, with a great deal of erudition in the answers to correspondents.) They go down to Tattersall's, and swagger in the Park, with their hands plunged in the pockets of their paletots.

What strikes me especially in the outward demeanour of sporting youth is their amazing gravity, their conciseness of speech, and careworn and moody air. In the smoking-room at the "Regent," when Joe Millerson will be setting the whole room in a roar with laughter, you hear young Messrs. Spavin and Cockspur grumbling together in a corner. "I'll take your five-and-twenty to one about Brother to Bluenose," whispers Spavin. "Can't do it at the price," Cockspur says, wagging his head ominously. The betting-book is always present in the minds of those unfortunate youngsters. I think I hate that work even more than the "Peerage." There is some good in the latter—though, generally speaking, a vain record: though De Mogyns is not descended from the giant Hogyn Mogyn; though half the other genealogies are equally false and foolish; yet the mottoes are good reading—some of them; and the book itself a sort of gold-laced and liveried lacquey to History, and in so far serviceable. But what good ever came out of, or went into, a betting-book? If I could be Caliph Omar for a week, I would pitch every one of those despicable manuscripts into the flames; from my Lord's, who is "in" with Jack Snaffle's stable, and is over-reaching worse-informed rogues and swindling greenhorns, down to Sam's, the butcher-boy's, who books eighteenpenny odds in the tap-room, and "stands to win five-and-twenty bob."

In a turf transaction, either Spavin or Cockspur would try to get the better of his father, and, to gain a point in the odds, victimise his best friends. One day we shall hear of one or other levanting; an event at which, not being sporting men, we shall not break our hearts. See—Mr. Spavin is settling his toilette previous to departure; giving a curl in the glass to his side-wisps of hair. Look at him! It is only at the hulks, or among turf-men, that you ever see a face so mean, so knowing, and so gloomy.

A much more humane being among the youthful Clubbists is the Lady-killing Snob. I saw Wiggle just now in the dressing-room talking to Waggle, his inseparable.

Waggle.—'Pon my honour, Wiggle, she did."

Wiggle.—"Well, Waggle, as you say—I own I think she DID look at me rather kindly. We'll see tonight at the French play."

And having arrayed their little persons, these two harmless young bucks go upstairs to dinner.

CHAPTER XL

Club Snobs

Both sorts of young men, mentioned in my last under the flippant names of Wiggle and Waggle, may be found in tolerable plenty, I think, in Clubs. Wiggle and Waggle are both idle. They come of the middle classes. One of them very likely makes believe to be a barrister, and the other has smart apartments about Piccadilly. They are a sort of second-chop dandies; they cannot imitate that superb listlessness of demeanour, and that admirable vacuous folly which distinguishes the noble and high-born chiefs of the race; but they lead lives almost as bad (were it but for the example), and are personally quite as useless. I am not going to arm a thunderbolt, and launch it at the heads of these little Pall Mall butterflies. They don't commit much public harm, or private extravagance. They don't spend a thousand pounds for diamond ear-rings for an Opera-dancer, as Lord Tarquin can: neither of them ever set up a public-house or broke the bank of a gambling-club, like the young Earl of Martingale. They have good points, kind feelings, and deal honourably in money-transactions—only in their characters of men of second-rate pleasure about town, they and their like are so utterly mean, self-contented, and absurd, that they must not be omitted in a work treating on Snobs.

Wiggle has been abroad, where he gives you to understand that his success among the German countesses and Italian princesses, whom he met at the *tables-d'hôte*, was perfectly terrific. His rooms are hung round with pictures of actresses and ballet-dancers. He passes his mornings in a fine dressing-gown, burning pastilles, and reading "Don Juan" and French novels (by the way, the life of the author of "Don Juan," as described by himself, was the model of the life of a Snob). He has twopenny-halfpenny French prints of women with languishing eyes, dressed in dominoes,—guitars, gondolas, and so forth,—and tells you stories about them.

"It's a bad print," says he, "I know, but I've a reason for liking it. It reminds me of somebody—somebody I knew in other climes. You have heard of the Principessa di Monte Pulciano? I met her at Rimini. Dear, dear Francesca! That fair-haired, bright-eyed thing in the Bird of Paradise and the Turkish Simar with the love-bird on her finger, I'm sure must have been taken from—from somebody perhaps whom you don't know—but she's known at Munich, Waggle my boy,—everybody knows the Countess Ottilia di Eulenschreckenstein. Gad, sir, what a beautiful creature she was when I danced with her on the birthday of Prince Attila of Bavaria, in '44. Prince Carloman was our vis-à-vis, and Prince Pepin danced the same *contredanse*. She had a Polyanthus in her bouquet. Waggle, *I have it now.*" His countenance assumes an agonized and mysterious expression, and he buries his head in the sofa cushions, as if plunging into a whirlpool of passionate recollections.

Last year he made a considerable sensation by having on his table a morocco miniature case locked by a gold key, which he always wore round his neck, and on which was stamped a serpent—emblem of eternity—with the letter M in the circle. Sometimes he laid this upon his little morocco writing-table, as if it were on an altar—generally he had flowers upon it; in the middle of a conversation he would start up and kiss it. He would call out from his bed-room to his valet, "Hicks, bring me my casket!"

"I don't know who it is," Waggle would say. "Who *does* know that fellow's intrigues! Desborough Wiggle, sir, is the slave of passion. I suppose you have heard the story of the Italian princess locked up in the Convent of Saint Barbara, at Rimini? He hasn't told you? Then I'm not at liberty to speak. Or the countess, about whom he nearly had the duel with Prince Witikind of Bavaria? Perhaps you haven't even heard about that beautiful girl at Pentonville, daughter of a most respectable Dissenting clergyman. She broke her heart when she found he was engaged (to a most lovely creature of high family, who afterwards proved false to him), and she's now in Hanwell."

191

Waggle's belief in his friend amounts to frantic adoration. "What a genius he is, if he would but apply himself!" he whispers to me. "He could be anything, sir, but for his passions. His poems are the most beautiful things you ever saw. He's written a continuation of 'Don Juan,' from his own adventures. Did you ever read his lines to Mary? They're superior to Byron, sir—superior to Byron."

I was glad to hear this from so accomplished a critic as Waggle; for the fact is, I had composed the verses myself for honest Wiggle one day, whom I found at his chambers plunged in thought over a very dirty old-fashioned album, in which he had not as yet written a single word.

"I can't," says he. "Sometimes I can write whole cantos, and today not a line. Oh, Snob! such an opportunity! Such a divine creature! She's asked me to write verses for her album, and I can't."

"Is she rich?" said I. "I thought you would never marry any but an heiress."

"Oh, Snob! she's the most accomplished, highly-connected creature!—and I can't get out a line."

"How will you have it?" says I. "Hot, with sugar?"

"Don't, don't! You trample on the most sacred feelings, Snob. I want something wild and tender,—like Byron. I want to tell her that amongst the festive halls, and that sort of thing, you know—I only think about her, you know—that I scorn the world, and am weary of it, you know, and—something about a gazelle, and a bulbul, you know."

"And a yataghan to finish off with," the present writer observed and we began:—

"TO MARY.

"I seem, in the midst of the crowd,
The lightest of all;
My laughter rings cheery and loud,
In banquet and ball.

192

My lip hath its smiles and its sneers,
    For all men to see;
But my soul, and my truth, and my tears,
    Are for thee, are for thee!"

"Do you call *that* neat, Wiggle?" says I. "I declare it almost makes me cry myself."

"Now suppose," says Wiggle, "we say that all the world is at my feet—make her jealous you know, and that sort of thing—and that—that I'm going to *travel*, you know? That perhaps may work upon her feelings."

So *We* (as this wretched prig said) began again:—

"Around me they flatter and fawn—
    The young and the old,
The fairest are ready to pawn
    Their hearts for my gold.
They sue me—I laugh as I spurn
    The slaves at my knee,
But in faith and in fondness I turn
    Unto thee, unto thee!"

"Now for the travelling, Wiggle my boy!" And I began, in a voice choked with emotion—

"Away! for my heart knows no rest
    Since you taught it to feel;
The secret must die in my breast
    I burn to reveal;
The passion I may not ..."

"I say, Snob!" Wiggle here interrupted the excited bard (just as I was about to break out into four lines so pathetic that they would drive you into hysterics). "I say—ahem—couldn't you say that I was—a—military man, and that there was some danger of my life?"

"You a military man?—danger of your life? What the deuce do you mean?"

"Why," said Wiggle, blushing a good deal, "I told her I was going out—on—the—Ecuador—expedition."

"You abominable young impostor," I exclaimed. "Finish the poem for yourself!" And so he did, and entirely out of all metre, and bragged about the work at the Club as his own performance.

Poor Waggle fully believed in his friend's genius, until one day last week he came with a grin on his countenance to the Club, and said, "Oh, Snob, I've made *such* a discovery! Going down to the skating today, whom should I see but Wiggle walking with that splendid woman—that lady of illustrious family and immense fortune, Mary, you know, whom he wrote

194

the beautiful verses about. She's five-and-forty. She's red hair. She's a nose like a pump-handle. Her father made his fortune by keeping a ham-and-beef shop, and Wiggle's going to marry her next week."

"So much the better, Waggle, my young friend," I exclaimed. "Better for the sake of womankind that this dangerous dog should leave off lady-killing—this Bluebeard give up practice. Or, better rather for his own sake. For as there is not a word of truth in any of those prodigious love-stories which you used to swallow, nobody has been hurt except Wiggle himself, whose affections will now centre in the ham-and-beef shop. There *are* people, Mr. Waggle, who do these things in earnest, and hold a good rank in the world too. But these are not subjects for ridicule, and though certainly Snobs, are scoundrels likewise. Their cases go up to a higher Court."

CHAPTER XLI

Club Snobs

Bacchus is the divinity to whom Waggle devotes his especial worship. "Give me wine, my boy," says he to his friend Wiggle, who is prating about lovely woman; and holds up his glass full of the rosy fluid, and winks at it portentously, and sips it, and smacks his lips after it, and meditates on it, as if he were the greatest of connoisseurs.

I have remarked this excessive wine-amateurship especially in youth. Snoblings from college, Fledglings from the army, Goslings from the public schools, who ornament our Clubs, are frequently to be heard in great force upon wine questions. "This bottle's corked," says Snobling; and Mr. Sly, the butler, taking it away, returns presently with the same wine in another jug, which the young amateur pronounces excellent. "Hang champagne!" says Fledgling, "it's only fit for gals and children. Give me pale sherry at dinner, and my twenty-three claret afterwards." "What's port now?" says Gosling; "disgusting thick sweet stuff—where's the old dry wine one *used* to get?" Until the last twelvemonth, Fledgling drank small-beer at Doctor Swishtail's; and Gosling used to get his dry old port at a gin-shop in Westminster—till he quitted that seminary, in 1844.

Anybody who has looked at the caricatures of thirty years ago, must remember how frequently bottle-noses, pimpled faces, and other Bardolphian features are introduced by the designer. They are much more rare now (in nature, and in pictures, therefore,) than in those good old times; but there are still to be found amongst the youth of our Clubs lads who glory in drinking-bouts, and whose faces, quite sickly and yellow, for the most part are decorated with those marks which Rowland's Kalydor is said to efface. "I was *so* cut last night—old boy!" Hopkins says to Tomkins (with amiable confidence). "I tell you what we did. We breakfasted with Jack Herring at twelve, and kept up with brandy and soda-water and weeds till four; then we toddled into the Park for an hour; then we dined and drank mulled port till half-price; then we looked in for an hour at the Hay-market; then we came back to the Club, and had grills and whisky punch till all was blue.—Hullo, waiter! Get me a glass of cherry-brandy." Club waiters, the civilest, the kindest, the patientest of men, die under the infliction of these cruel young topers. But if the reader wishes to see a perfect picture on the stage of this class of young fellows, I would recommend him to witness the ingenious comedy of *London Assurance*—the amiable heroes of which are represented, not only as drunkards and five-o'clock-in-the-morning men, but as showing a hundred other delightful traits of swindling, lying, and general debauchery, quite edifying to witness.

How different is the conduct of these outrageous youths to the decent behaviour of my friend, Mr. Papworthy; who says to Poppins, the butler at the club:—

Papworthy.—"Poppins, I'm thinking of dining early; is there any cold game in the house?"

Poppins.—"There's a game-pie, sir; there's cold grouse, sir; there's cold pheasant, sir; there's cold peacock, sir; cold swan, sir; cold ostrich, sir," &c. &c. (as the case may be).

Papworthy.—"Hem! What's your best claret now, Poppins?—in pints, I mean."

Poppins.—"There's Cooper and Magnum's Lafite, sir; there's Lath and Sawdust's St. Julien, sir; Bung's Leoville is considered remarkably fine: and I think you'd like Jugger's Château-Margaux."

Papworthy.—"Hum!—hah!—well—give me a crust of bread and a glass of beer. I'll only *lunch*, Poppins."

Captain Shindy is another sort of Club bore. He has been known to throw all the Club in an uproar about the quality of his mutton-chop.

"Look at it, sir! Is it cooked, sir? Smell it, sir! Is it meat fit for a gentleman?" he roars out to the steward, who stands trembling before him, and who in vain tells him that the Bishop of Bullock-smithy has just had three from the same loin. All the

CAPTAIN SHINDY'S MUTTON CHOP.

waiters in the Club are huddled round the captain's mutton-chop. He roars out the most horrible curses at John for not bringing the pickles; he utters the most dreadful oaths because Thomas has not arrived with the Harvey sauce; Peter comes tumbling with the water-jug over Jeames, who is bringing "the glittering canisters with bread." Whenever Shindy enters the room (such is the force of character), every table is deserted, every gentleman must dine as he best may, and all those big footmen are in terror.

He makes his account of it. He scolds, and is better waited upon in consequence. At the Club he has ten servants scudding about to do his bidding.

Poor Mr. Shindy and the children are, meanwhile, in dingy lodgings somewhere, waited upon by a charity-girl in pattens.

CHAPTER XLII

Club Snobs

Every well-bred English female will sympathize with the subject of the harrowing tale, the history of Sackville Maine, I am now about to recount. The pleasures of Clubs have been spoken of: let us now glance for a moment at the dangers of those institutions, and for this purpose I must introduce you to my young acquaintance, Sackville Maine.

It was at a ball at the house of my respected friend, Mrs. Perkins, that I was introduced to this gentleman and his charming lady. Seeing a young creature before me in a white dress, with white satin shoes; with a pink ribbon, about a yard in breadth, flaming out as she twirled in a polka in the arms of Monsieur de Springbock, the German diplomatist; with a green wreath on her head, and the blackest hair this individual ever set eyes on—seeing, I say, before me a charming young woman whisking beautifully in a beautiful dance, and presenting, as she wound and wound round the room, now a full face, then a three-quarter face, then a profile—a face, in fine, which in every way you saw it, looked pretty, and rosy, and happy, I felt (as I trust) a not unbecoming curiosity regarding the owner of this pleasant countenance, and asked Wagley (who was standing by, in conversation with an acquaintance) who was the lady in question?

"Which?" says Wagley.

"That one with the coal-black eyes?" I replied.

"Hush!" says he; and the gentleman with whom he was talking moved off, with rather a discomfited air.

When he was gone Wagley burst out laughing. "*Coal-black* eyes!" said he; "you've just hit it. That's Mrs. Sackville Maine, and that was her husband who just went away. He's a coal-merchant, Snob my boy, and I have no doubt Mr. Perkins's Wallsends are supplied from his wharf. He is in a flaming furnace when he hears coals mentioned. He and his wife and his mother are very proud of Mrs. Sackville's family; she was a Miss Chuff, daughter of Captain Chuff, R.N. That is the widow: that stout woman in crimson tabinet, battling about the odd trick with old Mr. Dumps, at the card-table."

And so, in fact, it was. Sackville Maine (whose name is a hundred times more elegant, surely, than that of Chuff) was blest with a pretty wife, and a genteel mother-in-law, both of whom some people may envy him.

Soon after his marriage the old lady was good enough to come and pay him a visit—just for a fortnight—at his pretty little cottage, Kennington Oval; and, such is her affection for the place, has never quitted it these four years. She has also brought her son, Nelson Collingwood Chuff, to live with her; but he is not so much at home as his mamma, going as a day-boy to Merchant Taylors' school, where he is getting a sound classical education.

If these beings, so closely allied to his wife, and so justly dear to her, may be considered as drawbacks to Maine's happiness, what man is there that has not some things in life to complain of? And when I first knew Mr. Maine, no man seemed more comfortable than he. His cottage was a picture of elegance and comfort; his table and cellar were excellently and neatly supplied. There was every enjoyment, but no ostentation. The omnibus took him to business of a morning; the boat brought him back to the happiest of homes, where he would while away the long evenings by reading out the fashionable novels to the ladies as they worked; or accompany his wife on the flute (which he played elegantly); or in any one of the hundred pleasing and innocent amusements of the domestic circle. Mrs. Chuff covered the drawing-rooms with prodigious tapestries, the work of her hands. Mrs. Sackville had a particular genius for making covers of tape or net-work for these tapestried cushions. She could make home-made wines. She could make preserves and pickles. She had an album, into which, during the time of his courtship, Sackville Maine had written choice scraps of Byron's and Moore's poetry, analogous to his own situation, and in a fine mercantile hand. She had a large manuscript receipt-book—every quality, in a word, which indicated a virtuous and well-bred English female mind.

"And as for Nelson Collingwood," Sackville would say, laughing, "we couldn't do without him in the house. If he didn't spoil the tapestry we should be over-cushioned in a few months; and whom could we get but him to drink Laura's home-made wine?" The truth is, the gents who came from the City to dine at the "Oval" could not be induced to drink it—in which fastidiousness, I myself, when I grew to be intimate with the family, confess that I shared.

"And yet, sir, that green ginger has been drunk by some of England's proudest heroes," Mrs. Chuff would exclaim. "Admiral Lord Exmouth tasted and praised it, sir, on board Captain Chuff's ship, the 'Nebuchadnezzar', 74, at Algiers; and he had three dozen with him in the 'Pitchfork' frigate, a part of which was served out to the men before he went into his immortal action with the 'Furibonde', Captain Choufleur, in the Gulf of Panama."

All this, though the old dowager told us the story every day when the wine was produced, never served to get rid of any quantity of it—and the green ginger, though it had fired British tars for combat and victory, was not to the taste of us peaceful and degenerate gents of modern times.

I see Sackville now, as on the occasion when, presented by Wagley, I paid my first visit to him. It was in July—a Sunday afternoon—Sackville Maine was coming from church, with his wife on one arm, and his mother-in-law (in red tabinet, as usual,) on the other. A half-grown, or hobbadehoyish footman, so to speak, walked after them, carrying their shining golden prayer-books—the ladies had splendid parasols with tags and fringes. Mrs. Chuff's great gold watch, fastened to her stomach, gleamed there like a ball of fire. Nelson Collingwood was in the distance, shying stones at an old horse on Kennington Common. 'Twas on that verdant spot we met—nor can I ever forget the majestic courtesy of Mrs. Chuff, as she remembered having had the pleasure of seeing me at Mrs. Perkins's—nor the glance of scorn which she threw at an unfortunate gentleman, who was preaching an exceedingly desultory discourse to a sceptical audience of omnibus-cads and nurse-maids, on a tub, as we passed by. "I cannot help it, sir," says she; "I am the widow of an officer of Britain's Navy: I was taught to honour my Church and my King: and I cannot bear a Radical, or a Dissenter."

With these fine principles I found Sackville Maine impressed. "Wagley," said he, to my introducer, "if no better engagement, why shouldn't self and friend dine at the 'Oval?' Mr. Snob, sir, the mutton's coming off the spit at this very minute. Laura and Mrs. Chuff" (he said *Laurar* and Mrs. Chuff; but I hate people who make remarks on these peculiarities of pronunciation) "will be most happy to see you; and I can promise you a hearty welcome, and as good a glass of port-wine as any in England."

"This is better than dining at the 'Sarcophagus,'" thinks I to myself, at which Club Wagley and I had intended to take our meal; and so we accepted the kindly invitation, whence arose afterwards a considerable intimacy.

Everything about this family and house was so good-natured, comfortable, and well-conditioned, that a cynic would have ceased to growl there. Mrs. Laura was all graciousness and smiles, and looked to as great advantage in her pretty morning-gown as in her dress-robe at Mrs. Perkins's. Mrs. Chuff fired off her stories about the "Nebuchadnezzar," 74, the action between the "Pitchfork" and the "Furibonde"—the heroic resistance of Captain Choufleur, and the quantity of snuff he took, &c. &c.; which, as they were heard for the first time, were pleasanter than I have subsequently found them. Sackville Maine was the best of hosts. He agreed in everything everybody said, altering his opinions without the slightest reservation upon the slightest possible contradiction. He was not one of those beings who would emulate a Schonbein or Friar Bacon, or act the part of an incendiary towards the

Thames, his neighbour—but a good, kind, simple, honest, easy fellow—in love with his wife—well disposed to all the world—content with himself, content even with his mother-in-law. Nelson Collingwood, I remember, in the course of the evening, when whisky-and-water was for some reason produced, grew a little tipsy. This did not in the least move Sackville's equanimity. "Take him upstairs, Joseph," said he to the hobbadehoy, "and—Joseph—don't tell his mamma."

What could make a man so happily disposed, unhappy? What could cause discomfort, bickering, and estrangement in a family so friendly and united? Ladies, it was not my fault—it was Mrs. Chuff's doing—but the rest of the tale you shall have on a future day.

CHAPTER XLIII

Club Snobs

The misfortune which befell the simple and good-natured young Sackville arose entirely from that abominable "Sarcophagus Club;" and that he ever entered it was partly the fault of the present writer.

For seeing Mrs. Chuff, his mother-in-law, had a taste for the genteel—(indeed, her talk was all about Lord Collingwood, Lord Gambier, Sir Jahaleel Brenton, and the Gosport and Plymouth balls)—Wagley and I, according to our wont, trumped her conversation, and talked about Lords, Dukes, Marquises, and Baronets, as if those dignitaries were our familiar friends.

"Lord Sextonbury," says I, "seems to have recovered her ladyship's death. He and the Duke were very jolly over their wine at the 'Sarcophagus' last night; weren't they, Wagley?"

"Good fellow, the Duke," Wagley replied. "Pray, ma'am" (to Mrs. Chuff), "you who know the world and etiquette, will you tell me what a man ought to do in my case? Last June, his Grace, his son Lord Castlerampant, Tom Smith, and myself were dining at the Club, when I offered the odds against *Daddylonglegs* for the Derby—forty to one, in sovereigns only. His Grace took the bet, and of course I won. He has never paid me. Now, can I ask such a great man for a sovereign?—*One* more lump of sugar, if you please, my dear madam."

It was lucky Wagley gave her this opportunity to elude the question, for it prostrated the whole worthy family among whom we were. They telegraphed each other with wondering eyes. Mrs. Chuff's stories about the naval nobility grew quite faint: and kind little Mrs. Sackville became uneasy, and went upstairs to look at the children—not at that young monster, Nelson Collingwood, who was sleeping off the whisky-and-water—but at a couple of little ones who had made their appearance at dessert, and of whom she and Sackville were the happy parents.

The end of this and subsequent meetings with Mr. Maine was, that we proposed and got him elected as a member of the "Sarcophagus Club."

It was not done without a deal of opposition—the secret having been whispered that the candidate was a coal-merchant. You may be sure some of the proud people and most of the parvenus of the Club were ready to blackball him. We combated this opposition successfully, however. We pointed out to the parvenus that the Lambtons and the Stuarts sold coals: we mollified the proud by accounts of his good birth, good nature, and good behaviour; and Wagley went about on the day of election, describing with great eloquence, the action between the "Pitchfork" and the "Furibonde," and the valour of Captain Maine, our friend's father. There was a slight mistake in the narrative; but we carried our man, with only a trifling sprinkling of black beans in the boxes: Byles's, of course, who blackballs everybody: and Bung's, who looks down upon a coal-merchant, having himself lately retired from the wine-trade.

Some fortnight afterwards I saw Sackville Maine under the following circumstances:—

He was showing the Club to his family. He had brought them thither in the light-blue fly, waiting at the Club door; with Mrs. Chuff's hobbadehoy footboy on the box, by the side of the flyman, in a sham livery. Nelson Collingwood; pretty Mrs. Sackville; Mrs. Captain Chuff (Mrs. Commodore Chuff we call her), were all there; the latter, of course, in the vermilion tabinet, which, splendid as it is, is nothing in comparison to the splendour of the "Sarcophagus." The delighted Sackville Maine was pointing out the beauties of the place to them. It seemed as beautiful as Paradise to that little party.

The "Sarcophagus" displays every known variety of architecture and decoration. The great library is Elizabethan; the small library is pointed Gothic; the dining-room is severe Doric; the strangers' room has an Egyptian look; the drawing-rooms are Louis Quatorze (so called because the hideous ornaments displayed were used in the time of Louis Quinze);

the *cortile*, or hall, is Morisco-Italian. It is all over marble, maplewood, looking-glasses, arabesques, ormolu, and scagliola. Scrolls, ciphers, dragons, Cupids, polyanthuses, and other flowers writhe up the walls in every kind of cornucopiosity. Fancy every gentleman in Jullien's band playing with all his might, and each performing a different tune; the ornaments at our Club, the "Sarcophagus," so bewilder and affect me. Dazzled with emotions which I cannot describe, and which she dared not reveal, Mrs. Chuff, followed by her children and son-in-law, walked wondering amongst these blundering splendours.

In the great library (225 feet long by 150) the only man Mrs. Chuff saw, was Tiggs. He was lying on a crimson-velvet sofa, reading a French novel of Paul de Kock. It was a very little book. He is a very little man. In that enormous hall he looked like a mere speck. As the ladies passed breathless and trembling in the vastness of the magnificent solitude, he threw a knowing, killing glance at the fair strangers, as much as to say, "Ain't I a fine fellow?" They thought so, I am sure.

"*Who is that?*" hisses out Mrs. Chuft, when we were about fifty yards off him at the other end of the room.

"Tiggs!" says I, in a similar whisper.

"Pretty comfortable this, isn't it, my dear?" says Maine in a free-and-easy way to Mrs. Sackville; "all the magazines, you see—writing materials—new works—choice library, containing every work of importance—what have we here?—'Dugdale's Monasticon,' a most valuable and, I believe, entertaining book."

And proposing to take down one of the books for Mrs. Maine's inspection, he selected Volume VII., to which he was attracted by the singular fact that a brass door-handle grew out of the back. Instead of pulling out a book, however, he pulled open a cupboard, only inhabited by a lazy housemaid's broom and duster, at which he looked exceedingly discomfited; while Nelson Collingwood, losing all respect, burst into a roar of laughter.

"That's the rummest book I ever saw," says Nelson. "I wish we'd no others at Merchant Taylors'."

"Hush, Nelson!" cries Mrs. Chuff, and we went into the other magnificent apartments.

How they did admire the drawing-room hangings (pink and silver brocade, most excellent wear for London), and calculated the price per yard; and revelled on the luxurious sofas; and gazed on the immeasurable looking-glasses.

"Pretty well to shave by, eh?" says Maine to his mother-in-law. (He was getting more abominably conceited every minute.) "Get away, Sackville," says she, quite delighted, and threw a glance over her shoulder, and spread out the wings of the red tabinet, and took a good look at herself; so did Mrs. Sackville—just one, and I thought the glass reflected a very smiling, pretty creature.

But what's a woman at a looking-glass? Bless the little dears, it's their place. They fly to it naturally. It pleases them, and they adorn it. What I like to see, and watch with increasing joy and adoration, is the Club *men* at the great looking-glasses. Old Gills pushing up his collars and grinning at his own mottled face. Hulker looking solemnly at his great person, and tightening his coat to give himself a waist. Fred Minchin simpering by as he is going out to dine, and casting upon the reflection of his white neckcloth a pleased moony smile. What a deal of vanity that Club mirror has reflected, to be sure!

Well, the ladies went through the whole establishment with perfect pleasure. They beheld the coffee-rooms, and the little tables laid for dinner, and the gentlemen who were taking their lunch, and old Jawkins thundering away as usual; they saw the reading-rooms, and the rush for the evening papers; they saw the kitchens—those wonders of art—where the *Chef* was presiding over twenty pretty kitchen-maids, and ten thousand shining saucepans: and they got into the light-blue fly perfectly bewildered with pleasure.

Sackville did not enter it, though little Laura took the back seat on purpose, and left him the front place alongside of Mrs. Chuff's red tabinet.

"We have your favourite dinner," says she, in a timid voice; "won't you come, Sackville?"

"I shall take a chop here today, my dear," Sackville replied. "Home, James." And he went up the steps of the "Sarcophagus," and the pretty face looked very sad out of the carriage, as the blue fly drove away.

CHAPTER XLIV

Club Snobs

Why—why did I and Wagley ever do so cruel an action as to introduce young Sackville Maine into that odious "Sarcophagus!" Let our imprudence and his example be a warning to other gents; let his fate and that of his poor wife be remembered by every British female. The consequences of his entering the Club were as follow:—

One of the first vices the unhappy wretch acquired in this abode of frivolity was that of *smoking*. Some of the dandies of the Club, such as the Marquis of Macabaw, Lord Doodeen, and fellows of that high order, are in the habit of indulging in this propensity upstairs in the billiard-rooms of the "Sarcophagus"—and, partly to make their acquaintance, partly from a natural aptitude for crime, Sackville Maine followed them, and became an adept in the odious custom. Where it is introduced into a family I need not say how sad the consequences are, both to the furniture and the morals. Sackville smoked in his dining-room at home, and caused an agony to his wife and mother-in-law which I do not venture to describe.

He then became a professed *billiard-player*, wasting hours upon hours at that amusement; betting freely, playing tolerably, losing awfully to Captain Spot and Col. Cannon. He played matches of a hundred games with these gentlemen, and would not only continue until four or five o'clock in the morning at this work, but would be found at the Club of a forenoon, indulging himself to the detriment of his business, the ruin of his health, and the neglect of his wife.

From billiards to whist is but a step—and when a man gets to whist and five pounds on the rubber, my opinion is, that it is all up with him. How was the coal business to go on, and the connexion of the firm to be kept up, and the senior partner always at the card-table?

Consorting now with genteel persons and Pall Mall bucks, Sackville became ashamed of his snug little residence in Kennington Oval, and transported his family to Pimlico, where, though Mrs. Chuff, his mother-in-law, was at first happy, as the quarter was elegant and near her Sovereign, poor little Laura and the children found a woful difference. Where were her friends who came in with their work of a morning?—At Kennington and in the vicinity of Clapham. Where were her children's little playmates?—On Kennington Common. The great thundering carriages that roared up and down the drab-coloured streets of the new quarter, contained no friends for the sociable little Laura. The children that paced the squares, attended by a *bonne* or a prim governess, were not like those happy ones that flew kites, or played hop-scotch, on the well-beloved old Common. And ah! what a difference at Church too!—between St. Benedict's of Pimlico, with open seats, service in sing-song—tapers—albs—surplices—garlands and processions, and the honest old ways of Kennington! The footmen, too, attending St. Benedict's were so splendid and enormous, that James, Mrs. Chuff's boy, trembled amongst them, and said he would give warning rather than carry the books to that church any more.

The furnishing of the house was not done without expense. And, ye gods! what a difference there was between Sackville's dreary French banquets in Pimlico, and the jolly dinners at the Oval! No more legs-of-mutton, no more of "the best port-wine in England;" but *entrées* on plate, and dismal twopenny champagne, and waiters in gloves, and the Club bucks for company—among whom Mrs. Chuff was uneasy and Mrs. Sackville quite silent.

Not that he dined at home often. The wretch had become a perfect epicure, and dined commonly at the Club with the gormandising clique there; with old Dr. Maw, Colonel Cramley (who is as lean as a greyhound and has jaws like a jack), and the rest of them. Here you might see the wretch tippling Sillery champagne and gorging himself with French viands; and I

often looked with sorrow from my table, (on which cold meat, the Club small-beer, and a half-pint of Marsala form the modest banquet,) and sighed to think it was my work.

And there were other beings present to my repentant thoughts. Where's his wife, thought I? Where's poor, good, kind little Laura? At this very moment—it's about the nursery bed-time, an while yonder good-for-nothing is swilling his wine—the little ones are at Laura's knees lisping their prayers; and she is teaching them to say—"Pray God bless Papa."

When she has put them to bed, her day's occupation is gone; and she is utterly lonely all night, and sad, and waiting for him.

Oh, for shame! Oh, for shame! Go home, thou idle tippler.

How Sackville lost his health: how he lost his business; how he got into scrapes; how he got into debt; how he became a railroad director; how the Pimlico house was shut up; how he went to Boulogne,—all this I could tell, only I am too much ashamed of my part of the transaction. They returned to England, because, to the surprise of everybody, Mrs. Chuff came down with a great sum of money (which nobody knew she had saved), and paid his liabilities. He is in England; but at Kennington. His name is taken off the books of the "Sarco-phagus" long ago. When we meet, he crosses over to the other side of the street; and I don't call, as I should be sorry to see a look of reproach or sadness in Laura's sweet face.

Not, however, all evil, as I am proud to think, has been the influence of the Snob of England upon Clubs in general:— Captain Shindy is afraid to bully the waiters any more, and eats his mutton-chop without moving Acheron. Gobemouche does not take more than two papers at a time for his private reading. Tiggs does not ring the bell and cause the library-waiter to walk about a quarter of a mile in order to give him Vol. II., which lies on the next table. Growler has ceased to walk from table to table in the coffee-room, and inspect what people are having for dinner. Trotty Veck takes his own umbrella from the hall—the cotton one; and Sydney Scraper's paletot lined with silk has been brought back by Jobbins, who entirely mistook it for his own. Wiggle has discontinued telling stories about the ladies he has killed. Snooks does not any more think it gentlemanlike to blackball attorneys. Snuffler no longer publicly spreads out his great red cotton pocket-handkerchief before the fire, for the admiration of two hundred gentlemen; and if one Club Snob has been brought back to the paths of rectitude, and if one poor John has been spared a journey or a scolding—say, friends and brethren, if these sketches of Club Snobs have been in vain?

CHAPTER LAST

How it is that we have come to No. 45 of this present series of papers, my dear friends and brother Snobs, I hardly know—but for a whole mortal year have we been together, prattling, and abusing the human race; and were we to live for a hundred years more, I believe there is plenty of subject for conversation in the enormous theme of Snobs.

The national mind is awakened to the subject. Letters pour in every day, conveying marks of sympathy; directing the attention of the Snob of England to races of Snobs yet undescribed. "Where are your Theatrical Snobs; your Commercial Snobs; your Medical and Chirurgical Snobs; your Official Snobs; your Legal Snobs; your Artistical Snobs; your Musical Snobs; your Sporting Snobs?" write my esteemed correspondents. "Surely you are not going to miss the Cambridge Chancellor election, and omit showing up your Don Snobs, who are coming, cap in hand, to a young Prince of six-and-twenty, and to implore him to be the chief of their renowned University?" writes a friend who seals with the signet of the Cam and Isis Club. "Pray, pray," cries another, "now the Operas are opening, give us a lecture about Omnibus Snobs." Indeed, I should like to write a chapter about the Snobbish Dons very much, and another about the Snobbish Dandies. Of my dear Theatrical Snobs I think with a pang; and I can hardly break away from some Snobbish Artists, with whom I have long, long intended to have a palaver.

But what's the use of delaying? When these were done there would be fresh Snobs to pourtray. The labour is endless. No single man could complete it. Here are but fifty-two bricks— and a pyramid to build. It is best to stop. As Jones always quits the room as soon as he has said his good thing,—as Cincinnatus and General Washington both retired into private life in the height of their popularity,—as Prince Albert, when he laid the first stone of the Exchange, left the bricklayers to complete that edifice, and went home to his royal dinner,—as the poet Bunn comes forward at the end of the season, and with feelings too tumultuous to describe, blesses his *kyind* friends over the footlights: so, friends, in the flush of conquest and the splendour of victory, amid the shouts and the plaudits of a people—triumphant yet modest—the Snob of England bids ye farewell.

But only for a season. Not for ever. No, no. There is one celebrated author whom I admire very much—who has been taking leave of the public any time these ten years in his prefaces, and always comes back again when everybody is glad to see him. How can he have the heart to be saying good-by so often? I believe that Bunn *is* affected when he blesses the people. Parting is always painful. Even the familiar bore is dear to you. I should be sorry to shake hands even with Jawkins for the last time. I think a well-constituted convict, on coming home from transportation, ought to be rather sad when he takes leave of Van Diemen's Land. When the curtain goes down on the last night of a pantomime, poor old clown must be very dismal, depend on it. Ha! with what joy he rushes forward on the evening of the 26th of December next, and says—"How are you?—Here we are!" But I am growing too sentimental:—to return to the theme.

The national mind is awakened to the subject of snobs. The word Snob has taken a place in our honest English vocabulary. We can't define it, perhaps. We can't say what it is, any more than we can define wit, or humour, or humbug; but we *know* what it is Some weeks since, happening to have the felicity to sit next to a young lady at a hospitable table, where poor old Jawkins was holding forth in a very absurd pompous manner, I wrote upon the spotless damask "S——B," and called my neighbour's attention to the little remark.

That young lady smiled. She knew it at once. Her mind straightway filled up the two letters concealed by apostrophic reserve, and I read in her assenting eyes that she knew Jawkins was a Snob. You seldom get them to make use of the word as yet, it is true; but it is inconceivable how pretty an expression their little smiling mouths assume when they speak it out. It any young lady doubts, just let her go to her own room, look at herself steadily in the glass, and say "Snob." If she tries this simple experiment, my life for it, she will smile, and own that the word becomes her mouth amazingly. A pretty little round word, all composed of soft letters, with a hiss at the beginning, just to make it piquant, as it were.

Jawkins, meanwhile, went on blundering, and bragging, and boring, quite unconsciously. And so he will, no doubt, go on roaring and braying to the end of time, or at least so long as people will hear him. You cannot alter the nature of men and Snobs by any force of satire; as, by laying ever so many stripes on a donkey's back, you can't turn him into a zebra.

But we can warn the neighbourhood that the person whom they and Jawkins admire is an impostor. We can apply the Snob test to him, and try whether he is conceited and a quack, whether pompous and lacking humility—whether uncharitable and proud of his narrow soul. How does he treat a great man—how regard a small one? How does he comport himself in the presence of His Grace the Duke; and how in that of Smith, the tradesman?

And it seems to me that all English society is cursed by this mammoniacal superstition; and that we are sneaking and bowing and cringing on the one hand, or bullying and scorning on the other, from the lowest to the highest. My wife speaks with great circumspection—"proper pride," she calls it—to our neighbour the tradesman's lady: and she, I mean Mrs. Snob,—Eliza—would give one of her eyes to go to Court, as her cousin, the Captain's wife, did. She, again, is a good soul, but it costs her agonies to be obliged to confess that we live in Upper Thompson Street, Somer's Town. And though I believe in her heart Mrs. Whiskerington is fonder of us than of her cousins, the Smigsmags, you should hear how she goes on prattling about Lady Smigsmag,—and "I said to Sir John, my dear John;" and about the Smigsmags' house and parties in Hyde Park Terrace.

215

Lady Smigsmag, when she meets Eliza,—who is a sort of a kind of a species of a connection of the family, pokes out one finger, which my wife is at liberty to embrace in the most cordial manner she can devise. But oh, you should see her ladyship's behaviour on her first-chop dinner-party days, when Lord and Lady Longears come!

I can bear it no longer—this diabolical invention of gentility which kills natural kindliness and honest friendship. Proper pride, indeed! Rank and precedence forsooth! The table of ranks and degrees is a lie, and should be flung into the fire. Organize rank and precedence! that was well for the masters of ceremonies of former ages. Come forward, some great marshal, and organize Equality in society, and your rod shall swallow up all the juggling old court goldsticks. If this is not gospel-truth—if the world does not tend to this—if hereditary-great-man worship is not a humbug and an idolatry—let us have the Stuarts back again, and crop the Free Press's ears in the pillory.

If ever our cousins, the Smigsmags, asked me to meet Lord Longears, I would like to take an opportunity after dinner and say, in the most good-natured way in the world:—Sir, Fortune makes you a present of a number of thousand pounds every year. The ineffable wisdom of our ancestors has placed you as a chief and hereditary legislator over me. Our admirable Constitution (the pride of Britons and envy of surrounding nations) obliges me to receive you as my senator, superior, and guardian. Your eldest son, Fitz-Heehaw, is sure of a place in Parliament; your younger sons, the De Brays, will kindly condescend to be post-captains and lieutenant-colonels, and to represent us in foreign courts or to take a good living when it falls convenient. These prizes our admirable Constitution (the pride and envy of, &c.) pronounces to be your due: without count of your dulness, your vices, your selfishness; or your entire incapacity and folly. Dull as you may be (and we have as good a right to assume that my lord is an ass, as the other proposition, that he is an enlightened patriot);—dull, I say, as you may be, no one will accuse you of such monstrous folly, as to suppose that you are indifferent to the good luck which you possess, or have any inclination to part with it. No—and patriots as we are, under happier circumstances, Smith and I, I have no doubt, were we dukes ourselves, would stand by our order.

We would submit good-naturedly to sit in a high place. We would acquiesce in that admirable Constitution (pride and envy of, &c.) which made us chiefs and the world our inferiors; we would not cavil particularly at that notion of hereditary superiority which brought so many simple people cringing to our knees. Maybe we would rally round the Corn-Laws; we would make a stand against the Reform Bill; we would die rather than repeal the Acts against Catholics and Dissenters; we would, by our noble system of class-legislation, bring Ireland to its present admirable condition.

But Smith and I are not Earls as yet. We don't believe that it is for the interest of Smith's army that young De Bray should be a Colonel at five-and-twenty,—of Smith's diplomatic relations that Lord Longears should go Ambassador to Constantinople,—of our politics, that Longears should put his hereditary foot into them.

This bowing and cringing Smith believes to be the act of Snobs; and he will do all in his might and main to be a Snob and to submit to Snobs no longer. To Longears he says, "We can't help seeing, Longears, that we are as good as you. We can spell even better; we can think quite as rightly; we will not have you for our master, or black your shoes any more. Your footmen do it, but they are paid; and the fellow who comes to get a list of the company when you give a banquet or a dancing breakfast at Longueoreille House, gets money from the newspapers for performing that service. But for us, thank you for nothing, Longears my boy, and we don't wish to pay you any more than we owe. We will take off our hats to Wellington because he is Wellington; but to you—who are you?"

I am sick of *Court Circulars*. I loathe *haut-ton* intelligence. I believe such words as Fashionable, Exclusive, Aristocratic, and the like, to be wicked, unchristian epithets, that ought to be banished from honest vocabularies. A Court system that sends men of genius to the second table, I hold to be a Snobbish system. A society that sets up to be polite, and ignores Arts and Letters, I hold to be a Snobbish society. You, who despise your neighbour, are a Snob; you, who forget your own friends, meanly to follow after those of a higher degree, are a Snob; you, who are ashamed of your poverty, and blush for your calling, are a Snob; as are you who boast of your pedigree, or are proud of your wealth.

To laugh at such is *Mr. Punch's* business. May he laugh honestly, hit no foul blow, and tell the truth when at his very broadest grin—never forgetting that if Fun is good, Truth is still better, and Love best of all.

NOTES

The papers Thackeray subsequently collected in volume form as *The Book of Snobs* first appeared (anonymously) in weekly instalments in *Punch* from 28 February 1846 to 27 February 1847, under the title 'The Snobs of England'. They were accompanied by Thackeray's own illustrations, a selection of which are reproduced in the present edition.

What began as fugitive satires might indeed never have been assembled into a book were it not for the immediate success of *Vanity Fair*, the monthly instalments of which began appearing over Thackeray's name in January 1847; this made the author a saleable commodity, and publishers Bradbury and Evans were happy to issue the *Punch* satires in book form. *The Book of Snobs* was published in 1848 in a printing of three thousand, and re-issued in 1855. Evidently it was popular with readers, though less so with the author himself, who subsequently conceived a thoroughgoing dislike of it.

The original chapters XVIII to XXIII were omitted from the book edition (cf. note to p. 88). They were written at a period of considerable political unrest; the Corn Laws were repealed, and Sir Robert Peel resigned as Prime Minister (29 June 1846). The excision of these pieces, and of one or two other local remarks of a political nature in other chapters, appears to have been prompted by a feeling that they were too sensitive; but possibly an awareness that satire too closely tied to topical reference loses its edge once the immediate occasion is forgotten was in Thackeray's mind as well. Readers interested in the complete text of the original serialization are referred to John Sutherland's exemplary edition of *The Book of Snobs* (St. Lucia, Queensland, and New York, 1978), to which the present popular edition is indebted; Sutherland's scholarship is exhaustive, elucidating from the newspapers of the time many references that had baffled previous editors and readers, and for help with material unglossed here the reader is referred to

Sutherland. In the notes that follow, words that can be found in any good dictionary are not glossed. *Ed.*

p. 11   *Professor Holloway*: Sutherland cites one Professor Holloway's pills, widely advertised at the time with a testimonial from the Earl of Aldborough, to the effect that "not even the waters of Carlsbad and Marienbad" had previously been able to effect a cure of his stomach and liver disorders (etc.).

p. 11   *the very article in question*: this sentence was followed in the original serialization by sideswipes directed at Sir Robert Peel (cf. note to p. 70) and at Daniel O'Connell (1775–1847), then leader of the Irish party. They were dropped, and some other references of a similar kind, when Thackeray's serialized pieces were collected in book form.

p. 11   *Derrynane Beg*: this was known to be one the poorest, most squalid places in Ireland.

p. 12   *Curtius*: among the legends of Rome was that of Mettis Curtius, who in 362 BC was said to have leapt on horseback into a chasm that had opened in the forum, which soothsayers claimed could be filled only with the most precious treasure in the city.

p. 13   *Horace*: cf. *Odes* I, iv, 13.

p. 15   *The Snob playfully dealt with*: in the serialization, this chapter was originally titled 'The Snob Socially Considered'.

p. 15   *Damon and Pythias*: Pythagorean philosophers of the 4th century BC whose names became synonymous with inseparable friendship.

p. 17   *the Silver-Fork School*: i.e. novelists who wrote about fashionable society.

p. 17   *it will be allowed ... a moral man*: in the serialization this read, "I flatter myself Silk Buckingham will at least say that *I* am a moral man". James Silk Buckingham

(1786–1855) was the founder of the British and Foreign Institute, regularly lampooned by *Punch*.

p. 19   *Sir Roderick Murchison*: author of a *Geology of Russia in Europe and the Ural Mountains* (1845).

p. 20   *Mr. James*: the historical novelist George Payne Rainsford James (1799–1860).

p. 22   *Mr. Squeers*: the schoolmaster in Dickens' *Nicholas Nickleby* (1838–9). Hawtrey was headmaster of Eton from 1834 till 1852, and Mrs. Ellis the author of *The Wives of England* (cf. p. 29).

p. 22   *Mr. Widdicomb*: John Widdicomb had recently been made master of ceremonies at Vauxhall Gardens.

p. 23   *Bradwardine*: a swipe at Sir Walter Scott, of whom this very anecdote is told by J. G. Lockhart in his *Life of Scott* (1837–8).

p. 24   *Lord John Russell*: Russell (1792–1878) became prime minister in 1846. Sutherland shows that Thackeray's ironic phrase in quotation marks alludes to Russell's manoeuvring in the period when the Corn Laws were repealed.

p. 26   *a noble marchioness*: the Marchioness of Londonderry, whose *Narrative of a Visit to the Courts of Vienna, Constantinople, Athens, Naples, etc.* was published in 1844.

p. 26   *black and other diamonds*: alluding to the (Durham) coalfields that were the source of the Londonderry fortune.

p. 26   *It is our fault*: the phrasing echoes that of Cassius in Shakespeare's *Julius Caesar*, I, 11, 139–40.

p. 26   *Kotoo*: more often seen as "kowtow" nowadays, the word refers to the Chinese ceremony of prostration (before the Emperor).

p. 30   *a German King-Consort*: while a prince of the Saxe-Coburg dynasty had indeed married into the Portuguese royal house, Thackeray is of course referring to Albert (1819–61), Prince Consort to Queen Victoria.

223

p. 31 *Calf's Head Club*: established after the execution of Charles I to perpetuate the memory of that event.

p. 42 *the Corsican invader*: i.e. Napoleon.

p. 46 *Young England*: a political group of the 1840s, of mainly conservative leaning, associated with Disraeli.

p. 46 *Laud*: William Laud (1573–1645), Archbishop of Canterbury, a high church anti-Calvinist extremist and wielder of considerable political power, whose actions occasioned unrest and misery in England and Scotland. He was tried for treason, found "guilty of endeavouring to subvert the laws, to overthrow the Protestant religion, and to act as an enemy to Parliament", and beheaded on Tower Hill. The background to Thackeray's observation here lies in the intellectual popularity of Catholicism in the 1840s; cf. note on Puseyism (p. 75 below).

p. 48 *Scharlaschild*: i.e. Rothschild.

p. 52 *Peninsular*: i.e. a veteran of the Peninsular War, that campaign of the Napoleonic wars fought in Portugal and Spain from 1809 to 1814.

p. 53 *Duke*: i.e. the Duke of Wellington.

p. 53 *Sobraon*: a Sikh camp taken by the British on 10 February 1846 (during an Indian insurrection against British rule).

p. 56 *Bell's Life*: a sporting periodical. Cf. also p. 188.

p. 59 *Ferozeshah*: an engagement during the Sikh war (cf. note to p. 53), on 21 December 1845.

p. 61 *Mr. Eisenberg, Chiropodist*: Sutherland has traced contemporary advertisements for this gentleman's services that carry a recommendation from the Bishop of Jamaica.

p. 61 *Sydney Smith*: the English clergyman and wit. Smith (1771–1845) co-founded the *Edinburgh Review*.

p. 62 *Puritani*: opera (1834) by Vincenzo Bellini (1801–35).

p. 63 *the clergyman ... a noble Duke*: the Duke of Buckingham, alerted by the clergyman requested to perform the ceremony, had interrupted the marriage of his daughter to a commoner. This was recent news (2 May 1846) and still a talking point at the time when this item in Thackeray's series was published on 23 May.

p. 70 *Sir Robert Peel*: Peel (1788–1850) was still Prime Minister when this number in Thackeray's series was published on 30 May 1846, but his government fell the following month. Disraeli (1804–81), powerful at that date but still a rising force, was at odds with Peel over a number of issues, especially the Corn Laws, and brought about his downfall. It is relevant in the present context that Disraeli was Jewish; there were campaigns at the time to remove disabilities on Jews, but *Punch* was far from sharing this liberal position, and indeed Thackeray added one of his more regrettable illustrations to this item (not reproduced in the present edition).

p. 71 *Crump ... President of the College*: William Whewell (1794–1866), who had taught Thackeray himself when he was at Cambridge, was now Master of Trinity.

p. 75 *Puseyism*: the English theologian Edward Bouverie Pusey (1800–82), Regius Professor of Hebrew at Oxford, was the leader of the Oxford Movement, and endeavoured to map ground on which a reunion of the Churches of England and Rome might be effected. Several of the most influential of those associated with him, such as Newman and Manning, indeed converted to Roman Catholicism. Cf. p. 132: "He used to preach those sermons in a surplice [...] He's a Puseyite."

p. 76 *Pelham's time*: i.e. the period of Bulwer Lytton's novel *Pelham* (1828).

p. 76 *high-lows*: laced boots reaching over the ankles. The straps not used by these youngsters passed from the trouser-bottoms under the soles of the boots.

p. 77 *Berlin glove*: i.e. one made of the fine knitting wool known at the time as Berlin wool.

p. 77 *Gyp*: a college servant.

p. 81   *N.P. Willis*: an American author of the day who offended English society by reporting publicly their private conversation.

p. 81   *the genteel novels*: of these society novels, only Samuel Warren's *Ten Thousand a Year* (1839) and Disraeli's *Coningsby* (1844) are still read at all. For the former, cf. also p. 162. Thackeray's characterizations of authors (now mostly forgotten) and periodicals in this chapter are heavily ironic.

p. 83   *a sum ... set apart*: the Royal Literary Fund had not impressed *Punch* by its generosity.

p. 84   *De Tocqueville and De Beaumont*: the French historian Alexis de Tocqueville and the writer Gustave de Beaumont both published accounts of travels in Ireland in the 1830s (the former as part of an account of both England and Ireland).

p. 85   *a certain great orator*: Daniel O'Connell. Cf. note to p. 11.

p. 87   *Hereditary Bondsmen*: the favourite phrase by which Daniel O'Connell addressed his Irish countrymen.

p. 88   *selection of Snobs ... political character*: this was no longer the case when the heavily political contributions were omitted from the book publication (cf. headnote above). To the editions of 1848 and 1855, Thackeray added the following footnote at this point: "On re-perusing these papers, I have found them so stupid, so personal, so snobbish—in a word, that I have withdrawn them from this collection.—THE SNOB."

p. 89   *bohea*: the term was once used of fine teas, but by Thackeray's time had come to be applied to the poorest of black teas. The word is derived from the Fuhkien Chinese.

p. 89   *Black Hole*: i.e. the Black Hole of Calcutta, a small dungeon in which Surajah Dowlah, Nawab of Bengal, confined 146 British prisoners in June 1756. It was so tiny and airless that all but twenty-two suffocated.

p. 90 *Ugolino*: confined in a prison tower in the *Inferno*, Canto XXXIII, in Dante's *Divine Comedy*.

p. 97 *Alexis Soyer*: chef at the Reform Club (Thackeray's club) and author of *Cookery or the Gastronomic Regenerator*.

p. 101 *battue*: Sutherland explains this as another "covert hit at Albert, who hunted in the German manner, driving the beasts together for a general slaughter".

p. 106 *Zollverein*: a Prussian-initiated customs union that created a free trade area in Germany, beginning in 1818 and growing throughout the 1820s and 30s to peak in the 40s.

p. 108 *Nicholas*: i.e. Russia's Czar Nicholas I (1796–1855), who visited England in 1844.

p. 114 *britzkas*: the britzka was an open four-wheeled carriage. The word entered English from Polish in the 1830s.

p. 115 *Carlists*: supporters of the Spanish pretender Don Carlos de Borbon (1788–1855).

p. 118 *Mr. Atkinson's shop*: a Bond Street perfumery.

p. 118 *kerseymeres*: i.e. cashmeres.

p. 122 *statue*: the equestrian statue of the Duke of Wellington was placed on 29 September 1846, the present instalment in Thackeray's series published on 10 October.

p. 123 *Mr. Green's balloon*: an attraction seen in London on 2 October 1846, and evidently a great talking point.

p. 131 *Barmecide*: in the *Arabian Nights*, a prince who serves an imaginary banquet, the dishes all being empty.

p. 135 *she*: other editions read "he". This emendation, Sutherland's suggestion, makes obvious sense.

p. 136 *Miss Crusoe*: *Punch* was at this time (the autumn of 1846) serializing *The Life and Adventures of Miss Robinson Crusoe* by Douglas William Jerrold (1803–57), one of the magazine's regular contributors.

p. 141 *Lord George Bentinck*: the sportsman and politician (1802–48), who had recently become more active in politics.

p. 147 *Hahnemann ... Priessnitz*: pioneers of homeopathic medicine.

p. 149 *martyrdom in our profession*: the sentence that followed these words was also cut from the book publication: "Ask Sir Edward George Earl Lytton Bulwer Lytton if there isn't, or any other eminent hand."

p. 158 *Malthus*: Thomas Robert Malthus (1766-1834), who argued that populations grow faster than the means of subsistence, and so called for sexual abstinence or birth control.

p. 166 *my favourite poet*: Horace.

p. 172 *Mr. Phelps at Sadler's Wells*: Samuel Phelps (1804-78) became manager of Sadler's Wells in 1844, and for eighteen years offered the London audience outstanding Shakespeare productions, often acting in them himself.

p. 173 *Lord Eldon's Life*: Horace Twiss, *The Life of Lord Eldon*, London, 1844.

p. 178 *Dr. Lemprière's elegant dictionary*: the great *Classical Dictionary* (1788) compiled by John Lemprière (c. 1765-1824), long a standard work and restored to celebrity by Lawrence Norfolk's 1991 novel.

p. 179 *Thalberg*: Sigismond Thalberg (1812-71), Swiss pianist and composer.

p. 180 *Chubb key*: the English locksmith Charles Chubb (1772-1846) patented important improvements in locks.

p. 181 *Blight's ... the "Contemplative Club"*: i.e. White's, Boodle's, Brooks's, and the Conservative Club.

p. 187 *Vanity Fair*: Thackeray's great satirical novel began to appear in monthly instalments in January 1847; the present item in Thackeray's taxonomy of snobbery appeared in *Punch* on 16 January 1847. The reader familiar with the novel will notice a degree of overlap in places.

p. 190 *the author of "Don Juan"*: i.e. Byron.

p. 192 *yataghan*: a Turkish dagger.

p. 197 *London Assurance*: a popular play at the time, by the Dublin-born dramatist Dion Boucicault (c. 1820–1890).

p. 206 *Paul de Kock*: French novelist (1794–1871) whose books were found to be easy, piquant reading.

p. 213 *a young Prince*: the election of Prince Albert to the chancellorship of Cambridge University aroused the scorn of Thackeray.

p. 213 *fifty-two bricks*: i.e. that number of instalments in the 'Snobs of England' series. Thackeray's editing of the text for book publication was at points cursory; here, he has remembered to correct the number to "45" in the opening sentence of this final chapter, but has overlooked this subsequent reference to "fifty-two".

p. 213 *Bunn*: Alfred Bunn, manager of Drury Lane theatre, had the habit of delivering the end-of-season speech from the footlights which Thackeray ridicules here.

p. 214 *one celebrated author*: again, Bulwer Lytton.

p. 214 *Van Diemen's Land*: Tasmania.